Praise for A SWARM IN MAY

"Mark Powers' suspenseful debut novel, *A Swarm in May*, utilizes his years as a physician and beekeeper to create a story that book clubs everywhere will compare to books like *The Secret Life of Bees* and *Where the Crawdads Sing*. Add the reality of racism in the South, and you have a story those readers will discuss late into the night."

–Dawn Reno Langley, Author of *The Mourning Parade and You are Divine: The Search for the Goddess in all of Us,* and President of Rewired Creatives, Inc.

"Damn you, Mark Powers .... I settled in to begin reading the book last night at 9:30. Around 3:30 AM I finished it. If that isn't an endorsement, then I don't know what is! The last book I did that with was *Where the Crawdads Sing*. Overall, I loved it. It is truly a page turner."

–Dr. Craig Rackley, MD, Associate Professor of Medicine, Duke University

"Hop on for a rollicking ride with Dr. Phineas Mann in this debut novel from Mark Anthony Powers! *A Swarm in May* is a gripping page turner you might have expected had John Grisham gone to medical school instead of law school. From bees to racism to ventilators in an ICU, Dr Powers shepherds us through the wonders and hazards of modern medicine—and life in general—in a troubled world."

–Dr. Lake Morrison, MD, Associate Professor of Medicine, Duke University

"I loved, loved, loved the book. This novel was absolutely fabulous! I thought at first that this would be a story just for beekeepers, but it is so nice that it's not. The ending was superb and so much fun! I think you have a winner here."

–Cynthia Speed, Certified Master Beekeeper and
Past President of Orange County Beekeepers

"Dr. Mark Powers' debut novel is both tender and funny. This tightly woven and well-paced adventure teems with entomologic and medical wonder while offering a gentle portrait of human connection. *A Swarm in May* provides the reader entrée into the heart and mind of a committed intensivist who must navigate uncertain terrain as his many worlds collide."

–Dr. Kim Talikoff, MD, Pediatrician, educator, documentarian, and beekeeper

"As an insider in both the medical and beekeeping worlds, Mark Powers' *A Swarm in May* is a fascinating novel that not only entertains but may teach you a few things!"

–Randall Austin, Certified Master Beekeeper and Piedmont Regional Director of the North Carolina State Beekeepers Association

"From the first day he steps into the intensive care unit, a cascade of events takes the reader on a thrilling adventure including medical mysteries, the ongoing legacy of racism, and the complex and fascinating lives of bees. It's hard to put this riveting book down once you start it."

–Tim Scialla, MD, Associate Professor of Medicine, University of Virginia

"While it is set in 1998, the racial themes explored are remarkably relevant today. I found myself empathizing with the characters, and the storyline kept me reading well past bedtime.

This novel reminded me that spending time in my garden and with my bees are some of the best ways to unwind and stay grounded, especially during challenging times."

–Dr. Carrie Donley, PhD, University of North Carolina Department of Chemistry and 2021 President of Orange County Beekeepers

"Fast-paced, captivating plot, great understanding of the world of bee-keeping. *A Swarm in May* intriguingly explores the parallels between the often disorganized community of man and the seemingly chaotic, but well-ordered and selfless community of honey bees."

–John Rintoul, Attorney and Past President of Orange County Beekeepers

"Mark Power's *A Swarm in May* is a great read filled with characters you immediately like and a story line that keeps you turning the pages. It brings together details of medical care in a teaching hospital, beekeeping, and racial tensions in a book that is a delight to read. I am already looking forward to Mark Powers' next book!"

–Jim Snapper, MD, Consultant Professor of Medicine, Duke University

"Mark Powers delightfully captures the joys of medicine and medical education in this fast-paced story of disease and intrigue in North Carolina. An especially great book for nurses and doctors of all ages!"

–Joseph Govert, MD, Professor of Medicine, Duke University

A SWARM IN MAY

Leoneda,

Your work inspires.

Mark Anthony Powers

A SWARM IN MAY

A NOVEL

MARK ANTHONY POWERS

A Swarm in May is a work of fiction. Other than the actual historical events, people, and places referred to, all names, characters, and incidents are from the author's imagination. Any resemblances to persons, living or dead, are coincidental, and no reference to any real person is intended. The author did his best to be rigorously true to honey bees including their biology and social behaviors.

Published by Hawksbill Press
www.hawksbillpress.com

Edited by Dawn Reno Langley, President of Rewired Creatives, Inc.
Book design by Christy Collins, Constellation Book Design
Author photo by Amy Stern Photography, www.amystern.com

ISBN (paperback): 978-1-7370329-0-8
ISBN (ebook): 978-1-7370329-1-5

Printed in the United States of America

for Marco

WEEK ONE

A swarm of bees in May is like a load of hay.
A swarm of bees in June is worth a silver spoon.
A swarm of bees in July isn't worth a fly.
ANONYMOUS, 17TH CENTURY

Opisthotonus.

This moment was the first time in Dr. Phineas Mann's twenty years of medicine he'd seen a patient posturing in the way described by the medical term opisthotonus. The pale old man had suddenly arched into a human comma flipped ninety degrees left, his round, wrinkled head face up, anchored at one end, and his legs curled down, heels digging into the Medical Intensive Care Unit mattress at the other. His face was grotesque with lockjaw, his teeth clamped powerfully on a plastic bite block, the only impediment to his chomping through the life supporting tube in his windpipe. His eyes were taped shut. The gown had fallen off his raised white chest, now hoisted a foot above the bed by the spasm, revealing ridges of taut muscles.

The ICU team had just witnessed the student nurse fleeing the room, terrified, tears welling up. The jarring noise of her explosive sneeze had triggered the patient's violent fit.

The room was kept as dark and quiet as an intensive care unit allowed. Any sudden stimulus could provoke the dangerous spasms induced by the deadly tetanus toxin. The only light came from partially dimmed vital sign monitors and the nurse's flashlight, and all alarms had been uncharacteristically turned off. Mechanical breath sounds still interrupted the silence every six seconds.

The patient's Registered Nurse, Lisa, showed Phineas a syringe. She whispered, "Dr. Mann, how much vecuronium do you want me to give?"

He was also whispering. "Start with 3 milligrams. We need to paralyze him before he fractures his vertebrae. And how much Versed is he on?"

"3 milligrams per hour. It *had* kept him well sedated."

"Let's help him sleep through this with an additional one-time dose of 3 milligrams."

Phineas leaned close to their patient's ear. "Sir, we're going to give you something to stop the spasms and to help you relax and sleep."

The arterial line monitor's blood pressure reading climbed to a frightening 240/120 and showed no sign of stopping. Phineas studied the flow chart. An hour before, blood pressure had been 70/40, and the nurse turned on a norepinephrine infusion to bring the reading up, but now the opisthotonus swung the man's pressure the other way.

Standing beside Phineas along the near side bed rail, two young doctors were ghostly, their eyes wide open in the excitement and dim light. "Looks like his BP is shooting up again. We better start nitroprusside to bring his pressure back down," Phineas murmured.

The nurse reached for the infusion pump controls. "It's a roller coaster. First, he's in shock, the next minute, it's accelerated hypertension."

Dr. Michael Downs, the Junior Resident in his second year out of medical school, sported a fresh blond crew cut that reflected the faint neon glow from the monitors. He shook his head slowly from side to side in awe. "Been like this since we came on service two days ago. After seeing him, *I'll* never miss *my* tetanus shot." He and his team's intern, Dr. Malcolm Carver, in his first year of internal medicine training, wore wrinkled scrubs, left over from the night's battles.

Their counterparts, today's on-call ICU house staff team, intern Dr. Ram Patel and resident Dr. Sadie Goldschmidt, both still in street clothes, watched from the even darker far side of the bed. Goldschmidt's long curly, dark brown tresses were pulled back and restrained. Patel's shiny black hair was neatly trimmed and combed. They nodded silent agreement.

They all watched the old man's backbone sink to the mattress as the paralytic gained control. His blood pressure trended toward a safer level. Phineas felt his own tense spine relax in sympathy. He let out a sigh of relief through pursed lips, and then pushed open the half-glass door. "Let's all step into the hall, so you can tell me the whole story."

From outside the old man's room number 10, Phineas could take in the entire Intensive Care Unit working area at a glance, the central nursing station with its desks and banks of vital sign monitors, the surrounding circle of closed doors to patient rooms, and the lone doctors' workroom, tucked behind the wall of illuminated screens.

It was Monday and Phineas' first day of a month-long rotation supervising the ICU teaching service. He would be the faculty's attending physician of record for May 1998, and the first two weeks would be without the usual pulmonary and critical care fellow to help with procedures and patient care. This month's fellow, Dr. Gabriela Morales-Villalobos, had gone off and gotten married and was taking a honeymoon. It had been many years since he'd covered this service without the help of a hard-working fellow. He tightened his shoulders and spine, raising him to his nearly six-foot height. Phineas was confident he could do it. He just wouldn't choose to. Homelife would suffer, and he'd hear about it.

The first day on service was the time for Phineas to impart important lessons young doctors might not think about. He began with, "We should always make sure patients are adequately sedated when we paralyze them. It can be terrifying otherwise. And I always assume they can hear me when I am speaking in the room." He thought about what had been said in front of his elderly patient and wished he'd set a better example. Phineas had done enough of this over the years to do better, even on the first day.

"Malcolm, please present his case for me."

Intern Malcolm Carver, a tall and lean young man, arranged his thin stack of index cards and stepped forward. His goatee was meticulously trimmed, and his shaved brown scalp reflected the bright overhead hall lights. "Dr. Mann, again, welcome aboard. Should be an interesting month. First case of tetanus in UNC Hospital in more than twenty years." He paused to glance at the face of each listener. "Enoch Jefferson is an 80-year-old Caucasian man, a semi-retired welder, who presented to the emergency room two days ago complaining of severe jaw and abdominal muscle spasms. While being assessed, he developed difficulty swallowing and shortness of breath. The senior surgeon they consulted for the abdominal tenderness astutely suspected tetanus, especially after he found inflamed and draining puncture wounds on an ankle. Mr. Jefferson reported that he'd been pecked there by a rooster."

Phineas couldn't stop himself from interrupting. "A rooster—and when was his last tetanus shot?"

"At that point he'd been in the ER for hours and could barely speak but managed to say that he'd never had one. Hadn't seen a doctor in over fifty years. Word got out that the ER had a case of tetanus. No one, except the senior surgeon, had ever seen a case, so the trickle of fascinated students, residents, and even professors of medicine wanting a peek turned into a flood."

Phineas guessed what came next and winced. "Not good."

Carver nodded vigorously. "It got noisy around poor Mr. Jefferson, noisy enough to trigger his first episode of opisthotonos. They had to sedate, paralyze and intubate him in a crisis mode...He's lucky he made it through it without any identifiable damage."

"And for the tetanus behind all this? What's been done for that?"

"The ER team gave him antitoxin—and his *first* tetanus vaccination. Then they called the ICU team to admit him. When I came on service the day after he was admitted, we had to restrict access to him. Too much commotion around him triggered another episode. Seems like everyone around here still hopes to see him do his thing."

RN Lisa leaned closer to Carver. "Don't ever be the most interesting case in a teaching hospital."

Like everyone else at the University of North Carolina Hospital, Phineas had heard about Jefferson, so he'd read up on tetanus. "This could go on for several weeks. We should request placement of a tracheostomy and a gastrostomy feeding tube."

Downs had been shifting his weight from one foot to the other. "Surgery's consulted. They should set those up for tomorrow or soon after."

"Good. We'll need to get consent from his next of kin."

Carver's eyes were wide open, their whites expressing dread. "I can try, but it should probably be you."

Why is he...? "I can do that. Who's his next of kin?"

"Jefferson's a widower, so it's his son, his only offspring. His son's not the first to tell me he thought I was an orderly. Now, whenever I approach him, he walks away." Carver clenched and unclenched his empty hand. "He has a stars and bars tattoo on his arm and wears an NRA hat."

"I'll talk to him, point out we're a team, and you're his father's doctor." This could turn into an unpleasant task, but his intern needed to be able to do his job. Phineas cringed inside that his first reaction was about *his* workflow, the hassle for *him*, and not the cruel and unnecessary burden a freshly minted young doctor was forced to carry.

The grimace on Carver's face suggested he hurt. "A nurse on evenings said he made a racist comment about me and said he didn't want me working with his 'Daddy.'"

"I'll talk to him."

"Name's Zebediah. Zebediah Jefferson."

Downs took a step closer to Phineas and whispered, "The nurse said he used the N-word." Carver bowed his head. The muscle along his jawline clenched as if he, a stoic man, had absorbed a blow.

Phineas' spine stiffened in sympathy. "I'm sorry, Malcolm. It's hard enough taking care of really sick patients *without* difficult families." *Oh man, I've got to deal with a throwback racist for the whole month?*

⬡⬡⬡⬡⬡

The first day on a service always felt endless for Phineas, whether it was the ICU, the pulmonary ward, or the consult service. His default mode, the compulsive approach, pushed him to read all the chart notes on all ten patients and review the labs, scans, and x-rays of each patient. Phineas wanted to be able to speak intelligently to the rush of families who would visit at the end of the day, to show them that he knew their sick loved ones well—and cared about them—which he did.

There was also his dedication to teaching, but he tried not to interrupt the team's daily work with too many comments and questions. They had a new patient to admit, procedures to perform, notes to write, and relatives to track down; and they were currently short their pulmonary fellow, Phineas' most valuable support.

Gabby Villalobos had warned him several months ago of her plans to take her yearly allotment of vacation during these first two weeks of May, two weeks she had banked since July of 1997, two weeks during which her extended family would arrive from Mexico, and she would get married and escape UNC for a honeymoon. She'd pledged to him that she would soon begin work with him on his asthma research, an invaluable extra mind and pair of hands. He'd just have to grit his teeth and handle things in the ICU without her for the next two weeks.

Ada James, the 75-year-old matriarch of a large Black family from Durham, had consumed a disproportionate portion of his day. She'd been in the ICU for almost two weeks and remained on life support. Her adult-onset diabetes had ruined her kidneys years ago, making her dependent on thrice weekly hemodialysis. In recent months her heart function had deteriorated to the point where, the instant she became dehydrated, she'd go into shock, especially during dialysis; or if the least excess fluid or demand burdened her failing cardiac pump, her lungs would flood. Even the work of breathing, normally a passive act, could stress her heart if any extra respiratory impairment was added. Her x-ray showed that the pneumonia that led to her hospitalization was improving, and her white blood cell count had come down to normal. Phineas hoped the ICU team would have the opportunity to remove her endotracheal tube and let her successfully breathe on her own before a surgical tracheostomy was advisable.

The James family had requested Phineas meet with them that evening. And Malcolm Carver had relayed with a grin that Ada James insisted, early in her stay through notes and gesticulations, that despite her tenuous condition, her luxurious black wig was to be on her head and perfectly arranged before all visitations.

That afternoon, Phineas found her propped up in bed wearing glasses and the groomed shoulder-length hairpiece. She held the television remote in her hand. He stooped over the sink to wash his hands, and the chatter from her television ceased. As he approached her bedside, she held up a clipboard with "nice to see you again" penciled across the top sheet.

He nodded. "You too. I believe I have some good news for you."

She raised her eyebrows.

He pointed at her ventilator. "I've gone over your tests and I believe there's a good chance you're ready to come off that thing and breathe on your own."

The corners of her lips curved into as much of a smile as the endo-tracheal tube in her mouth would allow. Her nurse stepped through the door. "Well, that's the first time I've seen her do that!"

Phineas gave her a moment to savor the happy news. "I'd like to learn your feelings about what we should do after the breathing and feeding tubes come out." He pointed at the tube in her nose that provided her nutrition.

Creases formed across her forehead.

"If we're right, and you do well off the ventilator, we just move on to rehab for you to regain your strength."

She nodded and her brow relaxed.

Now the hard part. "But if you start having breathing difficulties again, enough that we have to consider putting you back on the ventilator, then we have decisions to make."

She wrote, "Such as?"

"You've been on the ventilator long enough, that if we have to put the tube back in anytime soon, we suggest an operation to replace it with a shorter tube in your neck." He lightly touched the skin over her trachea. "Then you wouldn't have to have a tube in your mouth, and it would be easier to have you on and off the ventilator."

She was grimacing as she carefully printed, "You'd cut a hole in my neck?"

"A surgeon would, under anesthesia. At the same time, they could put a feeding tube directly in your stomach." He touched her left upper abdomen. "So, you wouldn't have to have it in your nose."

The tendons on the back of her hand stood out as she jabbed her finger at "hole in my neck". She glanced up at Phineas before she wrote, "permanent?"

He shook his head. "Usually not. Once you're off the ventilator for a while and doing better, it can be removed."

She wrote, "MY VOICE?"

"It can come back over time."

She shook her head and mouthed words Phineas couldn't interpret. He pointed at the clipboard. She took up the pencil and stared at the paper before she printed, "need it for singing in church". She looked up at him then back at her words and started writing again. "and for words of wisdom for my family".

"I understand. Think about it some more, and we can discuss it with them."

As she wrote this time, she pressed down hard enough that Phineas thought the pencil lead might break. "NO Hole" appeared.

He nodded. "Decisions are yours." *Now the harder part.* "So, if you needed the ventilator at some point in the future, you'd want us to replace the breathing tube to provide it?" He pointed at the endotracheal tube again.

She hastily printed "OR?". The forehead creases returned.

He considered different ways of answering and settled on, "Or not replace it and keep you comfortable with medications, while we treat you as best we can without the life support of the ventilator."

She stared at him for several seconds then out the window where clouds had drifted over the late afternoon sun. She picked up the pencil and wrote "I'm at peace with my dying." She tapped the lead on the paper several times then continued. "My family isn't."

She'd provided the marching orders. "So, Ms. Ada, if you need the ventilator in the future, we'll replace the tube to provide it."

She put down the pencil, nodded, and closed her eyes. Her head settled back into her pillow.

Phineas rested his hand softly on her forearm. "I'll let your family know you and I discussed this—and we'll be back soon." Ada's nurse glided in from the doorway, around the foot of the bed, and pulled up a chair. She grasped her patient's hand as Phineas washed his hands and departed.

At 6 PM Phineas circled back to Ada James' room and washed his hands for what felt like the hundredth time that day. He glanced in the mirror over the sink and noticed the beginnings of crows' feet. His black beard now contained faint brushstrokes of white on each side of his chin, reminiscent of their first dog Amos' aged face, his family's late and beloved Labrador retriever. A fleeting smile came and went at the memory and the reminder that he wasn't a young man anymore.

Her nurse had again positioned Ada James sitting upright. When she saw Phineas at her number 9 door, she waved. Two middle-aged women in pressed slacks and blazers stood at her bedside and turned worried looks in his direction. Their stylish greying hair and facial resemblance said "sisters." The closer of the two extended her right hand. "You must be Dr. Mann. We're the daughters. I'm Ruth and this is Rebecca." Her left arm gestured toward her sister who exclaimed, "Finally, a doctor with some grey hairs!"

Phineas grasped Ruth's soft, warm palm. "Nice to meet you. Is there more family who'd like to meet with me?"

"Oh yeah."

"We can use the family conference room."

"Already there. Now don't you let them worry you."

Huh? He released Ruth's hand. "Ms. James, I'll meet with your family, then come back to see you again."

Phineas held open the conference room door for the James sisters. The loud buzz of conversation inside immediately quieted. A multigenerational crowd had packed itself into the confined space down the hall from the ICU workspaces, and at least twenty pairs of eyes studied his face. Several stood, including a cluster of tall young men in the back corner behind the long table. Two wore red satin jackets and Chicago Bulls ball caps, like the ones in newspaper photos Phineas had seen of men reported to be gang members. Was this a reason to be concerned? Rising above them was a man with a solemn expression under a black durag. His matching t-shirt was stretched over a muscular chest and arms.

Phineas felt a tap on his shoulder. "You Dr. Ma-ann?" The words came from behind him in the hallway. The drawl gave his name an extra syllable.

He turned toward the voice and the odor of stale tobacco smoke, the source a compact, middle-aged, white man with a three-day growth of salt and pepper beard. His denim shirt displayed *Jefferson and Son Welding* over the pocket, and tiny burn holes peppered the front. The sleeves were rolled up past a Confederate flag tattoo on his right forearm. His sweat-stained camouflage patterned ball cap read "NRA". A faint whiff of alcohol made Phineas take a step back.

Whew! Doesn't need to wear his bigotry on his sleeve. It's embedded in his flesh.

"Yes, Sir. I'm Dr. Mann."

"Good. I wanna talk to you 'bout my Daddy, Enoch Jefferson."

Phineas held out his hand. "Glad you're here. I was going to look for you. We need to talk."

"Got that right." The man extended a hand that was laced with threads of healed burn scars. His index and middle fingers were stained amber from cigarette tar. "Zebediah Jefferson."

Phineas gripped Jefferson's callus-lined rough skin. "I'll meet with you right after my meeting with this family."

Jefferson peered inside the conference room, then at Phineas. Pockmarked eyebrows and parched lips pinched into a frown. "You gonna meet with *them* first?"

"I am. I'll look for you as soon as we finish."

"I *might* still be here." He squinted and shook his head slowly before he stormed away, hands balled into fists.

"I'll see you then." Phineas said to the man's back, before he stepped into the conference room and pulled the door closed.

Ruth offered him an empty chair next to her. "Smelled like trouble out there." She leaned close. "He was in the waiting room with us, then left. Our numbers may have overwhelmed the poor man."

Her soothing voice settled Phineas, and he forced a smile. Two children sitting across from him at the table were coloring in a shared book. He somehow felt more comfortable in this crowded room than he had alone with Zebediah Jefferson. "Thank you all for coming. I'm Dr. Mann. I've spent today getting to know Ms. James, so let me summarize her condition, then explain what we feel we should do next."

Ruth held up her hands, palms up. "The floor's yours. Tell us about Ms. Ada."

"You all know that Ms. Ada has needed kidney dialysis for years, probably from her diabetes." The sisters nodded. "And I'm sure you've been told that her heart has been gradually failing, what we call cardiomyopathy."

A voice from the back: "That's right."

"If anything puts more stress on her, the heart failure can cause fluid to back up into the lungs, and the pneumonia that brought her into the hospital did just that."

Another voice: "Tell it."

"All signs suggest that her pneumonia has improved on treatment." Phineas wondered if an "Amen" was coming next. "I believe we may have a chance to get her off the respirator tomorrow, if she stays stable overnight."

Rebecca clapped her hands. "Praise the Lord!"

"The hard decision will be what to do if she has difficulty after." Puzzled looks replaced smiles.

Ruth stared, on guard, then broke the silence. "You'd put her back on the ventilator, wouldn't you?"

"*I* would. *She* might feel otherwise at some point. We usually discuss performing a tracheostomy, if it looks like more time on the ventilator." He waited for his words to sink in. "She has indicated that she doesn't want that."

"Why wouldn't she?" Ruth's lips pressed into a straight line.

"It's an operation to move the breathing tube to an opening surgically created in her windpipe below her voice box. It makes it easier and safer to give her trials off the ventilator." Phineas considered offering to draw a picture on the chalkboard and rejected the idea as potentially too graphic for some—and time-consuming. He was tired after the long day.

Ruth had flinched at the word 'windpipe'. "So, what's her objection?"

"It makes speech difficult."

"And singing, I assume."

"Yes." He offered a single nod.

"I see." Ruth pulled her head back and tucked her chin as if to protect her own throat. "Would this be permanent?"

"If she continues to improve, we may be able to remove it eventually and let the site heal. Her voice should come back over time." He scanned the unrevealing faces around him.

Rebecca raised a hand. "What if she continues to refuse the operation?"

"We can still put a tube similar to what she has now back in, but eventually it tends to damage the vocal cords and windpipe. Or we can accept whatever happens off the respirator and keep her comfortable." Phineas blinked and waited.

"You mean let her die." After Rebecca's words all the pairs of eyes turned from her to Phineas.

"If that's what she tells us." The silence was a crushing weight. "This is always a difficult decision."

Ruth gestured at her family, sweeping her arm from left to right. "We'll need to talk about this—and talk with Mother. What time will you see her in the morning?"

"Would 9 or 10 work for you? That would be around the time we'd consider removing the tube."

"Rebecca and I will see you at 9."

"Does anyone have any other questions?" He hoped for none. It felt like their eyes were all drilling into him.

One of the young men in red stepped forward. "What if she doesn't want the tube put back in—and we don't agree with her?" Did his tone reflect anger or sorrow?

Phineas swallowed hard. "Since her mind is working, decisions are hers. But you can let her know how you feel." He stood slowly. "I'll confirm her wishes in the morning before we consider removing her breathing tube. Thank you all again for coming." He bowed his head slightly and opened the door.

The hallway on the way back to the ICU was empty. Zebediah Jefferson was nowhere to be found, not in the waiting room nor back in his father's darkened room. Enoch Jefferson's nurse looked up from the rolling table next to his closed door where she was documenting on his worksheet. "If you're looking for his son, he left in a bit of a huff."

"He say anything?"

"Said he'd be back tomorrow, and he expected you to meet with him. Not a happy guy. Probably going for another drink. Whew! Glad he left."

"Me too. Could be a long month."

⬡⬡⬡⬡⬡

Iris smiled at Stella, their yellow lab mix, who stared at her with electric blue eyes. Stella had been shuttling from Iris to son Jacob, to daughter Martha, and back to Iris. Any random noise: a car in the neighborhood, a woodpecker knocking on one of their hardwoods, the hospital's rescue helicopter throbbing overhead, sent Stella to the door whining for Phineas. His compulsive work habits always made him run late the first day on service. She knew the drill but couldn't resist checking the clock every few minutes. Iris wanted him to arrive home soon and deal with the surprise on the deck that so worried Stella.

Years ago, The Triangle Lab Rescue service had brought Stella by to see if the Mann's home would be a good fit for her after her extraction from an abusive owner. Stella had leaped out of the Rescue truck and nuzzled Amos, their ancient black lab, bringing him back to life. He'd been on a slippery slope in his dotage at thirteen plus years old. Stella had given him another good year, what Iris had hoped for.

Phineas had claimed that Iris must have felt an immediate kinship with Stella because of their dazzling blue eyes. The first time they had stared into each other's eyes, into what he called their "cerulean connection," they had entered an unannounced challenge to not blink first. Stella had eventually curled her lip and let out a frustrated yip before she'd slunk away. After that, Iris always blinked right away and gave Stella a vigorous patting. No need to stress the gentle dog, especially after Iris had established herself as the alpha female. When Phineas kidded Iris that she had wanted Stella so much because of her blue eyes, she teased back, saying she was not planning on bleaching her auburn hair. One blond per house was enough.

And Iris couldn't help but smile at the times almost twelve-year-old Jacob would go outside to call Stella in.

"STELLA! STELLA!"

Iris would watch the movie with Jacob someday.

The dog was more agitated than usual by Phineas' late arrival. She was afraid to go outside with the buzzing mass of honey bees drooping from a limb of a potted lime tree. Jacob kept a watch through the window, his bright white protective bee jacket in hand. He was itching for the chance to capture the bivouacked swarm before dark, and his mother had told him he had to wait for his father. Seven-year-old Martha glided by every few minutes and giggled her excitement, her chestnut ponytail bouncing along with the rest of her. Her azure eyes, flecked with gold, danced from Stella, to mother, to brother, to bees.

As the sun began painting a salmon sheen on the horizon, headlights crept down the long, winding driveway. Iris heard the car door shut and waited for the front door to open. Five minutes. Ten minutes. Phineas slipped through the door and quickly closed it. Iris rose from the table and planted a kiss on his cheek. "Glad you finally made it. We couldn't wait and ate without you." Stella whined and wagged her entire back end.

Phineas stooped to pat Stella and deposited his briefcase next to the table. He then wrapped his arms around Iris, as if starved for her more than food. "Sorry. Usual first day on service."

Jacob still stood by the porch door. He had already donned his jacket and pulled the screened hood over his thick dark brown hair. Phineas chuckled when he saw him. "I heard 'em...Looks like you're ready for action."

Jacob began rocking from his toes to his heels. "Come on! Let's get 'em, Dad." Jacob's big toes peeked out from under his baggy jeans.

"Uh, Jacob. Shoes."

"Do I have to? I have flip flops on."

"Yes, you have to. Real shoes."

"Oh, okay..." His son shook his head and glanced at the ceiling.

"Now that that's settled, how d'you want to do this?"

"Put 'em in an empty deep box with some comb."

"Good. Then?

Jacob was pulling on his long goatskin gloves. "Move it to the apiary after they're all in."

"Early tomorrow morning or tonight?"

"At first light, before they start foraging."

Phineas patted Jacob's shoulder. "I already put a deep box with a couple of frames of old comb on the deck. Let me get my jacket and a flashlight. Then, you're up to bat—and don't forget shoes."

Martha had an arm around Stella's neck. "Daddy, why did the bees swarm?"

Jacob rolled his eyes behind the hood's protective screen.

Phineas sent his son the briefest of disapproving looks before he turned to his daughter. "That's how one colony of bees becomes two, Martha. Half of the bees in a hive leave with the queen, while the remaining bees make a new queen. I'll tell you more after we take care of this gift of a new colony. Okay, Honey?"

Iris cracked open the window, so she and Martha could hear through the screen. They watched the two garbed figures set the box on a chair under the writhing dark amber cluster spotlighted by the flashlight's beam. It formed an upside-down triangle as big as a basketball, its weight pulling the tree's thin limb down at least eight inches.

Jacob held the end of the bee-covered branch firmly. "You ready with the cover, Dad?"

"Ready. Give it a hard shake."

Jacob jerked the limb over the box like he was cracking a whip, causing the mass of bees to land like an exploding water balloon in the wooden hive box. The buzz escalated to a roar. Bees began spilling over the edges before Phineas gently settled the lid in place over the bulk of them. The remaining few thousand bees began swirling around the hive box, an insect tornado, before they rushed to and through the entry slot at the bottom front.

"You must have landed the queen inside," Phineas announced. "The workers are following."

Jacob knelt close to the hive entrance. Bees landed on his jacket and hood during their stampede to join their queen. Phineas was in his teaching mode. "It's amazing how gentle bees usually are when they swarm. They're in a contented state with bellies full of honey for the trip to a new home. We won't find out the hive's real personality until after they settle in for a while." The two beekeepers watched until all but a few dozen stragglers were inside.

Iris left the window long enough to extract a foil wrapped plate from the oven, return to her viewing post, and hold it up for her husband to see. "Come eat your dinner, Phineas, before it becomes petrified. You kids can have ice cream while he eats."

Phineas brushed a few straggler bees off of his son. "You can tell me how you want to move them while we eat. And you get to name this colony." He stood next to the window and unzipped his jacket. "Hey Iris. Do I get ice cream too?"

⌬⌬⌬⌬⌬

The next morning at 7:30 AM, Phineas found Dr. Ron Bullock waiting for him at the ICU nursing station. Bullock, the Infectious Disease consultant assigned to inpatients for the month of May, pored over Enoch Jefferson's record. Tall and still athletic from competitive swimming, Ron had been an Infectious Disease fellow and a friend while Phineas did his pulmonary fellowship at UNC. They had worked together on many cases back then, as the AIDS epidemic began exploding.

Phineas donned his white coat. "Got any new wisdom for the team, Ron?"

"Naw. Just keep him alive until his tetanus resolves."

"Easier said than done. We're planning on a trache and G-tube. Expect it may be a few weeks before we can get him off the vent. You agree?"

"Yup. Hey Finman, I need a favor."

"Uh oh. Why am I getting a bad feeling?"

"I want you to be on TV with me. You can be a star."

"You're the one on TV all the time." Ron had frequently been asked for TV interviews as AIDS awareness evolved in the 80s, and the stations knew him well. The camera loved his clean-shaven, handsome face, and his loquacious personality and ability to make medicine understandable kept them calling. While Phineas disliked most public appearances, he suspected Ron would love to have a regular TV gig.

"WRAL wants to do a piece on tetanus. You just need to tell the public how sick folks can get with it. I'll talk about the importance of immunizations."

"You really need me?" Phineas knew he'd appear boring next to Ron. And being on the air was something he'd rather avoid, especially after all the trouble in New Orleans twelve years ago. He cringed at the memory of the many hours spent cloistered with his defense attorney, especially those rehearsing for his *60 Minutes* segment. He was sure he wouldn't get any rehearsal this time. "Can you at least tell me what they're going to ask me?"

"Like I said, describe the symptoms, and what you're doing for him. No names, of course."

"Of course." He couldn't come up with an excuse to get out of it. "When and where?"

"2 PM. They'll set up in the front of the auditorium where we have Grand Rounds. Thanks."

Phineas looked down at his dull green tie and resolved to dispose of it later. "Wish I'd worn a better tie."

◇◇◇◇◇

When Phineas entered Ada James' room, Ruth and Rebecca were waiting for him at their mother's far bedside in front of the single window. Despite the perfect Carolina blue sky, they stared at him with worry and expectation. Today's intern, Ram Patel, and resident, Sadie Goldschmidt, filed in behind him looking freshly groomed and lined up along the opposite bedrail. Phineas greeted the sisters before washing his hands in the room's sink. "Good morning. How are you?"

Their slacks and jackets were replaced by dark sweaters over somber colored dresses. Ruth answered softly. "We're fine. How's Mother?"

"I'm happy to report that your mother had a good night, and we feel today may be our best chance for her to come off the respirator."

Rebecca rose up. "Praise God!" Her voice was more spirited, hopeful.

Ruth followed. "Thank you, Doctor."

He introduced Drs. Patel and Goldschmidt. "When our team met with your mother earlier, she communicated that she would want us to put the tube back in if she got into difficulty. Right, Ms. James?"

She nodded vigorously and put her hands together. She closed her eyes tightly, and her lips looked to be praying. The shiny-black wig had been brushed into perfection for the big day.

Phineas gave her the moment then placed his hand on her forearm. "And she let us know that she doesn't want to make a decision about a tracheostomy now—if things don't go as well as we expect them to." Ada James nodded again, this time more slowly. She directed raised eyebrows at her daughters.

Ruth settled back into her chair with a look of relief. "The family's good with that."

Rebecca leaned over her mother, straightening sheets. "When will you do it?"

On that cue, Ava Jones, the respiratory therapist, entered the room. Phineas gestured to her and smiled. She signaled thumbs up and opened her equipment bag. Ava had restrained her long black hair in a braid tucked under a scrub shirt and covered most of her colorful tattoos with a brightly hued, long-sleeved cotton undershirt. A few vivid images managed to escape on her lower neck. Ava had joined the RT staff at UNC Hospital months after she learned that Phineas, her medical director at New Orleans' Baptist Hospital, had returned to Chapel Hill after charges against him were dismissed. Hurricane Jezebel had also displaced Ava from her Baptist job and trashed her New Orleans home. Phineas had put in a good word for her those years back.

He turned to the sisters. "Now is good for us. I'll find you in the waiting room as soon as we're finished."

Ruth and Rebecca each kissed their mother's cheek before they bustled out the door.

⬡⬡⬡⬡⬡

An hour later, Phineas found the sisters in the large generously windowed waiting room just outside the ICU's double metal doors. They sat across from each other, hands locked, eyes closed, mouthing prayers with the morning sun lighting up their faces. Two small children, too young for school, spotted his white coat and pressed against the women. Ruth and Rebecca rose to their feet and searched his face.

"It went well."

"Thank you, Jesus!" The two proclaimed to the ceiling almost in unison.

"She'll be wearing oxygen, and she'll be hoarse from the tube, so please only let her whisper for now."

Ruth brought her voice down almost to a whisper. "When can we go back?"

"Now is fine."

Rebecca stared at the children and pointed to the chair she had occupied. "You two sit there. One of us will be *right* back, so you *both* had better be in that chair."

The sisters exited the room and the children scampered into the indicated seat. They stared at Phineas with eyes wide and mouths puckered.

He lowered himself into the facing chair, accepting the breather. "So, what are *your* names?"

⬡⬡⬡⬡⬡

Phineas worried that he or his coworkers might let feelings about a family member affect their care of a patient. He couldn't let that happen. He found the interns and residents gathered in the workroom before the previous night's team went home.

He took a seat in the circle of chairs pulled into the room's center. "There's something I feel like I should say. You are all good people, and I know you always provide the best possible care for *all* your patients. There can be times when a family member, or even a patient, may offend us with their words. We can't let this prejudice us against someone we're caring for. We need to rise above and try to change by example."

Downs still wore rumpled scrubs, and his tired eyelids drooped halfway down like window shades lowered for a nap. He cleared his throat to speak. "Don't worry, Dr. Mann. We all talked about it and decided that, once we get him off the ventilator, Enoch Jefferson will be our nicest patient ever."

⬡⬡⬡⬡⬡

At the 2 PM television taping, Phineas' image stared back at him on the monitor next to the camera. Chelsea LaFever, of WRAL's Healthbeat and morning news program, sat on the left side behind a long table. Her long brassy blond hair and scarlet dress lit up the screen. Newspapers speculated as to how long it would be before she moved to a principal spot on the evening news, and then how long such a glamorous personality would stay with this local TV station before moving to a nationwide network program.

Bullock enjoyed the middle seat next to her, and Phineas occupied the right. Each wore their white coats, but Bullock's 6' 4" height and lean build made his look tailored and longer. Chelsea was smiling widely, ready for her audience. The cameraman silently counted down on his fingers, 5, 4, 3, 2, 1, and pointed at her.

"We have breaking news. A deadly disease from ancient times has shown up at the University of North Carolina Hospital. Tetanus. This is the first time there has been a case in North Carolina in decades. We have Dr. Ron Bullock from Infectious Diseases and Dr. Phineas Mann from the Intensive Care Unit with us today. Dr. Bullock, why haven't we seen this condition in a long time?"

Bullock directed his broad smile toward the camera. "Because tetanus shots have been part of routine healthcare for more than 50 years, and they completely prevent it."

"Then how did this patient get it?" Chelsea's face tilted toward him.

"I am told that the patient hadn't seen a doctor in a very long time and had never had a tetanus shot." His smile left him.

She pulled her shoulders back and perfected her posture. "How does a shot prevent it?"

"The shot causes us to make antibodies to the toxin that the bacteria in an infected wound makes. The toxin is what causes the symptoms. The antibodies bind to the toxin to prevent it from making us sick."

"What kind of a wound is necessary for this to happen?" Her nose wrinkled when she pronounced "wound."

"A cut or puncture, for example. I am told this patient was pecked by a rooster." Bullock stared at the camera, waiting for Chelsea's response.

Her perfect posture became even more erect. "Pecked by a rooster!" She turned toward Phineas. "Dr. Mann, how did you know this was a case of tetanus?"

Phineas smiled back at her before realizing he should face the camera. "I wish I could say that I made the diagnosis. Our astute surgeon, Dr. Frederick Cutler, figured it out after he was called to see the patient for abdominal pain. The tetanus toxin can cause pain from powerful muscle spasms, sometimes in the abdomen, and often in the face and jaw. Hence the old name 'lockjaw.'"

"So how then is it dangerous?"

"The toxin can also affect breathing muscles and swallowing muscles, and there can be total body spasms, so violent they can break bones."

Her golden hair twirled as her focus shifted abruptly from Phineas back to the camera. "Oh my! What can you do for someone who gets it?"

"A patient is given antitoxin, and a tetanus shot. But it can take several weeks for the symptoms to go away, during which we have to provide support on a ventilator. And blood pressure can be very high or low from one minute to the next, so intravenous medicines are needed to correct this. We have to sedate and often paralyze patients to keep them from fracturing the bones in their back."

Her perpetual smile faded. "I'm glad this has become a rare condition."

Bullock leaned into his table microphone. "This is why it is so important to keep up with vaccinations. Please everyone, review these with your doctor at your next checkup."

"Well, thank you, doctors. This is Chelsea LaFever with WRAL Healthbeat, reporting from UNC Hospitals. Make sure you get your tetanus shot!" She recovered her smile for the camera until the producer standing behind the cameraman announced, "That's a wrap."

Chelsea unfastened the clip-on microphone from her dress, leaned back and crossed her legs. "Thanks, guys. And Ron, you be sure to let me know whenever you've got something else big for me."

Ron cocked his head. "You know I always call you first, Chelsea."

Phineas raised his eyebrows at their suggestive flirtation. "Well, *this* guy needs to get back to work." *I'm so outta here.*

⬡⬡⬡⬡⬡

As Phineas decided where to start his Tuesday evening patient rounds, Enoch Jefferson's nurse, Lisa, waved him over to the central nursing station, where she was seated and writing on patient flow sheets while inspecting the extensive panels of monitors at intervals. Lisa had worked in the University of North Carolina Hospital's Medical Intensive Care Unit longer than Phineas. She'd reached a status where she only had to work the coveted weekday shifts, a schedule that kept her out of the sun, so her skin remained smooth and porcelain white. He'd seen her go from slender to portly with a succession of children over the years. She pointed her index finger at her patient's closed door. "He's here, and he's not alone."

Phineas swallowed and wiped his palms on his coat. "How's his son's mood today? And who's with him?"

"He seems a little better. Maybe behaving to impress the younger woman with him. She's wearing a nurse's uniform. Says she works at the Durham VA Hospital."

"Maybe she can help with him?"

Lisa surprised him with a doubtful expression. "We'll see."

"Anything new to report since earlier?"

"Still heavily sedated and paralyzed. Surgeons want to do his trache and g-tube first thing in the AM. Needs consents signed."

"You have the forms?"

She pulled the loose-leaf binder that held Jefferson's paper chart from the rack and extracted two documents. Phineas noted that the surgery resident had already filled in the blanks. Only the next of kin consent signatures were missing.

"I'll see if I can get these signed." He lowered his head and trudged toward Jefferson's room, took a deep breath, cracked open the door, and stepped into darkness. Two seated shapes on the other side of the bed gradually came into focus. The narrowing sliver of light from the door briefly produced a sparkle on the one of the visitors' chest. The sparkle became a cross when Phineas' eyes adjusted to the room's dimness. The other visitor, Zebediah, lacked his NRA hat, revealing a graying flat-top buzz cut. He came out of a slouch to a rigid posture. "Glad you could finally make it, Dr. Ma-ann."

The woman was half smiling, her head tilted to the right. "Well hello, Dr. Mann. Long time no see."

Phineas struggled to place her.

No! It can't be!

She had lost weight and her long hair now sported abundant waves of highlights, but there was no mistaking the face and the silver cross that still surfaced in sporadic nightmares.

Angela!

He thought he'd put her behind, buried her in a painful past. It had taken years for her to fade from his thoughts. The misery she created had been an agonizing boil that was finally lanced and allowed to heal twelve years ago, leaving a reminder scar. Was it to fester again?

He'd last seen her in February 1986, six long and agonizing months after her claims led to his arrest, slinking away from the New Orleans courthouse after multiple second-degree murder charges against him were dropped.

She, he, and hundreds of others had endured no power or plumbing together for five unrelenting miserable days and nights in the dark, sweltering, and fetid Baptist Hospital following the floods from Hurricane Jezebel. The glint from that silver cross had reflected his headlamp beams over and over in the gloomy hospital hallways. Angela had been watching him and was the one who reported him to the authorities for giving narcotics to suffering terminal patients who'd then died. She'd claimed that Phineas euthanized them.

Then, on the Sunday evening before his scheduled trial, she'd been humiliated on *60 Minutes* in front of a national television audience. She'd charged the camera and ranted about when she was a teenager, that her long-deceased father hadn't been given a chance for a miracle cure from God, and that doctors were letting their patients die without keeping them alive for divine interventions. Her tirade had revealed her deranged motives in bringing the charges against Phineas and abruptly concluded the program.

Had she figured out that Phineas, through his lawyer, had planted the seeds in Morley Safer for interview questions that germinated into her public embarrassment?

Phineas' mouth now felt so dry he could barely speak. "Angela? How?"

She clapped her hands together and cackled. "I saw you on TV today and just had to come by and say 'Hi!'"

Now he *really* wished he could have avoided today's TV spot. "How... how do you know the Jeffersons?"

"I didn't, until today. I met Zeb in your waiting room. I was thumbing through a really interesting article in *People* magazine, and he and I just got to talking about his Daddy and you—and he asked me to come back here with him. Now wasn't that nice?"

Nice. Not his feelings about either of them. "How long have you been in North Carolina?"

"Oh, a couple of years now. I got a great job in the Durham VA's Medical ICU. You know how much I *love* ICU medicine. And here I even get to see a rare case of tetanus in *your* ICU."

Phineas wanted to end this conversation. He glanced at the papers in his hand and leaned next to Enoch Jefferson's ear. "We're going to talk about you now, Mr. Jefferson." He stood erect and addressed Angela. "I need to talk with Mr. Jefferson about procedures for his father." Turning, he faced Zebediah. "Mr. Jefferson, do you want Ms. Portier to step out or stay while we talk?" He hoped for her immediate dismissal.

Zebediah stretched his neck to squint at the consent forms. "Yeah. I'd like her to stay. She knows more 'bout this stuff than I ever will...an' I trust her."

Wish I did.

Phineas arranged the forms on the bedside table and adjusted its height to Zebediah's level. He pointed at the first sheet. "This form is to give our surgeon consent to place a tracheostomy. That's an operation on your father's windpipe to create an opening for a short breathing tube. We can then attach it to the ventilator and remove the longer breathing tube in his mouth."

Zebediah winced. "You mean you're gonna have 'em cut a hole in his neck?"

"Tetanus probably won't get better for several weeks, and the tube he has in his throat now is uncomfortable and can eventually injure his airway and vocal cords. The tracheostomy also makes it easier to wean him off the ventilator faster. It can be removed after he is better, and the incision will heal."

"What's this other paper for?" He looked up from the consent form and stared at Phineas.

Phineas pointed at the clear plastic nasogastric tube protruding from Enoch Jefferson's nose. "We are feeding your father every four hours through this tube. It's rough on his nose, and the chance of the liquid feedings soiling and harming his lungs is higher than if we feed him through a tube placed directly in his stomach." He gestured at the old man's abdomen. "The surgeon can place a shorter tube here through a small incision, and we can remove the tube from his nose. It's called a feeding gastrostomy, and it can be placed at the same time as the tracheostomy. They should be able to do both tomorrow."

Zebediah sat back and looked up at Phineas. "Ain't he too sick for an operation? Must be risky."

Phineas needed to be honest but to avoid alarming the son, if he was going to get this done. "Any procedure has some risk. We believe the risks for these procedures is small and less than leaving in the tubes he has now. Our surgeons do these frequently. The list of risks is printed on these lines. Any operation lists bleeding, infection, and even death as risks." He pointed at a bold paragraph at the bottom of each page. "The chance of any of these happening is very low and less risk overall than continuing without these procedures in someone likely to be ill as long as your father is." He leaned over Enoch Jefferson. "If you're awake and listening, Mr. Jefferson, I'm asking your son to give permission for two procedures, so we can get these uncomfortable tubes out of your nose and mouth."

Zebediah squinted at the forms in silence before he pivoted on his seat to look at Angela. "Sound right to you, Angela?"

She placed her hand on his arm, next to the flag tattoo. "They're pretty routine procedures in your Daddy's circumstances, Zeb Honey."

Phineas felt a shiver run down his spine at their sudden familiarity. *Zeb Honey?* He offered Zebediah his pen.

"Okay, Doc. Now where do I put my John Henry?"

Martha appeared in faded t-shirt and cut-off jeans, materializing somehow out of thin air, at Iris' side. Iris was seated at her desk, immersed in her end of semester student grading, trying to make sure she was negotiating the university's new website correctly. Martha tugged at her mother's tee shirt. "Mom, we need to pick."

Iris had to force herself to look at her daughter and away from the lure of the computer screen. "What looks ready?" She knew she had to assume the dreaded mantle of harvesting vegetables and berries when Phineas was on service. During the other months, the garden was his and Martha's and was kept in the perfect order he craved. When he was on the ICU service, he could only make guest appearances on his garden stage, and his shy daughter missed working it with him.

Martha held up a bowl and a colander, her expert guess at harvest necessities. "I saw some raspberries and strawberries. Definitely snap peas, spinach and lettuce. And nice round radishes."

"Too soon for potatoes?"

Harvesting potatoes was Martha's favorite. Iris recalled that it had once been Jacob's, but he had outgrown the wonder of plunging a hand into soil and feeling around for the buried treasure of potatoes. Iris had once also briefly enjoyed it. Then she became too busy with career and kids. Phineas and Martha had yet to outgrow that simple pleasure.

Her daughter shook her head. "Geesh, Mom. Not even close. Not till the plants turn yellow."

"Okay, Girl, let's show Daddy what we can do." She sighed and logged out of the site for the University of North Carolina School of Social Work. Iris wanted to encourage Martha's initiative. It could be easy for her young daughter to settle into the role of silent spectator in their chaotic household, to exist in the long shadow created by her boisterous and cantankerous preadolescent brother.

Martha sprinted out the door with Stella trailing, as if the dog were pulled into a strong current. The Mann backyard operation had started with a couple of beehives soon after they bought the house in 1989. Right away, Phineas had planted blackberry and raspberry canes along the back fence that separated yard from forest. Then blueberry bushes and a fig tree. Then he built a raised bed for greens and tomatoes, then another, and another...

Iris had to admit that pulling fresh pea pods off their vines and selecting perfect lettuce leaves gave her a modest thrill—what Phineas called "the harvest high." But the weeding—Ugh! Once she'd experienced the guilt of ignoring Phineas' plantings for too long, and the tender shoots became smothered with weeds during his work-related absence. After a long day at work, he discovered this and silently labored to weed the garden and arrange the plants the way he liked them, needed them. In perfect order. Like when he cooked complicated dishes, calling his method "mise en place," everything in its place.

Iris knew his personality and had vowed to never let chaos reign again in his absence, so she knelt and pulled at tufts of whatever looked out of place, confident that if she mistakenly pulled one of Phineas' seedlings, he'd forgive her. And he always planted way too many seeds anyway, necessitating the painful thinning of the tiny overcrowded seedlings.

Stella, head down, commenced dutifully digging at her side, shooting sprays of dirt from her front paws between her splayed back legs. Iris grabbed Stella's collar and pulled her back. "Whoa, Girl. We're going to eat some of that."

Martha called Stella and rewarded her with a raspberry.

Iris laughed and warned, "Careful. She might learn to harvest those on her own. Then we won't get *any*." Stella rolled onto her back in the mulch and let out a contented groan.

⬡⬡⬡⬡⬡

On the first days of Phineas' months covering the ICU, Iris always expected him to be stooped over from the weight of the service on his shoulders, but this time, as he stepped through the door, his grim expression suggested dread more than fatigue. "You look like you've seen a ghost."

"I did."

Jacob looked up from his math homework and closed the workbook on the kitchen table. "What? You saw a ghost, Dad?"

Martha raced into the room. "A ghost? Where? In our house?" Her usual sunny expression had disappeared. Her eyes were round.

Hoping to calm her troops, Iris stepped close to Phineas to give him a quick hug and peck on his cheek. She turned back to face the children. "It's just an expression. No one saw a ghost."

He pulled out the chair next to Jacob and sat. "Close enough. I saw Angela Portier."

Iris collapsed into the seat across from Phineas. Painful memories of Angela Portier taunting Phineas in a restaurant began forcing their way back. The young nurse had been trying to send him to the Louisiana State Prison, claiming he'd euthanized patients after Hurricane Jezebel flooded their hospital. "Maybe it was someone who looked like her."

"No...She's lost weight and lightened her hair...but it was her."

Martha fidgeted while she stood next to Phineas. He put his arm around her and held her close. She looked straight into his eyes. "Who is Angela Por-tee-ay?"

Iris spoke softly to avoid alarming Martha. "She's someone we knew a long time ago. Why don't you kids go watch TV for a little while? Then we'll have supper."

Jacob looked even more puzzled. "You *want* us to watch TV?"

"Yes. Now. Scoot. Both of you."

Jacob whispered to Martha as they left the room. "She *never* wants us to watch TV."

Iris waited until she heard voices from a rerun of *The Cosby Show*. "Could she try to cause trouble here?"

Phineas still wore a glum face. "She acted friendly... *too* friendly."

"So, you *talked* to her?"

"Couldn't help it. She made friends with the son of one of our sickest patients. He's leaning on *her* now for advice."

"Ohhh, Phineas. I've got a bad feeling about this."

"I had a bad feeling about the patient's son even before *she* arrived and got involved."

Iris covered her face with her hands. She'd met Angela at the Baptist Hospital ICU Christmas party during their first holiday season in New

Orleans. Angela was chatty and barely out of nursing school. She begged Iris to call her to do things together. Iris was busy with her frail mother and a new job as a Tulane Hospital social worker and promptly forgot about Angela and everyone else at the party. Did she innocently offend Angela and contribute to her vendetta against Phineas? Did Angela decide that Iris considered herself too good for her?

Then there was Angela bringing murder charges against Phineas, charges that put them through six months of misery before they were dismissed. Was she somehow coming after him again, after she'd failed to destroy his life the first time?

⬡⬡⬡⬡⬡

The nightstand's digital clock announced 4:05 AM in neon red. Iris' gentle, rhythmic breaths beside him were the only sounds. Phineas stretched out flat on his back and stared at the ceiling. *Angela! Damnit!* He thought he'd seen the last of his accuser. It had been years since he'd finally ceased spending waking energy thinking about her, but that hadn't kept her from still sneaking into a random bad dream, one that always left him with his tee-shirt dampened with sweat.

Angela had come to his office during his first exhausted sleep after Hurricane Jezebel left New Orleans flooded and the hospital running on backup power. He'd worked at least forty hours straight in crisis mode before immediately dropping into deep sleep, almost a coma, on the floor of his windowless office. She'd awakened him with her penlight shining in his eyes, only to ask for orders for a sleeping pill for a patient. A sleeping pill! The first thing he'd seen was her silver cross dangling in his face. Had she been watching him then too?

He'd barely gone back to sleep when Ava, his trusted respiratory therapist, had shaken him awake, yelling that the generators had failed, that the entire hospital was without power. She needed him immediately in the ICU where all the ventilators were consuming their limited battery backup. He followed her into the hallway outside his office at the moment Angela returned, thus she'd witnessed Ava and him leaving his office and assumed the worst. In a bizarre rant, she accused him, in the midst of the pitch-black chaos, of infidelity.

That was when the real nightmare began. The disabled hospital was so hot! And the horrible ever-present stench after the plumbing failed and the toilets backed up. And the patients who deteriorated in the intolerable conditions. How they suffered! The disoriented ones had no understanding, only fear and agony. He'd given a few hopeless, terminal patients approaching their deaths precious doses of morphine. Then, after they passed on, Angela accused him of euthanasia and announced her intentions to report him to authorities. He'd hoped she was just sleep-deprived and temporarily irrational. Until he was arrested weeks later.

Phineas replayed the scene when he may have saved Angela's life. On the way to a helicopter evacuation from the crippled Baptist Hospital, a heart patient had suffered a cardiac arrest and collapsed in ankle-deep water. At the man's side first with the defibrillator, Angela was poised to shock him with the paddles fully charged. Phineas arrived just in time to convince her to wait until they dragged the unconscious man to a dry area. Phineas may have stopped her from shocking herself, maybe into her own cardiac arrest. If he hadn't been there, hadn't interrupted her, he might have never...been...arrested. He shook his head to clear those dark thoughts. They weren't who he was.

He thought he'd escaped her. First, after the five days of horror when the Good Samaritan, Malachi, rescued him in his flat-bottomed skiff outside the evacuated hospital's emergency room loading dock surrounded by foul, murky flood water. Then, the real escape months later, when his lawyer, Simon, burst into Phineas' pretrial breakfast, to announce that all the charges were dropped after Angela's unhinged performance on *60 Minutes*. Phineas was free—but would he ever *truly* be free? Would she let it out here in Chapel Hill that he'd once been charged with murder?

5:10 AM. Might as well get up. Get a head start on the day. What could happen that would be worse than what he'd already suffered through?

⬡⬡⬡⬡⬡

Ron Bullock waited patiently in a seat at the ICU nurses' station for Phineas to finish writing his note in Ada James' chart and to notice him.

"Hey Ron, what's up?"

"WRAL wants me to do another interview."

Phineas closed the chart. "I hope you're not here to ask me to be on again." *Once brought a demon from the past. Would Satan himself be next?*

"You're safe this time, but you still owe me."

Safe? Hah! If you only knew. "I thought I paid my debt with the last show."

Ron leaned on his elbows and grinned. "You did, for my contribution to your legal defense fund years ago. But there's also the current matter of my taking care of your mother-in-law. That's a recurring charge."

Phineas had to admit that Ron had done him a huge favor when he'd agreed to care for Sarah Jane and her recurrent lung infections after she'd moved to North Carolina. He suspected that while she challenged Ron on all his decisions, he found her feistiness entertaining, like the time she asked if he had even one antibiotic that wouldn't make her want to come back from the grave to haunt him.

Phineas had to ask, "What're you going to talk about this time?"

"Measles."

"Really? You got a case?" Hadn't heard that one in a very long time.

Ron's ever-present smile left him. "No, but we need to remind folks to vaccinate their kids."

"Thought getting a Measles Mumps Rubella vaccination was standard."

"It is, but some Brit published a paper claiming a link between autism and the MMR vaccine." Ron sounded disgusted.

"Was the study any good?" Phineas knew a colleague whose youngest child, a son, had autism. His behaviors disrupted the whole family's previously comfortable routines, throwing their lives into chaos.

Ron shook his head and frowned. "Naw—Only 12 kids. He claimed their autism came on after the MMR shot."

"How can he say it was the shot since the age for getting the MMR could be about when autism might show up?"

Ron nodded. "Precisely. The problem is the Internet."

"What's happening on the Internet?" Phineas had transitioned almost fully from hard copy journal research to scientific Internet search engines for his asthma studies. Even though it was 1998, he hadn't yet completely given up flipping through specific topics in the massive, printed volumes of *The Index Medicus*, the old school search method.

"Groups are promoting not vaccinating children, and the numbers are growing. It's still early—but could explode." Ron's hands flipped up in front of his face to simulate a bomb detonating.

"Scary," Phineas murmured.

"You're telling me. All it takes is a case, and a bunch of unprotected kids..." Ron raised his voice so loud that all the nurses near the station turned to watch and listen.

Phineas barely remembered having measles. By his mother's report, he and his sister were miserable. At least neither developed any of the possible serious complications. "Sounds like a good reason for you to go back on TV. Maybe it'll help."

Ron stood and addressed his audience. "The problem is, those against vaccination are feeding off each other on the Internet. *We* put stuff on it about the dangers of not getting shots, but they don't even look at our stuff, much less believe it. They only read what they want to hear."

"Well, good luck." Phineas put Ada James' chart in the rack and selected the next one. "So, you'll be on again with Chelsea LeFever?"

Ron winked. "Someone has to do it."

⬡⬡⬡⬡⬡

Phineas walked by Ada James room—then did a double-take. There she was, receiving one of her thrice-weekly hemodialysis treatments. Still, instead of reclining and resting during the procedure, she sat at attention, smiling, her wig primped into place, oxygen tubing under her nose. The size of a refrigerator, the dialysis machine's pumps were rotating slowly like miniature Ferris wheels, moving bright red cleansed blood back into her upper arm. The tall man who'd worn the black durag and stood silently in the back during the family meeting, deposited a light kiss on Ms. Ada's forehead after he arranged her blanket over her shoulders. He took the chair across the bed and looked from her face to the tubes full of flowing bright red blood.

Phineas entered her room, not sure of the visitor's connection. "Ms. James seems quite pleased to see you."

The visitor stood and offered his hand. His now uncovered shaved scalp rose a head above Phineas, and he had at least forty pounds on him, much of it in his broad shoulders. "I'd hope she be glad to see her first grandson. She helped raise me. I'm Jericho."

Phineas shook the meaty hand. "Nice to meet you. Your grandmother seems to be holding up fairly well without the breathing machine, so far."

"You're not gonna send her outta' here yet, are you?" His expression morphed from at ease to concerned.

"Not yet. We want to see her stable in the ICU for at least a couple more days."

Ada James waved her free hand. "You boys worry too much." Her weak voice was raspy. "I feel fine, just tired...Dialysis always takes it out of me for a while."

Jericho shook his head at her. "Now you listen to your doctor. You need to get stronger before you leave the ICU."

As per his routine, Phineas inspected her lunch tray. A forkful or two was missing from the chicken with rice and the once green beans, now boiled to an olive hue. "Looks like you didn't think much of the main course."

"Sorry." She shook her head. "They do their best, but I'm spoiled."

He couldn't blame her. None of it looked appetizing. A spoon was planted in a half empty chocolate pudding cup. "I hope you can do better with your eating, Ms. James. You need calories and protein to heal, and we still need to regulate your insulin."

"Dialysis takes my appetite," she answered softly. "I'll do better with supper. Maybe they'll put some salt and spices in it."

"The dieticians are pretty stingy with salt for kidney and heart patients."

"Wish they'd add salt to my tray on my dialysis days. They take it and any extra fluid off with that machine anyway, so why not let me have some to give the hospital food a little taste?"

"Good point. I'll talk to our dietician. See what she can do."

Jericho took a step toward the door. "Hey, Doc, got a minute to talk outside?"

Ada James shot him a wide-eyed look, her head tilted forward. "Now don't you boys be sayin' things about me behind my back!"

"Don't worry Gramma. I wouldn't dare." He strode into the hallway.

Phineas followed. "She's really enjoying your visit."

"Thanks, Doc. Family's happy." He collected his thoughts. "I think I need to warn you about something."

"Oh?" Didn't he just say the family was happy?

"That dude with the NRA hat and the flag on his arm."

Phineas tried to keep his expression even. "The visitor to Room 10? Has he done something?"

"Just stare and look mean, so far. But I saw his truck in the parking deck. Side said Jefferson and Son Welding."

"Must be his."

"It's nasty." Jericho scowled. "White Power bumper sticker. Gun rack...I peeked inside and saw an ammunition clip on the floor, stickin' out under the seat, might have been one of those high-capacity ones. Hard to tell."

Phineas considered whether he should or could do anything and came up empty. "Let me know if he does or says anything, and I'll let security know."

"I'm not worried 'bout me, and my brothers can take care of themselves." His powerful hands had transformed into fists.

Phineas now understood he was indeed being warned.

"I heard him tell that nurse lady he was with that his Daddy *better* get better..." Jericho whispered. "I didn't like the way he said it."

"Thank you, Jericho. I appreciate your concern." Phineas shook Jericho's hand again. "You probably want to get back to your grandmother."

Phineas lingered in the quiet hallway, his heartbeat pulsing in his ears. Just how dangerous was Zebediah Jefferson to him and his team—and to Ada James' family? Jericho didn't come across as wanting to cause trouble. Should he bring security into it, or would that raise everyone's tension and fan embers into flames?

⬡⬡⬡⬡⬡

Phineas spotted Jacob pacing on the lawn next to the driveway. His son had collected the hive smoker, the crate of pine needles Phineas kept for fuel, and hive tools, the flat metal devices for prying components of the hive apart. Their beekeeping jackets lay nearby next to the garage doors. Jacob's long goatskin gloves dangled from his jeans' back pocket. He'd clearly received the message that Phineas had finished rounds and was on his way home.

"Looks like you want to inspect the swarm hive."

"It's been four days. We should look for eggs and the queen."

"Remember, she may not start laying right away. The workers shake her for days to shrink her abdomen before they swarm, so she's light enough to fly. Her ovaries, where eggs come from, need to get back to full size." Jacob started to frown, causing Phineas to soften. "Okay. Lemme say 'Hi' to your mother and Martha. Then I'll change my clothes and be right out. You can light the smoker."

"All right!" Jacob grabbed a handful of dry pine straw and stuffed it in the metal canister as Phineas hurried inside.

Returning in jeans and t-shirt, Phineas donned his beekeeping jacket as Jacob enthusiastically pumped the metal smoker's bellows to belch long white clouds from its conical spout.

Phineas laughed. "Hey! Save some fuel for the hive. Remember to give them only enough smoke for them to get a whiff. We don't want to fumigate them."

"Yeah. Sure, Dad. Ready?"

"Ready." They strode to the backyard apiary, three hives tucked on the edge of the woods in the back of their lot. Trees to the west mostly shaded the southeast facing hives from the hot late afternoon sun. Each morning, the dawn's rays warmed the workers and sent them out on their foraging missions. Father and son took inspection positions behind the box containing the swarm, well out of the colony's bees' flight path from the hive's entrance in its front.

Jacob gave a gentle puff at the entrance then pried open the outside cover. It produced a soft 'pop' as it came loose from the bees' propolis seal, the organic glue they manufactured. Dark, some almost black, bees marched over the inside cover. A troubling number lifted their stingers in a warning posture. Jacob pumped the smoker, sending a cloud through them. Many retreated through the ventilation hole in the inside cover onto the ten frames underneath, each a removable sheet of wax comb surrounded by wood frames suspended in the protective wooden hive body. Jacob inserted the hive tool under the edge of the wooden lid and levered it loose, making another 'pop'. Worker bees erupted from the frames and began colliding with the outside of Jacob's veiled hood. A few hit Phineas' hood in warning. Jacob responded with a defensive plume of smoke and stepped back.

Phineas peeked into the spaces between frames as more agitated workers were pouring out. "They're pretty spicy today. Better put on our gloves." He began pulling his on.

"Ow!" His son shook his hand and began scraping the back of it with the sharp end of the hive tool. He puffed smoke onto his hand to mask the alarm pheromone that came with the venom and hurried to glove up.

Phineas asked, "didja get the stinger out?"

"Yeah. Let's keep going." Jacob lifted a wooden frame from the center of the box with his gloved hands. He held it so the evening sun's shallow rays shone into the cells. "I see eggs!" He handed it to Phineas.

Phineas regretted he hadn't thought to put on one of the several pairs of reading glasses scattered around the house. Was his mind still drifting to Jericho's warning? He squinted hard and imagined he might see the tiny eggs in a small central patch of comb. "Wish I had your young eyes." He hated to admit he couldn't still discern the tiniest details without corrective lenses. Several bees bounced off the screen over his face. Others searched his sleeves for openings to his skin. He'd better give his undivided attention to the matter at hand and leave hospital matters behind for now.

Jacob was holding another frame. "I found the queen!" He held it over the hive and angled it so the side faced Phineas. She scrambled across its face to the other side, dragging her long abdomen, her main distinguishing feature. Finding her among the tens of thousands of worker bees always elated Phineas. Jacob looked and sounded delighted.

Phineas pointed the end of the frame he held at the hive. "Better slide that frame in carefully. Don't want to hurt her. She's clearly grown back to reproductive size." He watched Jacob replace the queen's frame then handed him the other.

Bees continued to dive-bomb them. The steady buzzing had risen to the crescendo roar of a jet's turbine engine, a sound that never ceased to thrill Phineas. He suspected his son had caught the same bug—knowing that the threat of thousands of venomous warriors was at their fingertips, but continuing to work, even under attack. Phineas felt a sting through his jeans.

"Ow! Put the top on and let's get out of here." He made his way toward the driveway and lowered his pants to inspect the sting site on his thigh. When he buckled his belt, he was not surprised to see the stinger embedded in the denim pant leg. He hollered back to Jacob, "That is one defensive hive! If they don't settle down by the end of the month, we may need to replace the queen with one who will make gentler workers."

Jacob reassembled the hive covers and followed. He unzipped his jacket and expanded his proud prepubescent chest. "I can handle 'em."

Phineas caught sight of Iris peeking around the corner of the house, her long hair in a ponytail, with Martha, like a shadow attached to her heels, gliding on the humid evening air. Their daughter chanted, "I see London. I see France. I see Daddy's underpants."

Iris was laughing. "And why is my husband taking off his pants while beekeeping?"

Jacob studied the pink, swollen area on his hand. "We both got stung."

After convincing himself that no stragglers had hitched a ride, Phineas slowly peeled off his jacket. He shoved a wad of green leaves into the smoker spout to smother the fire. "They got riled up pretty quickly."

"Just spirited females responding to two males barging in with noxious smoke." Iris had taken on a professorial tone.

"It was more than that. They're angrier than average. We might have to requeen."

"You're talking regicide in my backyard? Don't even think about 'requeening' in the big house."

Phineas chuckled at Iris' joke as he watched Jacob gathering the equipment. "Jacob, did you notice your bees' color?"

"They're a lot darker than our other bees."

"You're right. Our other bees are Italians, and they're golden."

"Think the swarm might be Africanized killer bees?"

"No way. First of all, Africanized bees are only along the Texas border, at least so far in 1998. And second, if they were Africanized bees, they'd still be chasing and stinging us, hundreds of 'em. Besides, those bees are said to usually be golden colored also."

A silent Martha gripped her mother's t-shirt, while Iris was eavesdropping. "So what kind is the swarm?"

"Dark bees could be from Carniolan, Russian or German races. Doubt they're Carniolan, 'cause Carniolan bees are supposed to be very gentle. German bees were once supposed to be mean, but it's thought there aren't many pure German bees left in the U. S., since they're mostly all interbred now. German bees were the first honey bees brought to North America by European settlers. The American Indians hated to spot them on flowers, because they knew white settlers wouldn't be far behind. They called those mean honey bees the 'white man's fly.'"

Jacob asked, "What's race mean in bees? And what's interbred?"

"In bees, race is where they first came from long ago. I suspect your swarm colony has Russian roots giving it its darker color, and Russian bees are said to be 'testier' by some. I've never worked with them." He draped his jacket over his arm. "What's interbred? You know queens mate with at least a dozen drones from other colonies located at a distance, so there's a lot of bee variety in the genes in a hive. Preserving many different inherited traits in a colony helps with its chances of survival. A mean gene could come from any race of bees."

"If you say so." Jacob put his hand over his mouth, acting out a yawn. "So, you're sayin' color doesn't tell you if they're gonna to be good bees or bad bees?"

"I couldna' said it better. Okay, lecture's about over. It's also possible they are overly defensive because they swarmed from a hive where they were treated poorly. Bad beekeepers can teach bees to be aggressive. If that's the case, they might behave better with time and our gentle handling."

Phineas opened the smoker to make sure the embers had been extinguished. "So, Jacob, have you come up with a name for your hive yet?"

Jacob hunched his shoulders and shook his head.

Iris approached and answered for him. "Well, you guys always give them female names, right? And the other two are Grace and Charity."

"Workers are all females, Mom."

She folded her arms. "And these ones are angry females."

Phineas and Jacob waited expectantly for her next words.

"So, name it Jezebel."

Phineas winced at another reminder of that nightmare, surprised that that Iris would bring it up. Angela's surfacing must have made her think of it.

Jacob looked puzzled. "Who's Jezebel?"

Phineas answered, "An evil Old Testament character. She...uh...met a gruesome end."

"Cool! Then Jezebel it is."

Phineas wasn't going to be the one to tell Jacob that Jezebel turned her people against God and was then devoured by wild dogs as punishment, but he couldn't stop Jacob from looking it up on his own—and he probably would. Jacob knew how to find things on the Internet.

A thunderclap forced their attention to the darkening sky. Phineas saw a second bolt in the distance behind Martha's silhouette.

He hurriedly began gathering the beekeeping equipment. "Let's get inside. Maybe this is why Jezebel's bees were so grumpy. They know a storm is coming."

⬡⬡⬡⬡⬡

Iris kept an eye on Jacob while he groused about having to load the dishwasher. She had avoided telling him how he was conceived on the eve of Hurricane Jezebel, and then born as she and Phineas planned their return to Chapel Hill in 1986 following Phineas' terrifying legal ordeal. She hadn't figured out how to let him know that his father'd had the charges of second-degree murder dropped just three months before he was born. And Jacob's twelfth birthday was approaching in less than three weeks.

It was such a relief to leave New Orleans. After the widely seen and provocative *60 Minutes* episode that led to Phineas' charges being dismissed, locals sometimes recognized him and stopped him on the street or in the grocery store. Most expressed support for his dedication in the crisis. A few made uninformed and unpleasant accusations. One burly man approached them on a city sidewalk and called Phineas a murderer then spat at him.

Iris' life simplified when her mom sold the family home and moved from New Orleans to Durham. One visit to The Croasdaile Retirement Community was all it took to convince her mom that spending her golden years dining and chatting with newfound friends would be happier than alone in the New Orleans' Garden District, as the city struggled to recover from devastation.

Phineas had detailed to Iris his trips back to Chapel Hill to set up his office and find them a residence, and how the trips had put him back in contact with their cherished prior landlord, Jackson Lee. The octogenarian had helped them find a suitable rental house and then quietly moved his beehives onto the back of its lot before the Manns moved in. Iris chuckled at the memory of his greeting her during their move. She'd had baby Jacob in her arms. Mr. Lee had lost an inch in height and wore the same overalls she remembered.

"Well look at you! You've been fruitful and multiplied since I last saw you."

"Hi Mr. Lee. It's great to see you. Meet Jacob."

He leaned in for a closer look. "Well, hey Jacob. Sure does favor his Daddy, don't he?"

At that point their first dog, a black Lab named Amos, emerged from his house inspection, spotted, and charged Jackson Lee, almost bowling the skinny old man over. He knelt and allowed the old dog to smell and lick him. Amos was beside himself at their reunion and sprinted circles around them, his butt tucked low to the ground.

"Moves purty well for an old dog."

"I haven't seen him move like that in years."

"Knows he's home."

Iris summoned a mock frown at that point. "Pretty sneaky putting your beehives back there."

Jackson Lee grinned wide enough that she could see he'd lost a molar on each side. Only then did she notice how frail he'd become. "I remembered how much Phineas like watching when I worked 'em."

"Uh huh..."

"And I ain't getting any stronger. Lost my friend, Moses, last year. Remember him? Shore do miss 'im." His Black friend had tilled the Manns' garden space with his mule each spring during Phineas' residency and fellowship. "Could use some hep liftin' 'em at times. Won't be a bother."

"Uh huh..."

"Thought I mentioned the hives'd be here to your husband, when he was here before. Might've slipped my memory."

She watched him shift his weight from one foot to the other before she decided to let up on him. "That's all between you and Phineas. I'm certainly not going to mess with them."

Phineas immediately purchased a veiled bee jacket and soaked up honey bee knowledge at the old man's side. And before long, the annual honey harvest became a tradition, a day of celebration.

Iris wept for days after Jackson Lee was found in his car off the road in a cornfield. Lee's daughter, Maude, told them that the ambulance crew had found her right-handed father's left foot on the brake, his left hand clutching the steering wheel, and his eyes pegged to the left, all signs he'd steered out of oncoming traffic while suffering a massive stroke.

The loss of Jackson Lee brought back painful memories of Iris' father's death only four years earlier, the death that sent her mother, Sarah Jane, into a near terminal tailspin of depression, the depression that had brought Phineas and her to New Orleans and his ill-fated first job after fellowship, the job that ended with Jezebel—and his arrest for murder.

After Jackson Lee's death, they had learned of the custom that someone has to tell the bees when their caregiver dies. An Orange County beekeeper friend had produced a passage outlining the traditional ceremony. Iris watched Phineas honor the ancient rites and announce to the hives that Jackson Lee had passed on, and that he, Phineas Mann, would assume the sacred responsibility of being their keeper. He draped the suddenly roaring hives in black cloth and walked from hive to hive tapping each three times with Jackson Lee's old hive tool while chanting:

"Honey bees, honey bees, hear what I say!
Your Master Keeper has passed away.
But his friends now beg you will freely stay.
And gather honey for many a day.
Bony bees, bony bees.
Hear what I say."

She and Phineas had stared in amazement when each hive suddenly became silent after his words.

⬡⬡⬡⬡⬡

As he began reciting the Thursday morning rounds update in front of Enoch Jefferson's door, Intern Malcolm Carver wore a cautious smile and stood up straight. "Mr. Jefferson had no opisthotonus episodes yesterday. We needed less of the meds to control his blood pressure fluctuations. He's requiring no extra oxygen, and his tube feeding is going well. Kidneys and bowels are working fine. Labs are stable."

Phineas clasped his hands behind his back in a professorial posture. He raised his eyebrows. "Think it's time to begin weaning him off paralytics?"

"We could try."

"Let's go see him then decide."

The ICU team was grateful to find no surprises from Jefferson's examination or in his nurse Lisa's bedside update. Carver whispered to her, "We want to begin inching down his vecuronium infusion ever so slowly."

Her brow creased in the middle. "Why do you want to go and stir things up on *my* shift? He's been so calm the last few days." Her tone and her volume, louder than prescribed, revealed her apprehension.

Phineas answered her softly, "Let's step back outside."

Lisa now looked sheepish. "Sorry. Haven't had my second cup yet."

"No problem. He may not be ready to come off the meds, but we won't know when he is ready, unless we try at intervals. Being on long-term paralytic infusions could lead to a lengthier recovery, especially if it causes a second muscle problem, a myopathy."

"Got it. I'll start weaning. Baby steps."

"Thanks. Good. Let's keep rounding, Team."

⬡⬡⬡⬡⬡

After wrapping up morning rounds, Phineas found his way down the long windowless, off-white corridors to the UNC Hospital security offices in the building's basement. He knocked on a metal door labeled Chief of Security. From inside, a disembodied male voice bade him to come in.

As Phineas entered, the plump chief stood and offered Phineas a soft, pale hand to shake before he motioned him to sit across from him at his cluttered desk. The nameplate read Captain Alton Vickers.

"What can I do for you, Dr. Mann?"

"I'd like to get your thoughts on a possible problem." A problem he hadn't faced before.

"Fire away."

Where to start? "An ICU patient's family member saw an ammunition clip in another ICU patient's son's truck. It might have been a high capacity clip. They weren't sure."

The chief picked up a Carolina blue plastic pen and began jotting notes on a legal pad. "Where was the truck, and did they see a weapon? Ammunition?"

"Hospital parking deck. No weapon. I didn't ask about ammunition." *Probably should have.*

"It's not against the law to *own* a high-capacity clip. You just can't buy one since the 1994 law. Anything else?"

"It's my guess that the man who drives the truck, Zebediah Jefferson, may have violent tendencies."

"Based on?"

"My conversations with him, and what else the other family saw—a White Power bumper sticker."

Vickers' eyes narrowed. "Would the 'other family' happen to be African American?" The corner of his mouth twitched.

"Yes. Does that matter?" Phineas clenched his teeth at the question.

The officer put down his pen. "Just getting all the information. Anything more?"

"No."

"So there hasn't been any conflict, and no one has clearly broken any laws, as far as I can determine. We have no information to say there was an illegal ammunition clip. And all you have is hearsay, maybe even a racial ax to grind."

"I felt I should give you a heads up, before anything happens." Phineas didn't think he deserved to feel foolish. "Should you do anything now? Can you?"

"Tell you what. Let us know when both families are visiting, and we'll have someone in a uniform present in the ICU. Sound good to you?" A token gesture.

"We'll let you know."

⬡⬡⬡⬡⬡

It was Thursday evening and Jefferson's nurse, Lisa, was waving at Phineas from her seat at the nursing station. He had arrived for his walk-by to look at the ICU patients before checking the waiting room for family, and before he could head home. Lisa was documenting data and observations on a patient's sizable paper flow sheet. She whispered just loud enough for him to make out: "Son's in there."

Phineas approached her, to be close enough to keep their conversation private. "I guess that's good. Anything change?"

Lisa shook her head slowly. "Not so far."

"And the dose of paralytic?"

"Down to less than half." She put down her pen and drummed her fingertips on the desktop in the rhythm purposed for grand entrances. "I reminded his son to keep it quiet."

"Smart. Guess I'd better go in now." He took a slow breath in an attempt to settle expected tension.

"She's in there too." She pressed her lips together in a tight line.

"She?"

"The VA nurse." Lisa's raised eyebrows suggested that she hoped for a reaction from Phineas.

Muscles along the sides of Phineas' neck tightened. Still, he had to admit that Angela's presence hadn't been an issue, yet. He kept his tone casual. "She here much?"

"About every time I see the son." Still studying him.

Phineas nodded weakly at Lisa before he stepped toward Jefferson's door. *What is Angela's purpose here?* He composed himself again, then stepped into Enoch Jefferson's darkened room and spoke softly to his patient. "Mr. Jefferson, we're going to talk about you." Then to the son. "Good evening. How are you doing?" .

Angela glanced at Zebediah and whispered, "We're fine. How are you?" while he groused, "How long 'fore he's better?"

As Phineas' eyes adjusted to the dim light, the two figures gradually came into focus. Angela's bright white nurse's uniform dominated Zebediah's olive camo patterned t-shirt.

Phineas scanned the tracings on the monitors over the head of the bed. "He hasn't had any new problems yet. The tetanus toxin's effects can take weeks to fully clear." He paused for a few seconds. "But we have begun reducing his paralytic medication, hoping he'll tolerate a lower dose."

Angela grasped Zebediah's hand and beamed. "That's wonderful news, Zeb."

"Sittin' here most every evenin's getting old, even with your comp'ny." Not even a hint of a smile.

"Don't you worry. I can sit with him while you take breaks."

Phineas had to make a conscious effort to conceal his troubled reaction to her offer.

Zebediah stood. "I'm agoin' out for a smoke. Be back after. This place gets to me."

Sometimes it gets to me too.

Angela stood and let Zebediah squeeze by her. "So, Dr. Mann, how's Iris? It's been forever since I talked with her. How many children do you have? I remember she was pregnant last time I saw her—back in New Orleans." She said it like that terrible time deserved only casual conversation. Not a hint of contrition.

"She's fine. Two children. Excuse me. I want to see if he has any more questions." Phineas escaped from the room and caught up with Zebediah as he was passing the nurses' station.

"Mr. Jefferson, did you have more questions?"

Zebediah spun around and stared at Phineas. "Naw. Just so's he keeps getting better, I won't be getting upset."

What does that mean? "We're doing our best to get him through this."

"Like I said. Keep him getting better. And don't be lettin' them young doctors at him." He spit out his words as if to prove his manhood, his dominance.

"We're all on his team. And they're here 24/7 watching him." Phineas clenched his jaw.

"Just so's it's just watchin'." Zebediah turned and pushed through the heavy double ICU doors.

Lisa looked up from her charting. "Well, that could have gone worse."

Phineas shrugged his response as Ava appeared from an adjacent room, her black leather respiratory therapist valise in hand. "Hey, Dr. Mann."

"Hey, Ava. Everything all right by you on Mr. Jefferson?"

"No ventilator issues." Then she lowered her voice and stepped closer to Phineas. "But I don't like *her* sitting in there with him. I don't trust the bitch—and she don't like me much either."

Lisa dropped her pen. "You know her?"

"We go way back. Same with Dr. Mann."

Lisa's expression went from startled to puzzled. "Dr. Mann?"

Phineas closed his eyes and shook his head. He had spoken against creating prejudice for patients. He needed to protect their objective care. Yet he knew that Ava always had his back.

Not long after her move to Chapel Hill, Ava had confessed she hadn't yet followed Phineas' advice to have HIV testing, advice offered when her tattoo artist husband was diagnosed with a terminal AIDS illness, Kaposi sarcoma. Phineas had then arranged for her care with Infectious Disease specialist, Ron Bullock, who began her on the latest treatments, as potent as Magic Johnson's. Ava still seemed to believe that the two men had pulled her back from the abyss.

He turned to face Lisa. "Long story, Lisa. Do me a favor. I know Jefferson's not your only patient, but when his son leaves that woman in there with his father, find a reason to go in there whenever you get the chance."

Lisa squinted at him then picked up her pen, as if to write down his answer on Enoch Jefferson's chart. "Sure thing. What are you thinking?"

"Just a feeling." *Not a pleasant one.*

She restarted her documenting on the flow sheet before she responded. "Okay, whatever you say" She glanced up at him with an afterthought. "Oh, by the way, your resident, Downs, called. He and the intern are at The Rat 'celebrating TGIF a day early,' since they're on call tomorrow. Said you should stop by."

Well, that's a first. "They want *me* to join them?"

"Sounded like they want to talk."

⬡⬡⬡⬡⬡

When he called to inform Iris of his planned detour on the way home, she hadn't sounded pleased. She reported she'd been both supervising homework and putting dinner together. He had offered resident stress and teamwork building as excuses. Duty.

At least there was a parking space right down the street from "The Rat." On this simmering weekday evening, Phineas took note that Silent Sam, the sculpture of a rifle bearing Confederate soldier, would guard his weathered Toyota SR5 pickup truck as well as entry into the University of North Carolina campus. The image of Zebediah Jefferson's tattoo flashed through Phineas' thoughts, before he quickly blocked it out.

The smell of pizza and stale beer greeted him as he slipped through The Rathskeller's basement entrance. The crowd was thin, so he easily spotted Michael Downs sitting in a booth in the back. Downs waved him over. Malcolm Carver and a young Black woman sat across from him, their fingers wrapped around half-empty glasses of beer. Most of an extra-large pepperoni pizza covered the table.

"Have a slice, Dr. Mann?" Downs asked.

"Thanks. Better save my appetite for dinner. Wouldn't want to hurt the Missus' feelings."

Downs lifted the metal pizza pan. "Come on. One slice won't hurt. You *have* to be hungry."

"Well maybe just one." He held out his hand to the young woman. "Hi. Phineas Mann."

Her palm was cool and dry. A modest diamond set on a thin gold ring was on her other hand.

"Patrice. Nice to meet you." Her tone was warm, but business-like.

Long and lean with shoulder length cornrows, she wore a cobalt blue and lemon-yellow dress—a "dashiki," Iris had called it, after purchasing one for hot Carolina days. Phineas loved the way its fabric concealed yet caressed Iris' graceful figure.

Malcolm studied Patrice with obvious pride. "Patrice is my fiancé. She just passed her PhD exams and is working on her dissertation. We're getting married in August."

Downs waved at the waiter for another pitcher and glass. "Dr. Mann's wife is the other Dr. Mann. She has a PhD and teaches in the School of Social Work."

Phineas folded a floppy slice of pizza lengthwise. "Congratulations, Patrice. What are you studying?"

"African American Studies."

"And your thesis?"

"It's on the political situation before the Wilmington Massacre of 1898."

Phineas drew a complete blank on her reference and felt ignorant. "Afraid I don't know about that history. I grew up in Vermont and have been pretty much immersed in medicine since I came south."

"It's not *in* the history books. One of many critical events purposely left out. Whenever you're ready, I can explain it to you." Her tone exuded confidence.

Downs poured a glass of beer and slid it in front of Phineas. "Appreciate you coming, Dr. Mann. We thought you might be tied up."

"I hurried over after I met with Jefferson's son. I was lucky to find parking close by, right across the street and under the watchful eyes of Silent Sam."

Downs' gaze shifted to the ceiling. Carver began to scowl. "Two disagreeable topics."

Phineas felt uncharacteristically clueless. "I understand about Zebediah Jefferson. But Silent Sam?" He'd only heard the legend that Silent Sam was supposed to fire his musket if a virgin coed happened by. Best not to mention that.

Patrice spoke with the gentle but firm tone of a kindergarten teacher. "You should read about Julian Carr and his speech at the 1913 graduation day dedication of Silent Sam. The same Carr for which Carrboro is named."

"What'd he say?" Phineas couldn't help, but immediately regretted, asking.

"The original owner of Bull Durham tobacco bragged about horse whipping a 'negro wench' in public for insulting a white woman. And he *thanked God* for efforts to keep 'the purest strain of Anglo-Saxon race in the South,'" Patrice answered him, her voice climbing. "He and the United Daughters of the Confederacy were KKK supporters, and they paid for the statue. At the same time, and it was then *50 years after The Civil War was supposed to have ended slavery*, countless similar statues were erected across the South, aimed at further pushing Jim Crow policies to suppress Blacks. The monuments were not for people to remember the heroism of soldiers but were and continue to be an ongoing 'whitewashed' revisionist narrative of one race enslaving another."

Phineas felt as if a tempest had blown through him. "I didn't know—and clearly need to read about it."

"I'll have Malcolm bring you some of my work." Her gentle tone again. A kind smile appeared to forgive that gap in his education.

Downs forcefully cleared his throat. "So, what are we going to do about Jefferson's son?"

Carver and Patrice regarded Phineas expectantly.

"Malcolm, has he interfered with your care of his father?"

"Not yet."

"Then try to keep your good work the same. We know when he usually comes in. I'll make it a point to try to come by at those times and fill him in on his father. If he happens to come in the room when you're with his Dad, talk to him as you would anyone. It'll be his choice how he responds."

"And if he's insulting?"

"Then we talk to administration about someone to act as a mediator, and about limiting his visiting. It'll be his loss."

Patrice was now wringing her hands. "Dr. Mann, we're *used* to rude and insulting. It's Malcolm's safety *I'm* worried about."

"I've let the head of hospital security know about Jefferson's son. He doesn't think we have anything to act on at this point. If you detect any threat, anything at all, we go right back to security and to administration. That sound okay?"

Did they lack confidence in the head of hospital security? The memory of Jericho's warning was troubling, but Phineas had already struggled with whether to mention the ammunition clip in Jefferson's truck and decided against it. Letting a rumor like that out might negatively impact the old man's care and create chaos whenever the son showed up.

Three blank faces stared silently at Phineas. Did they think he was being cavalier, that he wasn't taking their concerns seriously enough, that he didn't care about Malcolm's safety? He stood and reached for his wallet. "You guys are doing a great job. I appreciate it. We'll get through the month—and I think you'll learn plenty." He found only two ones and a five and dropped it all on the table. "This cover me? I should get home before my kids' bedtimes."

Downs half-smiled. "Our treat, Dr. Mann. Thanks for coming." He scooped up the bills and extended his arm to hand them back to Phineas, who was waving on his way out The Rat's' door.

⬡⬡⬡⬡⬡

Phineas began chewing the first bite of a peanut butter and honey sandwich. He had just arrived from Saturday ICU rounds and was looking forward to Jacob's game.

"Dad, will you pitch me a round of Stella ball batting practice before the game?" Jacob, his gear bag at his feet, sported his freshly laundered bright shamrock green Cubs Little League baseball shirt, clean grey pants, and a soiled batting glove. He offered his father three tennis balls.

"Sure. Soon as I finish lunch."

Phineas was usually asked to coach third base when he could get to games. For some of them, he could slip away from the hospital for the seven innings and return to finish work after the last pitch. He'd be the only dad in slacks and a button-down shirt, worn in case the beeper on his belt sent him urgently back on duty.

After the last bite of his sandwich, Phineas found Jacob tossing their Labrador retriever tennis balls in the driveway, each enthusiastically retrieved and dropped. His son's back was to the garage door, their batting practice backstop. His bat lay on the ground nearby. Martha watched from the side deck, a silent spectator.

Jacob gingerly handed Phineas the three balls. Two were soaked in Stella's slobber.

Phineas shook off the loose drool. "Hope you can hit my spitball." Stella took up a vigilant posture next to Phineas before he delivered his first pitch, an easy one.

Jacob slammed a fly ball into the woods, sending a comet tail of dog spit behind it. Stella bolted in the flight direction, intermittently sniffing and circling around the landing spot until she pounced. She then pranced back and proudly released the ball at Phineas feet, wagging her thick yellow tail. A faster pitch, another shot into the woods, another retrieval, and so on over and over, until Stella lay panting, having taken refuge in the shade under the porch, still chewing on the last hit ball.

Phineas chuckled. "Looks like batting practice is over for today, Buddy. You're ready. Let's go get 'em." Jacob began packing his gear.

Martha descended from the porch and sauntered close to him as he began rinsing Stella slobber off his hands at the hose bibb on the side of the garage. Martha's hands were clasped behind her dragging Jacob's first metal bat, tiny compared to his current 30-inch version. Her head was bowed ever so slightly as she shyly asked, "Will you pitch to *me*, Daddy?"

Iris leaned on the porch railing, watching. She appeared keenly interested in his response. “I suggested she ask. We’ve still got five or ten minutes before we need to go.”

“Sure thing, Sweetheart. Jacob, grab your glove for fielding practice. Stella’s spent.” Phineas held up the two remaining balls. “Martha, go ahead and stand where Jacob was batting.”

His shy daughter took a tentative position in the imaginary batter’s box facing directly at Phineas. She was wearing a too long and faded Cubs t-shirt, a Jacob hand me down from two seasons ago. She always seemed to pick out clothing that matched her surroundings, whatever allowed her to silently fade into a comfortable background. Her ponytail was tucked through the back of a Durham Bulls cap.

Phineas took the three steps to her and turned her to a more correct sideways stance. Then he arranged her hands on the bat’s handle. “There, now you look like a professional.” He lobbed a soft underhand pitch to her strike zone. She chopped down at it, missing by almost a foot.

Jacob took off his glove and groaned. Phineas shot him his version of “the look” to keep him silent. “Better get ready, Jacob.” Phineas held up the other ball. “Martha, now show me some flatter swings.” After a few practice swings, she began to look like she had a chance to hit something, and Phineas knew where her bat would be in the strike zone. He aimed his next gentle lob there.

She whacked the tennis ball on a lively bounce straight at Jacob, who could only duck and deflect it from his face with his loose glove. Stella shot out from under the porch and fielded Jacob’s error.

Phineas clapped. “Nice one, Martha. Ready for another?”

Iris blew him a kiss.

Could that be a hint of later pleasures?

At the first stop on Sunday morning ICU rounds, Downs and Carver leaned over the sides of Ada James' bed and shared worried expressions. She was sitting upright, perspiring, and laboring to breathe between rattling coughs. Her nasal oxygen tubing had been replaced by a facemask that delivered high levels of supplemental oxygen. Yet her oxygen levels, measured by finger probe, registered as barely adequate. James' dark scalp and patchy, matted white hair were on troubling display. Her groomed wig rested on the Styrofoam head perched on the windowsill.

Phineas sensed the beginnings of a lump in his throat, a breakdown in the separation between patient and caregiver, a separation needed for optimal thinking. He forced himself to be as unfeeling and objective as possible. "When did she get like this?"

James' weekend nurse stood at the foot of the bed clutching the two-by-three foot clipboard and paper flow sheet. "She's been like this since I came on thirty minutes ago. Her night nurse recorded an elevated temp of 38 at 4 AM. Respiratory has been turning up her oxygen since then."

Carver grasped James' hand between both of his. He leaned close to her ear and asked, "Ms. James, can you tell us what doesn't feel right? Any pain?"

Her neck muscles tightened with each breath. "No pain. Just...can't... breathe."

"We're going to examine you now, okay?"

Her head tilt granting permission was barely detectable. The three doctors took turns applying their stethoscopes to her back, then her heart. They studied her neck veins, her fingernails, and searched for edema. Carver leaned close to her ear. "Ms. James, I'm going to confirm what we found with Dr. Mann, so you can hear it. okay?" She signaled again with a single nod.

"She feels hot to the touch. I hear crackles on her left side. Her heart exam hasn't changed, except for the higher rate, and she doesn't seem to have an excess of fluid. Labs show her white count has increased to 14,000." He turned back to her. "Ms. James, I'm worried you may have pneumonia." She looked up at him with tired but startled eyes. He turned to her nurse. "Please recheck her temperature. And we need to look at this morning's chest x-ray."

Phineas agreed with a quick dip of his head. "Let's do that right now, so we can get antibiotics started. Has she been able to raise any sputum?"

Her nurse shook her head. "She's too weak to cough it up."

The three doctors gathered at the x-ray viewing boards in the room next to the ICU. Carver scrolled through the panels until he found her illuminated images. "There's a new density behind her heart. Looks like pneumonia."

Phineas leaned close. "I agree. And I don't think there's heart failure, so an early dialysis won't help her. Let's go back and get antibiotics going STAT. She'll probably need to go back on the ventilator."

Only minutes later when they returned, Ada James appeared in more distress. Phineas spoke slowly to her, "You told me before that if you became unstable again, you'd want us to put the tube back in your throat. Pneumonia can be treated, so unless you've changed your mind, we'll get ready to put you back on the ventilator."

When she tried to speak, no sounds came out. Her neck muscles tugged at her collarbones with each breath and rattling cough. She closed her eyes and slowly bowed to indicate her acceptance.

Phineas spotted respiratory therapist, Ava Jones, vigilant in the doorway. "Ava, please send a blood gas." He turned to James' nurse whose lips were pressed together, suggesting she was as worried as he was. "Have you seen her family?"

"Sunday morning. They're bound to be on their way to church."

"Do you have a cell number for one of them?"

"The grandson, Jericho."

By the time Jericho and the daughters arrived, the blood gas had confirmed suspicions of a dangerously high carbon dioxide level; the team had sedated Ada James then quickly inserted an endotracheal tube. She finally rested supine and allowed the machine to do all the breathing work. Ava suctioned ropes of olive-colored sputum for cultures as the first doses of antibiotics ran into Ms. James' veins.

Phineas, with Downs and Carver at his side, met her people in the hallway by her room. Jericho led the trio. The powerful man was striking in a charcoal grey suit and silver silk tie. Ruth pressed an embroidered handkerchief into her eyes with white-gloved fingers. Her church attire included a light grey suit and one of the most elegant hats Phineas had seen in person. Almost two feet wide, it featured a black silk bow, a luxurious black feather, and loosely arranged netting with black polka dots. Rebecca wore royal blue. Her stylish hat, smaller and adorned only with a bow, was less extravagant than her sister's.

Carver took a step toward them before speaking. "She's resting now. We've sedated her and the ventilator is supporting her. Her x-ray showed pneumonia that wasn't there two days ago. She's had the first doses of antibiotics, and cultures were sent."

"Thank you, Dr. Carver." Ruth was staring up into Phineas eyes through her hat's netting. "So, what happened, Dr. Mann? She looked okay last night."

Phineas looked from Jericho to Rebecca to Ruth. "Patients who have been on ventilators and have diabetes are at increased risk for pneumonia. We'll need to treat the pneumonia for several days at least, before we try to take her off the ventilator again." He bowed his head. "I assure you that we're all disappointed and saddened by this development."

Ruth put her hand on Phineas' forearm and gave it a gentle squeeze. "The rest of the family will be coming in soon. We know you can't meet with each person individually, so why don't you tell the three of us what you want to convey to the others, and we'll be here to pass it on. You have other sick folks to also care for."

"That would be most helpful. Thank you."

Jericho shook Carver's hand in both of his. "We know you're doing what you can, and we appreciate it."

Rebecca leaned close to Phineas. "Now Dr. Mann, we know you're working hard here, but try not to forget that today's Mothers' Day. I'm sure you've *also* got someone to remember."

Yikes! Did he ever! He'd sent an early card to his mother, figuring it had to get all the way to Vermont, and he might forget once he came on service. He should call her later. But he'd also promised Iris weeks ago that she could bring Sarah Jane over, and he'd cook a celebratory meal for them. That pledge had slipped by him during all of the month's ICU drama. He'd need to shop on the way home for dinner, flowers, and an all-important card for his beloved.

⬡⬡⬡⬡⬡

As soon as Phineas opened the front door, Stella blocked the opening, wagging her entire back end and trying to push her nose into the grocery bag. "Uh uh, Girl. Not for you." He held the cake box high to protect it.

Iris and Sarah Jane had bookended Martha on the sofa, listening to her read. Iris stood and accepted the flowers and card he'd found on the way home and rewarded him with a kiss full on his lips. "How lovely! Thank you, Phineas. I better get these in some water."

Sarah Jane accepted her hug sitting down. She remained thin but had managed to gain healthy weight on her retirement center's meals after Ron Bullock treated her chronic lung infection. She no longer piled her hair high, going for a stylish, easy-to-care for cut, instead. And she'd allowed her natural silver-grey color to replace her formerly perpetual bright platinum.

"We're hearing about Curious George, and I'm definitely heading to the bookstore this week to look for some literature aimed a bit higher for this bright daughter of yours."

Jacob shuffled into the living room. "Can we play Stella ball, Dad?"

"Maybe after dinner, if we still have daylight. I need to cook now. Want to help me? Since it *is* Mothers' Day?"

"Maybe next time. I'm kinda busy." He escaped back to where he'd come from. Phineas breathed relief that he didn't have the extra burden of supervising his son in the kitchen, as he hustled to prepare the impromptu meal.

He'd battled in a crowded Whole Foods for the ingredients he arranged into a grid of neat piles on the countertop. Then he washed and cut up the potatoes and asparagus before drizzling them with olive oil and sprinkling freshly ground salt and pepper on them. He rubbed the salmon fillet with a Za'atar facsimile, Iris' favorite Mediterranean herbs and spices combination for fish. After firing up the Weber grill, he checked the clock and calculated the exact times he'd start each of the items, and when they should come off. He wrote these numbers on a sheet of scrap paper.

Iris slipped into the kitchen and embraced her chef husband, pinning him against the cabinets. The smell of her lavender soap replaced that of their dinner's herbs as he savored the soft skin of her cheek against his, her silent promise of later romance. She scanned the precise piles of food and murmured, "Some things never change." He knew she enjoyed teasing him about his compulsiveness, a trait that had served him most times in his career but had once been a handicap back in New Orleans, when his workload and sleep deprivation were crushing both of them.

He responded, "Mise en place. I stick with what works."

Before everyone was served, Sarah Jane fixed Phineas in a penetrating gaze and said, "So Phineas, Iris tells me that pitiful young nurse, Angela, has returned to darken your ICU door."

Phineas passed the platter of herb speckled orange-red fillet to Sarah Jane. "Have some salmon, Sarah Jane. Why don't we talk about something more pleasant on Mothers' Day? What have you been up to lately?"

Phineas noticed Jacob's puzzled look at Martha, and that she returned it. Was it time for him to explain to his children why he had once been charged with multiple murders, before they found out on their own?

WEEK TWO

"Like lightning, now, Charity bent from her saddle, and seizing a stout stick, she wheeled around to the other side of the hedge that protected the hives like a low wall. Then, with a smart blow, she beat each hive until the bees clouded the air...

As Charity galloped off at high speed she heard the shouts of fury from the soldiers, who fought madly against the bees. And, of course, the harder they fought, the harder they were stung. If they had been armed with swords the brave bees could not have kept the enemy more magnificently at bay."

FROM *HOW THE BEES SAVED AMERICA, AMERICAN BEE JOURNAL* 57, NO. 9 (1917)

On Monday evening, Phineas steeled himself for his meeting with Zebediah Jefferson. The son hadn't arrived during Phineas' weekend rounds, and he felt like he'd been spared.

RN Lisa stepped out from Jefferson's room and closed the door. "They're waiting for you." She chanted it in a sing-song delivery.

"They?"

"Zeb and Angela." Her pairing felt too easy. "Cute couple."

Cute. God help us! "Any changes in his condition?"

"Not since you were by earlier. Still off the paralytic. Still on Versed for sedation."

"Wish me luck." He took a deep breath and stepped into darkness.

"Well, hey, Dr. Mann! How are *you* today?" Angela's perky whisper greeted him from one of the chairs on the far side of Enoch Jefferson's bed.

"I'm fine, and I'm happy to report that Mr. Jefferson has had a quiet couple of days." He bent to whisper to his patient. "Sir, Dr. Mann here. I'm going to talk to your son about you now." He stood and turned toward the visitors. "We took him off the medication that he was on to paralyze him, and he hasn't had any of those dangerous tetanus spells."

Phineas' eyes adjusted enough to make out their faces. Angela's displayed a broad grin, her teeth almost bright white. "Well, that's wonderful news! Don't you think so Zeb?"

Zebediah's tight lips and squint under his ball cap brim revealed no pleasure. "How much longer's he gonna be in the hospital?"

Phineas had to regroup after the unexpected inquiry. "That's a good question. Unfortunately, it's way too soon to estimate a date. We still need to reduce his sedation and let him have trials of breathing on his own. Could be weeks before he can leave here."

Zebediah groaned. "I don't much like settin' in this place—even with Angela here. Sorry, Angela. Rather be elsewhere. Don't like hospitals. Makes me even more ornery than usual."

She gave his hand a squeeze. "I'll help you get through this, Zeb Honey. Things are going well. No complications so far, right Dr. Mann?"

Zeb Honey! Damn. "That's right. So far."

Phineas shuddered inside at the notion of Zebediah being more "ornery than usual." That tattoo, the white power bumper sticker, and an ammunition clip already felt like way too many raised red flags.

⬡⬡⬡⬡⬡

Iris strode toward Phineas' truck and pulled the driver's side door open before he'd finished gathering his papers and work mail. Her brow hooded over her eyes in a pained expression.

"You need to talk to Jacob."

"Now? What's he done? Grand theft? He's too young to have gotten a girl pregnant—at least I think he is."

Her lack of a response confirmed that his sorry attempt at humor hadn't worked. She planted her hands on her hips. "He's been on the Internet."

"Porn?" A discussion Phineas would rather avoid. He was standing on the driveway, his truck door still open.

"Worse." She jabbed his chest with both index fingers. "He searched YOU."

He recoiled from her manicured points. "Me? He interested in my asthma research?"

"He read about the murder charges after Jezebel—then he asked me how come I'd stayed with you after that."

Damn Internet! "Oh. Shoot. What have you said to him?" Phineas slammed the truck door harder than he needed to.

"That the charges were dropped because you did nothing wrong. He didn't read any of the later articles." Her bitter tone made clear her frustration. She touched the back of her hand to her eye.

Trepidation replaced Phineas' hunger pangs and the gnawing emptiness in his gut gave way to writhing coils of snakes locked in combat. Jacob had seen his father called a murderer in the press, on the all-powerful Internet. How could he ever undo that damage? "You want to sit down with him before or after dinner?"

"I think we should get this over with. He said he hasn't told Martha about it, so I told him not to."

"Right. Good."

"I'll get Martha started on her homework, then join you and Jacob. He's waiting for you in his room." She composed herself now, submerging the emotional outburst.

"I'm on my way." *I'd rather take a beating.*

"Phineas, one more thing."

"What's that?"

"I looked at his search history."

"And?"

"The stuff that showed up was pretty sensational. Lots of early horrible stuff. And each article outdoing the last. Seems like news sources print a lot less when it's decided no one did anything wrong. They never undo the harm they've done." Her tone and another wipe of her eyes confirmed that her frustration persisted.

"The media world we live in. Clearing someone's name doesn't sell. I doubt it's going to get any better." He wondered if they were ever going to be allowed to put that painful time behind them. Five days in a Hell named Baptist Hospital following a devastating hurricane, only to be thrown in the Parrish jail on his return to New Orleans following his evacuation. Then the months out on bail preparing his defense with endless rehearsals trying to summon an actor he was not hard-wired to be. The terror as his trial approached. All because of the malicious actions of Angela Portier. And now, thanks to her return, his son thinks he's a murderer.

In the hallway, Phineas stood and collected his thoughts. Jacob had been a quick study when they'd purchased their first computer, an Apple MacIntosh. He was fearless at trying things on it, and he'd had more time than his parents to explore its capabilities. He, or one of his friends, had early on changed the error indicator from its noxious beep to a high-pitched, singsong, "Oooh...Don't *do* that!" Phineas had made that discovery when trying to figure out how to accomplish some new task. With each blunder, the irritating message repeated. Iris had been drawn into the room by the computer's siren pleas. Despite Phineas' rising frustration, she'd found the scene too hilarious to stifle her mirth.

Phineas wondered what new computer capabilities and knowledge his son now possessed.

Jacob had propped himself up on two pillows on his twin bed. He closed an *Avengers* comic book when Phineas entered.

"Hey, Jacob. How was school today?"

His answer was flat, his expression suspicious. "Okay. The usual."

Phineas turned around Jacob's desk chair and sat cowboy style, leaning his arms on its back. "Your Mom said you found me on the Internet."

Jacob pushed himself into his pillows and lowered his chin. He stared at Phineas without speaking.

"I didn't do anything wrong. The bad stuff you read was before everything came out. It was to sell newspapers." Phineas kept his tone as even as he could.

"The articles said you gave people drugs and they died. They said you were arrested for murder—for four murders." His son's voice trailed off, as his jaw quivered. He had to be thinking he'd lost the father he thought he knew, or perhaps more frightening, that his friends might find out.

"Those horribly sick patients were close to death and suffering terribly when I gave them something to help their pain. I didn't kill them. Their medical conditions did." Phineas' explanation felt too superficial for the charges, but how could he help Jacob comprehend the difference between easing someone's suffering and euthanasia?

Jacob continued staring at Phineas. "Okay." He didn't look convinced.

Iris slipped in through the door and closed it softly behind her. She sat on the end of the bed. "Your father did heroic work after the hurricane—and nothing wrong. He cared for countless really sick patients in darkness and intense heat—with no power, plumbing, or communications for five days and nights."

She raised her eyebrows and leaned closer to Jacob. "I gather you found Angela Portier's name in your searches?"

"Yup."

"You might not have read that the authorities decided they couldn't believe what she said about your father." Iris seemed to have steadied herself.

"So why were you so upset when she showed up?" The way Jacob asked reminded Phineas of those difficult pretrial rehearsals with his attorney twelve years ago—the ones when he answered anticipated questions from a prosecutor in his usual flat, factual way—the ones when his defense attorney poked him over and over with the tip of a fishing rod, to remind him he needed to express sadness, to show emotion. His attorney had said, "Phineas, it's a short stroll from unfeeling to cold-blooded, and you know what word usually follows cold-blooded."

Phineas shuddered at the memory.

Iris closed her eyes before she let out a deep sigh. "Those were awful times for us, and she's a reminder."

"She a problem now?"

Iris answered, "We don't have any reason to think so."

Jacob appeared to soften. "Okay. I'm good...mind if I still name my hive Jezebel? I like the way it sounds."

The unexpected question allowed Phineas to chuckle. "Sure. Why not?"

He was certain his son was only letting them off for the moment; that he hadn't fully bought their explanations but was uncomfortable with the discussion and ready to tuck it all away for now. But Phineas felt a need to lance this boil before it festered.

"Jacob, let's sit down and go over those news stories and show you when and why the charges were dropped. Okay?"

"Later. I'll let you know when. Dinner ready? I'm hungry."

Phineas reluctantly accepted his son's stalling. "Yeah, it's ready." He'd try again soon.

"Dad?"

"Yeah?"

"I'll never want to be a doctor."

When Phineas was out of work between his arrest after Jezebel and the dropped charges six months later, he'd wondered over and over why *he'd* wanted to be a doctor. Then, out of a Carolina Blue sky, came the gracious offer from his former chief, Dr. Kornberg, an offer to return to work at the University of North Carolina, a place where his six years of residency and fellowship training had been a time of rich learning, and of tenderness with Iris in their first years of marriage.

Today, Iris' strong defense of Phineas to Jacob demonstrated that she still had his back, as she always had in the past. Like twenty years ago when, on top of her own responsibilities as a newly minted full time hospital social worker, she'd nurtured him through his exhausting internship and kept up with bills and taxes and the other mundane necessities of their life. At the end of his fellowship, she'd had to take over her family's New Orleans home after her father's unexpected death, and to rally her mother out of her steep decline into a near terminal depression.

The year prior to Jezebel, Phineas had again needed her to steer their ship, when he was abruptly left as the sole intensive care specialist covering Baptist Hospital's ICU and forced to try to function in a constant sleep deprived fog.

Iris then became the sole source of income for them and Sarah Jane in the social work chaos that followed the devastating hurricane. He was out of a job, and she labored long hours despite constant nausea and fatigue during her pregnancy with Jacob.

And now, now she kept the engine that was their home humming. She was there when he couldn't be. Tonight, she showed him again that she always had his back, and Jacob's, and Martha's, and Sarah Jane's.

⬡⬡⬡⬡⬡

Tuesday morning rounds were about to commence, when Phineas found an alarmed Malcolm Carver waiting at the ICU's metal double door.

"Something happened to Jefferson overnight."

"Something?"

"A few hours ago. He started grimacing, like he was in terrible pain.

Sadie and Ram said his face looked different than the lockjaw. Then he began retching, so they gave him something for nausea. Then the diarrhea started. And his urine looked dark, so they sent some for analysis and gave him extra fluids. He got so fidgety that they started the paralytic back."

"He didn't have opisthotonus?"

Sadie Goldschmidt exited the staff restroom and joined them. Still in the night's pale blue scrubs and with her thick hair pulled back, she looked puzzled behind wire-rimmed eyeglasses that had replaced contact lenses. "Dr. Mann, I saw his tetanus before, and this looked different. Before, it looked like the muscle spasms were the main event. This time it looked like pain came first—and I couldn't localize it." She shook her head. "We sent labs and repeated x-rays. No change, except his kidney function was off a bit, and his red cell count a little lower. We don't know what caused it."

"Let's go see him." Phineas' first guilty thoughts were how a setback meant dealing with Zebediah and Angela for longer than he'd hoped, that he likely wouldn't be rid of their misery anytime soon. He could already hear the son's grumbling and accusations. Would threats follow? He forced himself to think about his complicated patient objectively and what could have happened to him. What would suddenly cause pain they couldn't localize? And the minimal laboratory findings? The possibilities were endless without more to go on.

Patel, also still in wrinkled scrubs from his night in the ICU, came from the doctors' workroom followed by Downs, who was starting his day in dress shirt and tie. Both hurriedly drained Styrofoam coffee cups and tossed them into a hallway trash bin.

The team examined a medically paralyzed Enoch Jefferson from head to toe and found no signs of an acute abdominal crisis or sepsis, no bedsores, no clues whatsoever. They pored over the flow sheet and noted only a three-hour decline in urine output starting between 2 and 3 AM. After the extra intravenous fluids, the urine flowing in Jefferson's catheter was now clearer than the prior urine in the collection bag.

Goldschmidt pointed at the urine in the bag. "We sent a sample for urinalysis. It only showed some hemoglobin. Figured it was likely related to bladder trauma from his catheter."

"Possibly. Better send a hemolysis workup. Maybe one of his medications damaged some of his circulating red cells. And have the lab save samples of his urine and serum, in case we think of more tests."

Carver opened Jefferson's chart to the order page. He looked up at Phineas. "One of us should call his son."

Just how I wanted to start my day. Phineas sighed. "It should be me. You write the orders and keep thinking. I'll try him now."

After eight rings, he reached an answering machine. The voice on it wasn't Zebediah's. It was an old man's. "Hey. Y'all have reached Jefferson Welding. We're likely busy with our torches, cutting or welding somethin'. Leave us a message after the noise."

Phineas had not anticipated hearing Enoch Jefferson's voice for the first time. The old man sounded weary, like he'd recorded it at the end of a long day. Not mean or angry. Phineas thought about what a father had to be like to raise a son like Zebediah, then realized that the recorder was waiting for him.

"Mr. Jefferson, this is Dr. Mann at UNC Hospital, calling about your father. Please call the hospital operator and have me paged."

⬡⬡⬡⬡⬡

With morning in its last minutes, Phineas took a seat at the nursing station to write notes in patients' charts. Malcolm stepped out of the resident workroom and handed over Enoch Jefferson's. "I just finished my note. His son call back yet?"

"Not yet. I suspect I'll have to tell him this evening." Phineas swallowed at the anticipated discomfort.

"Page me if I'm not in the unit, and I'll come ASAP." Malcolm pressed his lips together.

Phineas nodded. "I appreciate that. Having numbers might help."

"I wish my being in the numbers would. If you think me being there will make it worse, I can stay out here."

"He needs to know that we're a team and that you have my support."

Malcolm nodded. "Thanks." He extracted another two charts from the rack and turned toward the workroom door. As he pulled it open, Phineas saw only vacant chairs.

"Looks empty in there."

"Easier to crank out notes without anyone to distract. Michael wanted to look up something in the library." Writing daily notes was a big box to check off on the duties list. Finishing them was a weight lifted off a hospital doctor.

Phineas hesitated before he asked, "Mind if I join you in there to write my notes?"

"Not at all, as long as you don't mind me picking your brain, when I have questions."

"It's there for the picking." Phineas scooped up Jefferson's chart and followed Malcolm inside then settled into the worn vinyl seat of one of the standard-issue metal chairs. "So, other than the unpleasant challenges Jefferson's son presents, how has the rotation been so far?"

"It's what I expected. Good cases. Michael and I work well together, and he's been good about teaching—brings me lots of Xeroxed articles—more than I have time to read." He looked thoughtful for a few seconds, like he realized he should say something else. "And we appreciate your teaching. It's been good, especially how much you're involved with the patients and their families."

"Thanks for that, and you'll get even more when Gabby Villalobos gets back next week. Anything I can do better?"

"I'll let you know if I think of something. We get way more teaching from attendings here than I did in medical school. Most of them were too busy putting out fires all over the hospital."

"Remind me where that was?"

"Boston University."

"Ahh, City Hospital. I was at Tufts across town." Phineas had heard war stories about crazy-hard working conditions and really sick indigent patients at City Hospital.

"City Hospital and University Hospital merged right before I started clinical rotations. We rotated back and forth depending on the service. Very different experiences."

"I can imagine. What made you decide to come to North Carolina?"

"Patrice. She thought she needed to do her PhD in African American Studies in the South. She came here after finishing college at Harvard a year before I finished med school, so I listed UNC and Duke as my top residency match choices, and here I am."

"What are some of the differences from Boston for you? It's been twenty years since I was there."

"Differences? Medical or personal?"

"How about personal first, then medical? Since they say on TV that we're supposed to be in the 'southern part of Heaven'."

"Hmph! Personal. Let's see." He massaged his goatee. "Chapel Hill is okay. Pretty small and tame next to the South End of Boston...Driving. Didn't have a car in Boston. Didn't want or need one there. Now we live close enough that Patrice walks to school, and I walk to the hospital, but we did buy a used car, and we drive for groceries and stuff, and to explore the area a little, when we have time. I let her do most of the driving now though...ever since I got pulled over."

"What? Should I ask what happened?" Phineas felt like he may have crossed into being nosy. But why would Malcolm have mentioned it, if he wasn't supposed to respond?

Malcolm put down his pen and briefly squeezed his hands into fists. "It was a couple of months after I started my internship. We were out in the county one night coming home from dinner at another intern's house, and, for no apparent reason, a cop pulled me over. Made me get out, spread 'em, and put my hands on the car, while they patted me down and searched the trunk." Malcolm closed his eyes and took a deep breath. "Patrice was yelling at him, saying I hadn't done anything, that I was a doctor." He looked up at Phineas, as if searching his face might provide a means to erase the terrifying event and keep it from happening again. Or was Malcolm judging Phineas' comprehension of what he felt?

The slightest smirk surfaced on Malcolm's face. "The guy said, 'Yeah, sure, and I'm Dean Smith.'" He turned his gaze to the floor. "When I started to reach for my wallet with my UNC Hospital ID, he pulled his pistol. I thought he might shoot me right then and there."

Phineas cringed. "My God! That's still going on here in 1998? Sounds like it's more dangerous for you than the big city."

"You know the deep sleep you have when you're dead tired after you've been up for thirty-six hours? Sometimes then, I dream about that night. I always wake up in a sweat after he aims his pistol at me—right before he pulls the trigger. I can tell he's going to, because his eyes narrow, and his finger twitches." When Malcolm glanced back up his shoulders were slumped. "Patrice does most of the driving now if it's dark, or if we're outside of town." He picked up his pen, leaned over an open chart, and started writing. He was biting his lower lip.

Phineas took the cue and reviewed Enoch Jefferson's progress notes and added his concise summary. He closed the chart and waited for Malcolm to finish the note he was working on. "Malcolm, how about in the hospital? Aside from Zebediah Jefferson, how has it been in UNC Hospital?"

Malcolm shrugged. "Mostly okay. Like I said, the teaching's good. Most of it. A couple of attendings have treated me differently than the white interns though. Like they trusted me less, like they're not sure what to expect from me. Feels like I have to prove my competence over and over and over." He slid the next closed chart along the desk to Phineas.

The answer embarrassed Phineas. "Sorry to hear that. Have you given any feedback on that to anyone in the Chairman's office?"

Malcolm again displayed the beginning of a smirk. "Do you really think there's a way to do that anonymously? They'd know it was me, and you know there'd be retribution in some way. Maybe not to my face or right away, but whoever I complained about would find a way to affect my career."

His response troubled Phineas. Could any of his colleagues be that malicious? Wouldn't they want to be better teachers? Better people? "We just haven't trained enough Black doctors here yet. Our Chairman tells me they're trying to recruit more Black medical students to apply here for the residency match, but that's only been in the last several years, and some applicants are understandably hesitant about programs in the South. I think once we can accomplish that, it'll help with some of the biased faculty." Phineas cracked open the next patient's chart and began scanning notes, in case Malcolm had shared all he wanted. "Your work has been excellent in the ICU, despite the challenges of people like Zebediah Jefferson."

"He's not the first. Other families and patients here have asked for a white doctor. Even poor, uneducated and uninsured, down and out folks." He shook his head and glanced at the ceiling. "It even happened with a Black patient. Like he couldn't believe I'm as good. When I introduced myself, he said he didn't come to Chapel Hill to see 'another colored man.'"

Ouch! "I can't imagine how frustrating that has to be."

"Frustrating, sure. And it hurts. I was considering pursuing a career in the public health sector, to see if I could make things better, especially for those people, or should I say, 'my people'?" He stared into Phineas' eyes, probing. "Now I'm not so sure. Maybe I should just specialize and settle into a comfortable practice."

"Some patients have trouble trusting doctors in general. Don't you think that some patients might trust you *more* than a white doctor?"

Malcolm nodded his head slowly. "Yeah. I've seen that, and I've had some older Black patients tell me how proud they are of me, how they're rooting for me."

Malcolm's last statement aside, his revelations were more than Phineas had anticipated. What would *his* residency have been like twenty years ago, if *he* were Black? The most stressful days in *his* career never had the additional burden of systemic racism. He'd always been encouraged, even coddled at times. His white face meant he'd never had to justify his position as a doctor.

He wished he could promise that it would be better for Malcolm going forward, but he knew he couldn't. "I hope you keep your dream alive, Malcolm."

"If I do, Patrice will be a big part of the reason. I don't get a lot of encouragement otherwise. She's amazing. She's telling history the way it was, not the way it's in the books. She wants to change things."

Phineas wanted to offer a glimmer of hope. "I had a recent encounter that might be encouraging."

Malcolm lifted his eyebrows, an invitation to continue.

"I referred a very Southern white lady, probably a one-time debutante and a long-time patient of mine, for consultation to a gastroenterologist who happened to be Black. When she came back to see me in follow-up, she thanked me profusely for the referral and said something you might appreciate."

"What was that?" Malcolm tilted his head forward, waiting.

"She said that when he walked into the room and she saw he was Black, she realized that he had to be an incredibly smart and dedicated doctor to have risen to where he was, despite all the barriers that had been placed in front of him."

Malcolm was silent for a moment, like he was turning the story over in his mind. "Wish there were more who think like she does." If the anecdote about one exceptional white person had helped, it wasn't obvious, and it *was* the only time Phineas had heard a white patient express *any* understanding of the extra burdens Black doctors carried.

"So do I, and I know that going over all this hasn't been easy, but thanks for sharing, for educating me."

The pupil had become the teacher, and Phineas was embarrassed at how much he still had to learn, and he was ashamed of how oblivious he was to all Malcolm and other Blacks had to endure every day. If Phineas was to be a better doctor, teacher, and human being, he needed to somehow see and understand their extra challenges and their history.

Malcolm *had* to be wondering why he needed to explain all of this to a supposedly well-educated university faculty member—his teacher.

⬡⬡⬡⬡⬡

Zebediah Jefferson didn't call back. To try to get the anticipated unpleasantness with his son over as soon as he could, Phineas made it a point to start evening rounds earlier than usual.

When Phineas pushed open the double ICU doors, the enticing fragrance of fried chicken surprised him. A half-eaten drumstick rested on a paper plate next to RN Lisa, who sat at the central nursing station writing on a flow sheet. "Better get yourself some of this chicken before everyone else eats it. Carver and Downs are in the workroom with full platters. And sides."

"Okay...Anything new on Jefferson?"

"Same as earlier. Paralyzed and sedated. Blood pressure has been acceptable." Her eyes motioned toward Jefferson' door. "They're waiting for you in there."

Guess I'll be ready. "Thanks."

Phineas opened the workroom door just as Carver took a bite from a golden-crusted thigh cradled in his fingers. Downs was busy cutting into a breast with plastic cutlery. Carver immediately set his portion on a paper plate and found a napkin to wipe his mouth. "Hello, Dr. Mann. We weren't expecting you yet. Have some chicken."

Free food was irresistible when Phineas was a cash-strapped intern, so he understood the young men's fervor. "Who's our benefactor?"

"Ada James' family. Turns out her grandson, Jericho, has a business. He sent all this by." Carver gestured at two tall paper tubs, one open and revealing a mound of coleslaw; and two large, open and oil-spotted cardboard clamshell boxes held golden fried chicken pieces and hush puppies. He peered through the plastic cover of the unopened tub and from the white meringue on top, guessed dessert was banana pudding.

"He has a restaurant?"

Malcolm grinned. "A garage."

"Excuse me?"

"He cooks all this in his garage. People call in orders. His cousins—you remember the guys in the red jackets—told me he has quite a local following when they delivered it. Business cards are in the box."

The door cracked open and Ron Bullock's inquisitive face poked through ahead of his immaculate white coat. "I smelled food."

Phineas laughed. "The locusts are invading! Help yourself, Ron."

"Thanks, Guys. Been a long day and I'm starving."

"How's the measles thing going?"

Bullock picked up a plate and began surveying the offerings. "Still trying to stay ahead of the antivaxxers on the Internet; before herd immunity wanes and we have an outbreak." The infectious disease specialist unfolded a paper napkin and used it to extract a breast and a drumstick then purposed another napkin to grip the plastic serving spoon before plating sides.

Carver's head snapped back at Bullock's words. "Measles! They taught us in medical school that it was a thing of the past." Ron explained about the British article and the growing movement against vaccination.

Phineas pocketed one of Jericho's business cards and stepped toward the door. "I'm going to face Jefferson's son now. Save me a piece. I'll have a taste after—just so that I can properly thank the James family."

Carver reached for his piece of chicken. "Make sure you try the sauces, especially the honey mustard."

Phineas lingered, feigning patience with the hungry young men. He began tapping his foot. "Anyone care to join me?"

Carver and Downs glanced at each other with sheepish expressions. Phineas waited while they wiped their hands. Carver stood and buttoned his white coat. "Sorry. Of course, we'll come with you."

Phineas led them out of the workroom. "Lisa said Jefferson's been quiet all day on his meds. Any new clues for what happened earlier?"

"No, Sir," Downs answered. He and Carver looked uneasy when they reached Jefferson's door.

Phineas lifted his hand, ready to push it open. "Ready?" Carver and Downs nodded, and Phineas led the way. The three lined the near side of the bed and squinted in the dim light. Phineas smelled sweat and stale tobacco smoke layered with the bleach-like odor of ICU disinfectant. He surveyed the monitors and his patient and absorbed the added tension in the room. Every six seconds, the mechanical wheeze of the ventilator penetrated the silence. He spoke close to their patient's ear first. "Mr. Jefferson, Drs. Mann, Carver and Downs here. We're going to talk to your son about you."

He turned to the visitors seated across the bed from them. "I hope you received my message. I called this morning to let you know that your father had a setback."

When Zebediah Jefferson shifted his weight to lean forward, his denim shirt was dark with perspiration around the neck and under the arms. "I came soon as I heard it. What's 'a setback' mean? What in hell happened to Daddy?"

Angela wore her nurses' whites with the top unzipped to where a silver cross, resting on the beginning of her cleavage, bobbed as she twisted toward Zebediah and said, "Now, no need to curse, Zeb." She turned her attention to Phineas and adjusted her top. "I came as soon as Zeb called me. What have you been able to determine, Dr. Mann?"

"The residents found him during the night looking like he was in severe pain. Then he had diarrhea. Our tests have been unrevealing so far. We were concerned he might start the violent spasms again, so he was treated for pain and placed back on the medication to paralyze him."

"So, nothing else to explain it?"

"No Ma'am."

Angela sat back in her chair and folded her hands, as if she was reflecting on a biblical passage in church.

Zebediah stared at Carver's face. "I don't like this place—and then havin' to come here to make sure y'all are lookin' after Daddy—and I find y'all hiding and eatin' fried chicken...You young doctors is spoilt. Daddy made sure I wasn't spoilt." He pushed his right fist into his left palm and cracked his knuckles. "Like I said before, he better get better 'fore this place gets on my last nerve."

Under the burden of Zebediah's glare, Carver transferred his weight from one foot to the other and back again.

Angela placed her hand on Zebediah's. "Now Zeb. A body's got to have sustenance. Let's you and me go pray for your Daddy. You can show me the church where you were raised."

Zebediah groaned. "One *more* place I'd rather not be."

"Then I say it's high time I went there with you."

A gurgle came from under Enoch Jefferson's sheet, and a stench filled the room. Zebediah stood, his eyes still locked on Carver. "Les go, Angela. They need to clean his mess up."

When Zebediah pushed open the room's door, Lisa's evening shift replacement nurse, Dorothy, stood at attention outside. Her uniform was brilliant white against flawless expresso brown skin, and her straightened hair was cut short. Her eyes became round saucers as Zebediah slowed his departure long enough to bark at her. "You need to wipe his ass. He's shit hisself."

⬡⬡⬡⬡⬡

For the second time that evening, the aroma of cooked chicken greeted Phineas, but this time it saturated his senses as he stepped through his own front door. Iris squatted in front of the open oven, her flushed face reflecting its heat.

"I think it's done. Hope you're hungry. I baked chicken and potatoes."

"Famished. Thanks, Darlin'." Phineas felt no need to inform her he'd already feasted on chicken, deep-fried to crispy perfection and smothered in delicious sauces. Or that he'd also enjoyed a heaping helping of banana pudding, modest consolations after the unpleasantness of Zebediah Jefferson. If Phineas confessed to this, Iris' beautiful, flushed face would fall, and he'd hear how she'd toiled to put food on their table.

As she pulled a pan out of the oven, she turned her cheek up for a kiss. "Why don't you wash up and rally the troops. Ask Jacob to set the table."

Phineas sneaked a look at the pan of Shake and Bake chicken that she set on a trivet before she hugged him with oven mitts. He whispered in her ear, "Do you think I'm *that* hot?"

She burst into laughter. "Absolutely. How was your day?"

"Not a good day in the ICU. The patient Angela's been visiting had a setback."

Iris wrinkled her nose. "So, you're probably stuck with her a while longer?"

"'Fraid so. Can't say more. Patient confidentiality." He wanted to say more.

Jacob shuffled into the kitchen. "I'm hungry. When's dinner?"

Iris pointed at the empty table. "Your timing is perfect. I need you to set the table while I put the food out."

"Maybe I should do some more homework until it's all ready." He began slipping away.

She clapped the mitts together. "Hold it right there, young man. Wash your hands and set the table now. Homework after we eat and clean up dishes."

During dinner, Phineas' thoughts kept straying to his burdens in the ICU, especially the mystery of Enoch Jefferson's decline. He had to force himself to focus on family. He watched Jacob for a conversation opening when his son's mouth wasn't full. "So, Jacob, is there much activity in the hives?"

"I watched them a little while this afternoon. Lots of foraging flights from all three with the nectar flow. Then I got chased away. I'm pretty sure it was Jezebel's workers that pinged me when I stepped close." Phineas was pleased that Jacob was understanding the meaning of the beekeepers' term 'pinging', the warning taps bees use to let an intruder know their presence is not going to be tolerated for long, before the stinging begins.

"So, they're still pretty spicy?" Phineas envisioned Martha and Iris squatting in the garden to harvest berries and vegetables while bees foraged around them. "Martha, have they bothered you?"

Crunching on a mouthful of snap pea pods, she shook her head with enthusiasm.

Jacob buttered his potato. "I'll say they're spicy. When can we requeen? I'll find the old one and pinch her as soon as we have a new one."

"We probably should if they're still aggressive. Bees are usually on their best behavior now, during the tulip poplar nectar flow, since they have plenty of food. Unfortunately, I won't have time until June when I go off service." Phineas couldn't imagine when he'd have enough of a break to purchase a new queen and then find the old queen to execute her, to 'pinch' her in beekeepers' parlance. He searched for a tidbit that would keep Jacob's interest.

"Did you know that angry bees have been used in warfare?" He had not long ago finished reading a book on honey bees' roles in history.

Iris pursed her lips at him. She might not be thrilled with his direction.

Jacob looked up from his plate, a mouthful of baked chicken filling his cheeks. "How?" He mumbled.

"During ancient times, bees were lobbed in brittle clay containers into enemy strongholds in order to root out troops. And our own colonial troops even used bees against the British in the Revolutionary War."

Jacob paused his chewing. "Now *that's* cool!"

Iris narrowed her eyes at Phineas. "Jacob, no more talking with your mouth full."

⬡⬡⬡⬡⬡

Iris turned off the house's lights, one by one, until she reached him in the living room where Phineas was reclining with a thick sheaf of papers on his lap; his reading glasses perched on the bridge of his nose. Stretched out on her pillow on the floor next to him, Stella was snoring. Phineas could sense Iris peering over his shoulder before she spoke. "That doesn't look medical. What're you reading?"

He turned his head to answer her over his shoulder. "My intern's fiancé gave me some of her PhD thesis writing. It's about The Wilmington Massacre of 1898."

Iris looked puzzled. "What inspired her interest in what you're reading?"

"I met her that night I stopped at The Rathskeller before coming home. Her name is Patrice. She's a PhD candidate in African American Studies and told me about her thesis. I confessed complete ignorance on the topic, so she sent a copy of an early draft. It's very good, if you're interested." Phineas took off his glasses. "She's worried about her fiancé, who is also my intern—and is Black. Malcolm's taking care of the racist's father."

"Should she be worried?" Her concern replaced her puzzlement.

"We're all on edge around him. This evening when we met, he glared at Malcolm through the whole meeting. And he looked and sounded angry, but angry seems to be his default mode."

Iris' hands rested on his shoulders. "So, what do you know about this guy?"

"Well, he has a confederate flag tattoo, a White Power bumper sticker, an NRA hat, and he owns firearms." He extended a new finger with each detail. "And he seems constantly angry." He held up his thumb.

She squeezed his shoulders. "Shouldn't you let hospital administrators and security know?"

"I talked to security already—and he hasn't really done anything yet."

"They shouldn't wait..." Her voice had risen. "... till he does." Then softened to a level that wouldn't awaken Jacob and Martha.

Phineas pivoted his torso enough to look into Iris' blue eyes. "I'd hoped his father would get steadily better and we could avoid it. Then something...and we don't know what it was...happened to the old man. Looks like he'll be in the ICU longer than I hoped. And whatever happened has inflamed his son."

"Are you sure just talking to security is enough? *You* need to stay safe too." Eyes still blazing, Iris leaned in to kiss his cheek, before she stood tall and studied his face.

Phineas reassembled the papers in his lap and deposited them on the table next to his chair. Iris glanced at the pile. "Tell me about Wilmington."

"I haven't finished all of it yet, but I can tell you I was ignorant on the subject when I started reading. Before 1898, Wilmington was a city with a biracial government and successful Black businesses, including the main newspaper. Then, on one day before the election, encouraged by articles and cartoons in the Raleigh News and Observer, hundreds of heavily armed white vigilantes marched through the town murdering Blacks and burning their properties. The whites had a Gatling gun on a wagon and killed many—maybe hundreds of Black citizens. The rest fled into the swamps."

Iris winced. "How horrible! I didn't know." She stared into his eyes. "You *are* going to tell me what a Gatling gun is?"

"The first machine gun, a powerful weapon in those times, and one that only the army was supposed to have. After the violence, the white supremacists installed their men in the Wilmington city government in a coup d'état, and it didn't stop there. Their movement spread all the way to the state and federal government and gave birth to Black voter suppression and Jim Crow. A brutal event a century ago in North Carolina is still ruining the lives of millions of Black US citizens and continues to create people like my patient's son."

"Think white supremacists could take power again?"

"I suppose it's possible—or at least they could commit more acts of violence. The Ku Klux Klan is still strong in North Carolina—outside of liberal Chapel Hill. You've seen the articles about their very public demonstrations, and some were not so far from here."

"I want to read her paper. Sounds like everyone should read it, because it's not in the history books *I* read in school."

Stella rose from her pillow and rummaged under it with her snout, until she extracted a long white athletic sock. She bowed before Phineas and Iris, stretching, sock dangling from her mouth, tail wagging.

Iris knelt next to Stella and pried her jaws open to extract the sock. "Give me that, Girl. C'mon." She began studying the sock for holes. "She's started sneaking into Jacob's room and stealing his smelly socks."

"Must like the bouquet."

She wrinkled her nose. "In case you haven't noticed, his smell *is* changing. Adolescence has definitely begun."

"I noticed. Hope we're ready for it."

"Stella takes them into the backyard and deposits them in your tiny patch of lawn."

"At least we know where to find them."

Iris stood and shook her head at Stella, who begged with her eyes for the sock. "If it were that simple. Problem is that Jacob doesn't pick them up before he mows the lawn. Told me we didn't tell him that was part of the job. I had to buy him a new pair of baseball socks last week for his game after the mower shredded his."

"Now he knows it's part of the job. If he can't see his way to pick up his dirty socks from his floor or the lawn, *he* buys the next pair."

She tilted her head toward him and squinted. "You do recall that his twelfth birthday is a week from Saturday?"

Phineas had to dig under the deluge of recent events to bring that memory to the surface. “Of course. What do you want me to do?”

“I’ll take care of a present. Can you do food?”

“Tell me how many. I’ve found a takeout place I think will be good, and they deliver.” He extracted the business card from his pocket. It read *Gramma’s Cookin’* above a phone number and *Home Cookin’ Delivered to your home.* “What are you going to get him?”

“Besides socks, he wants a video game.”

“Which one?”

She frowned. “He’d prefer one called Mortal Kombat, but I told him that’s a nonstarter. He said he’ll let me know other options. Any ideas?”

“If I think of something, I’ll be sure to let you know.”

“Great. I predict a last-minute shopping trip. Come on. Time for bed.”

Stella whined and padded to the front door. She turned her head and looked from Phineas to Iris expectantly.

Iris followed to let her out. “Either she needs to go, or she’s going to look for a replacement sock. You go ahead to bed. I’ll be in after I let Stella back in.”

⬡⬡⬡⬡⬡

Iris found Phineas flat on his back between the sheets, eyes closed, face relaxed, snoring softly, clearly too tired to stay awake for her. He’d have to rise before dawn again tomorrow, yet even these months attending on the ICU were better than his time at Baptist Hospital in New Orleans. Back then they’d paged him so many times every night, that she had to move into the guest room or be too tired to function at her job. Now as a UNC faculty member supervising house staff, it was rare that he was paged after they went to bed. She lifted his shoulder and rolled him onto his side after she slipped under the covers. Her brain continued to churn on full alert.

Iris had also been sleeping better since they’d moved back to North Carolina, at least until the news of Angela’s return last week. After Iris finished her PhD in 1992, she'd joined the UNC faculty and was soon promoted to assistant professor. Being on the faculty meant that she no longer had to be in the front lines performing onerous social work duties for tragic, desperately challenged patients, like during the AIDS epidemic they'd both faced in New Orleans. Now, she only filled out discharge forms, investigated insurance coverage, and went through the process of finding a bed in a nursing home as occasional teaching examples. Instead, Iris wrote lectures and research papers, and graded her students, who formed an insulating layer between her and patients' miseries.

The satisfaction she felt in her motherhood role continued to surprise her, but she often felt like she was tasked with generating the energy and gravitational pull of a sun to keep Martha, Jacob, Phineas, and her mother healthy and in their correct orbits, especially these months when Phineas was covering the ICU.

When Phineas was a resident and fellow at UNC, before children, she'd had time for hobbies and to read novels. She'd pursue creative activities again someday. Maybe return to the pottery wheel and the soothing feeling of wet clay turning in her hands. Maybe try her hand at clay sculpture. Maybe mosaics. Maybe combine them into sparkling art.

It had felt like Jacob processed the information they'd given him about the charges against Phineas but didn't fully accept it. She'd been planning to explain it all to him eventually; she just hadn't settled on a time or approach. She'd wanted to protect Martha and him from it as long as she could and had waited too long, allowing him to find out on his own without any guardrails. She swallowed and blinked back a tear for her mistake. Jacob had promised he wouldn't tell Martha. Gentle, sweet Martha. Martha wasn't ready yet and wouldn't be for quite a while. She hoped he'd keep his promise.

Why had Angela surfaced after so many years? Could she have had a secret schoolgirl crush on Phineas, felt rejected, and now returned slender and blond, for him to have a fresh look? That seemed doubtful. Was it even remotely possible she held no grudges against him? Or against her?

Back in New Orleans in 1985, Phineas had explained that Angela possessed some sort of fringe religious belief that obliged her to try to keep patients alive until all resuscitative efforts failed, alive even if they were hopelessly suffering and lacked any chance at regaining an acceptable quality of life. He said her views came after she lost her father from a hopeless terminal lung condition when she was a teenager; that she believed he'd been denied a chance for a miracle cure, for *her* miracle. Phineas had concluded that this was why, after he provided morphine to ease the suffering of terminal patients during the miserable aftermath of Hurricane Jezebel, she'd pursued murder charges against him.

Iris must have suppressed until now the memory of the last time she'd seen Angela in person. It was an angry scene she and Angela created in a French Quarter bistro with Phineas and Simon, Phineas' lawyer, as onlookers. Angela had burst through the door and taunted Phineas, teasing that he should enjoy good food while he could, because there wasn't going to be any in prison. A shocked and pregnant Iris had exploded from her chair and called the bitch a bitch.

Angela was out for revenge. Iris felt it in every tired bone.

⬡⬡⬡⬡⬡

After Wednesday morning rounds, Phineas found Ada James' daughters, Ruth and Rebecca, once again in the ICU waiting room, their Sunday finery replaced with casual weekday attire. Jericho hurried into the room in a crisp grey work shirt and pants, and black industrial shoes. His shirt pocket advertised JJ's Office Cleaning. Phineas shook his large hand, appreciating the restraint in his grip, the restraint from its potential crushing strength.

"How's the James family today?"

"Depends," Ruth answered. "How's Mother doing?"

"We're making slow progress. Her white blood cell count is trending in the right direction and she's had no fever for 48 hours, so the antibiotics seems to be helping."

Rebecca half smiled before her spontaneous reaction to any good news faded, and she again looked concerned. "That sounds positive. How much longer do you think she'll have to be on the respirator?"

"At this point, I can only make an educated guess. She's tolerating feeding through the tube, she doesn't need as much extra oxygen, and her x-ray hasn't worsened."

They studied his face and waited for his guess, as if mere words would determine Ada James' fate. "We might begin letting her do more of the work of breathing by the weekend."

"Praise God," Ruth responded.

Rebecca followed with, "And thank you, Dr. Mann. We're grateful for your team's care of Mother."

"You're certainly welcome." He looked up at Jericho James, who leaned close to Ruth and Rebecca so as not to miss a word. "Mr. James, thank you for the delicious food you sent by yesterday. It lifted the spirits of the whole team."

A wide smile lit up the big man's face. "Call me Jericho… Glad you liked it. They're Gramma's recipes. She taught me."

"I was surprised to hear you cook in your garage."

"That's just until I can save up enough to get the food truck I got my eye on. And once I get that all handled, I'll try to sell my cleaning contracts and do lunch *and* dinner menus from the truck at busy locations I got picked out." He took a deep breath and exhaled slowly. "Might be a while though. I gave up on trying to borrow. Know how hard it is for a Black man to get a loan?"

Phineas remembered the first Chapel Hill bank he went to as a strapped intern in July of 1977. The affable loan officer just handed him cash and told him to pay him back when he could. "You must be having some long days."

"Jericho and his cousins clean offices from 11 PM till they're done. After they get some rest, he buys fresh food and cooks. His cousins deliver till it starts to slow around 10." Ruth flashed a proud grin as she looked up at her nephew. "No one can match Jericho's batter fried chicken—or his dipping sauces."

"Best I've had," Phineas responded, while trying to not display amazement at Jericho's considerable workload and undeterred ambitions. "I'd like to place another dinner order for the ICU next week, and I want to pay for this one. Will Tuesday around supper time work again?"

"We can certainly make that happen. Same order?"

"It was perfect. How much do I owe you?" Phineas reached through the slit on the side of his white coat for his wallet.

Jericho held up his hands, palms out. "Just pay when it comes. Cash or check."

"Any chance you can make a home delivery the following Saturday for my son's birthday?" *And make me a hero with my family?*

"Tell me what, when and where."

"Do you do seafood too?"

"Shrimp and flounder, and we have other vegetables: collards, beans and deep-fried okra. You like okra, Dr. Mann?" He pulled a worn leather wallet from his back pocket and extracted one of several folded pieces of paper. "Here's our menu. You can keep it."

Phineas quickly studied the Xeroxed sheet. "So, the okra's battered—then deep fried?"

"Just like Gramma's."

Fresh saliva began to pool under Phineas' tongue. One good thing he'd escaped New Orleans with was a taste for okra.

⬡⬡⬡⬡⬡

Late afternoon rounds were completed earlier than Phineas had anticipated. There had been only one new ICU admission to be tucked in, and Enoch Jefferson's visitors hadn't yet arrived by the time the team rounded. The resident and intern were gathering their dinners and night's provisions in the hospital cafeteria before returning to review and chart the day's progress or lack of it. The only new data was Jefferson's blood panel, which suggested a minor portion of his red blood cells had ruptured, i.e., hemolyzed, at the time of his setback. They reviewed his medications and the lengthy list of possible causes of this hemolysis and had come up empty.

Phineas scanned the workstation for Enoch Jefferson's nurse, Lisa, without locating her. He wanted to check if there had been any last-minute changes in the elderly man's condition before he left the hospital. Phineas cracked open the patient's door and heard hushed women's voices. The hallway light shone on Lisa's back as she stood at the near bedside and on Angela, who was leaning back into one of the two chairs on the far side. Her crossed legs extended straight out with her feet concealed under the bed.

Lisa turned her head to look at him. "Speak of the devil. We were just talking about you."

Phineas saw no path of escape. He stepped through the doorway and pulled it closed. Even after his eyes adjusted, he felt exposed and vulnerable in the darkness. "Did I miss Mr. Jefferson's son?"

"Naw. He had to go to some kind of club meeting with a bunch of his friends," Angela answered. "Said he'd be by later."

What kind of club does HE belong to? Probably not stamp collecting.

Lisa cocked her head at an angle. "Angela's been telling me about how you two worked together in New Orleans."

"I imagine you're finding *that* interesting."

"I sure am! Sounds like you had lots of excitement there."

"Well, that was a long time ago, and a hurricane put an end to it, and now I'm here." He wanted to close down *that* conversation but wondered how much Angela had told of her deranged side of his story. Who knew what she would include?

Lisa took the hint. "I need to get more tube feed and some flush solution for Enoch. I'll let you two catch up." She stepped into the hallway and closed the door. Being left alone with Angela was not what Phineas had wanted.

Silence followed except for the ventilator breaths at six second intervals. Angela's stare suggested she was going to wait for him to speak first. He cleared his throat. "I'm curious... How did you decide to come to North Carolina?" He couldn't say her name. Just the thought of it painfully tightened the muscles along the back of his neck and skull.

"Well, you know what it was like in New Orleans after Jezebel washed away Baptist. Job prospects there were slim—and usually fell through after they met me—after they recognized me from TV." She paused and narrowed her eyes like she was waiting for him to respond. "I could only get the jobs no one else wanted. Third shift in a nursing home got old."

"Sorry to hear that."

"I'm sure you are, especially now that I'm here." She knew how he felt about it.

"Why all the way to Durham?"

"The VA lists job openings nationally. I saw an opening in the Durham VA ICU, and I'd heard through the grapevine that you and Ava had come to North Carolina, so I figured it must be a good place to live."

"And has it been?" Maybe Angela would decide to look elsewhere in the VA system, now that she's in it.

"Oh yes! And now I've met Zeb. My social life was pretty empty after all the Jezebel mess." She began fingering the silver cross on its thin strand. "I know you don't think he's much, but it's nice to finally have a man interested in me."

"It's none of my business, but he seems pretty angry when he's here." *Scary angry, actually.*

She uncrossed her legs, planted her feet, and leaned forward. "I can handle him. I know what I'm doing. And you're right...It's none of your business."

Lisa pushed through the door, a large syringe of clear liquid in one hand and a bag of thick cream-colored fluid in the other. "So, are you two enjoying getting caught up?"

Angela laughed out loud. "Lisa Honey, it's been an absolute blast shooting the breeze with Dr. Mann here. We have *so much* history together."

The history that Phineas wanted buried forever. "I guess I'll have to speak with Mr. Jefferson's son tomorrow. Please let him know that I stopped by." He still couldn't say her name to her face. He began inching toward the door.

"You can be sure I will." A smirk came and went in an instant.

Phineas picked up his pace on the way out the of the ICU and headed straight for the adjacent hospital parking deck, removing his white coat and folding it over his arm as he hustled. Deep breaths of warm outside air partially settled the tension he'd contained in Jefferson's room. He kept moving with the single-minded realization that, with the lengthening May days, this could be a rare opportunity during the hectic month for him to decompress while enjoying precious daylight time in his garden. This thought brought him much needed comfort.

He found his pickup truck in its usual location on the third level, where early morning arrivers could be assured of spots. There was no line at the concrete block exit kiosk, where the familiar attendant waved Phineas through when he saw the color-coded faculty hangtag on his rearview mirror.

Traffic out of town on Airport Road moved better than he expected as he passed by the modern police headquarters, an architect's statement in grey cement. Good to know how accessible the place was. He hoped he'd never need it. He'd seen all he needed of the inside of police stations after his arrest for murder so many years ago.

When he opened the front door, Stella was waiting at attention, her thick yellow tail wagging. Martha looked up from a jumble of papers on the kitchen table with Stella's whining. "Daddy's home!" She scrambled from her chair and accepted a bending hug from him.

Iris turned from the counter. "Well, didn't expect you this early. I'm just gathering dinner ingredients. Should be ready in plenty of time for us to get to Jacob's game."

Whoops! With Phineas' focus on escaping Angela and on enjoying the pleasures of gardening, Jacob's evening game had escaped him. He was grateful that Iris had everything on the home front under control. "I thought I'd do a little work in the garden before that." At that moment, he resolved to fill out a personal calendar at the beginning of his ICU months and look at it every morning. He should have learned that by now. Next time he'd do it for sure.

As he kissed Iris' cheek, she put down a paring knife. "Take Martha. I'll call you when dinner's close."

He winked at Martha, whose sunny smile rewarded his efforts to hurry home. "Martha, I just need to change my clothes and I'll meet you there. Why don't you grab the colander? And where's Jacob?"

Iris turned back to the salad fixings. "In his room. He's supposed to be doing his homework. Go do your gardening."

Honey bees reflecting the aesthetic early evening light came and went from the hive entrances like shooting stars high over Martha's and Phineas' heads. Father and daughter were a silent team in the four raised beds, she gathering produce and he on his knees weeding what didn't belong. If only he could eliminate certain people from his life as easily. People who created conflicts for his team of doctors. People who unearthed past miseries from sites where Phineas had buried them.

Having the whole backyard production in perfect order deeply satisfied Phineas. Working the rich soil drew the ICU stress out of his core, the outside air cleansed his lungs, and Martha's enthusiasm and happiness were contagious. She and her ponytail bounced from one plant to the next, pausing now and then to nibble a snap pea pod or study a bumblebee on a blackberry blossom. She began humming a tune he vaguely recognized from the movie *Mulan* he'd taken her to in April.

He probed the soil along the carrots and noted that some were fat enough to harvest. "Martha, want to pull a few carrots?" She happily obliged.

Stella announced Jacob's arrival with a single loud whine. His baseball uniform promised her the cherished duty of retrieving his batting practice offerings. "Hey Dad, can we play some Stella ball?"

"I can get there sooner if you lend a hand—and it's good for *everyone* to get some dirt on their hands once in a while."

Jacob's shoulders slouched forward. "Huh! I'll get dirt on my hands when I steal second base, and third." He pivoted and sauntered back toward the garage.

Phineas spotted Stella snatching ripe raspberries off the canes. *When did she start doing that*? "Stella! Shoo! Those aren't for you."

⬡⬡⬡⬡⬡

Saturday morning in the ICU came too early for Phineas. He and Iris had to outlast a willful Jacob, who had been determined to stay up late on a Friday night, while they were hoping for quiet pillow time together. Iris finally pulled rank and sent the stubborn nearly 12-year-old to bed at 11, before she and Phineas could slip between the cool sheets of their king-sized bed and enjoy each other's warm caresses.

Phineas was in the middle of covering a head-tilting-back, gaping yawn when Downs and Carver arrived for duty with droopy eyelids that made them look wearier than Phineas felt. The young men cradled the obligatory large Styrofoam cups of steaming coffee.

Phineas thought back to his training years as he pushed his hands into the sleeves of his lab coat. "TGIF?"

Downs winced and swallowed the hot liquid. "Bars were epic. He's Not Here was rockin'."

"Big turnout?"

"*Lots* of house staff. You shoulda' come."

"If your leader was there, it might not've been 'rockin'.'"

The double ICU doors parted with Ram Patel and Sadie Goldschmidt, in Carolina blue scrubs, guiding a rolling stretcher. A shock of white hair was all that was visible of the blanket-covered patient. He or she was receiving life-supporting breaths that the respiratory therapist squeezed from a bag through an endotracheal tube. The chart-carrying ER nurse completed the transport team. She hefted a stack of fat manila folders held together with thick rubber bands.

Jeff, the weekend ICU charge nurse, approached the group. "Put him in seven." After a college football injury had ended Jeff's athletic career, he'd changed his major from physical education to nursing. His time as a patient had enticed him into the medical field. The other nurses were glad to have his upbeat attitude and his lifting strength.

Patel eyed Carver and Downs. "Man, you guys have looked better. Sure you're ready to work?"

Phineas was skimming the ER clipboard. "Hey, I know this guy."

"He's a frequent flyer," Patel responded. "I found your name on some prior admissions."

"So, what happened this time?"

"About the same as the last time...and the time before. He gets bronchitic symptoms and more short of breath, and even though he's been told not to, he turns his oxygen way up and suppresses his respiratory drive. Then, as you'd predict, he retains lots more carbon dioxide, enough to put him to sleep. When he can't be roused, his wife calls 911. His CO2 was 112 this time, not even *close* to his record. Antibiotics, steroids, bronchodilators, and weaning his vent and oxygen have always worked, so I ordered the same. Sputum cultures were sent from the ER."

"Chest x-ray?"

"Just big emphysematous lungs. No pneumonia or heart failure."

"Sounds good. How was the rest of your night?"

"No surprises, but we did join the less than exclusive ranks of the Zebediah-offended." Patel shook his head.

Anger began seeping onto the blank slate of Phineas' usual upbeat early morning mood. "Oh no. What'd he say *this* time?"

"He told the evening nurse that he didn't want 'any more of them thar colored doctors messin' wit' his Daddy'." The accent Patel mimicked was rural Southern with a hint of the Asian subcontinent.

"Or Jew ladies," Goldschmidt added with a snarl.

Patel raised his hands, palms up and shrugged. "Looks like he's fired everyone but Downs and you, Dr. Mann."

"We'll see how long he keeps *me*. You all just keep up your good work." Phineas finished buttoning his white coat. "We'd better get started on rounds, so you can go home and get some sleep."

It then occurred to him that the pulmonary fellow, Dr. Gabriella Morales-Villalobos, was scheduled to return Monday from her honeymoon. Would her warm and winning ways soften the stone heart of Zebediah Jefferson, or would her Mexican roots add heat and oxygen to his smoldering fires?

WEEK THREE

He is not worthy of the honeycomb that shuns the hive because the bees have stings.

From The Tragedy of Locrine by W. S. 1595

Dr. Gabriella Morales-Villalobos waited at the ICU nurses' station as Phineas arrived for Monday morning rounds. She chatted with the interns and residents of the team in her immaculately white and pressed lab coat. A sharp line of demarcation encircled her eyes where sunglasses had kept the golden skin its original hue. The rest of her face was a rich bronze. Her shiny black hair, which nearly reached her slim waist at pulmonary division social events, was restrained in a tight bun.

As soon as she noticed him, Phineas proclaimed, "You came back! I was beginning to worry you'd decided you preferred the beach to the ICU."

She took on a wistful expression. "Who says I don't?"

"Well, I'm sure glad you're back. We can use your help." He turned to his intern. "Malcolm, where do you want to start?"

Carver shuffled his thin deck of index cards. "Where we usually start. With Jefferson in 10." He summarized the patient's initial presentation,

ICU course and last week's mysterious worsening for Villalobos. "I am glad to report that he's improved from his sinker last week, and he's almost back off of the paralytic infusion."

Phineas took a step toward Jefferson's door before turning to address their returning pulmonary fellow. "We'll need to fill you in on issues with his son."

The weekdays nurse, Lisa, was waiting for them outside the room. "Weekends reported that he and his nurse friend were here early last evening. Night shift's verbal handoff was that he was almost unrecognizable in a tie and coat. It seems she'd dragged him to a church. Can you believe it?"

Carver extended his arm to push the door open. "May God help us."

Phineas turned toward Lisa. "Think they're actually dating?"

"He's acting like he's courting her, while she seems to be leading him around by his nose."

Phineas offered, "Maybe it's been a while for him, and he might be really lonely now, with his father here."

"Doesn't explain why *she* has an interest in *him*." Lisa wrinkled her nose. "She's not bad looking and a professional, but *that guy*—maybe it's pity dating."

The team streamed into the room and gathered around Jefferson's bed in the low light. Phineas let a paralyzed Enoch Jefferson know they were speaking of him before he whispered to Villalobos, "Sorry you didn't get to see the opisthotonos—but we're hoping it doesn't happen again."

Carver, Villalobos, and Phineas took turns examining Jefferson before stepping back into the hallway. Carver announced softly, "I'd like to try him off paralytics today. If he tolerates that, we can begin weaning his sedation."

Phineas nodded his agreement. "Lisa?"

His nurse looked dubious. "I can try again."

Starting with Room 1, they pressed on from room to room, introducing Villalobos to the conscious patients and examining each of them. The final occupied room, Room 9, contained Ada James. Phineas spotted her daughters, Ruth and Rebecca, through the door's window. They were hovering over her, Rebecca inspecting and straightening her bed linens, and Ruth adjusting and brushing Ms. Ada's glorious wig.

Carver's face brightened when he saw them. "Wish all our patients had a Ruth and a Rebecca." He glanced at his index cards. "Ms. Ada had a quiet weekend. White count is better, and her chest x-ray has started to improve. I think we can start to wean the ventilator."

Phineas nodded to the hemodialysis nurse, as she pushed her bulky machine through the double ICU doors. "We can reduce the ventilator support after Ms. James' dialysis. Let's go see her."

The sisters surveyed the team as they entered. Ruth held her hand out to Villalobos. "So, we have a new doctor. I'm Ruth, one of the daughters, and this is Rebecca."

"Gabriella Morales-Villalobos. Pleased to meet you."

Ruth's eyes opened wide as she released Villalobos' hand. "Oh my. I'm not sure I can remember all that."

"Dr. V will be fine."

Rebecca also extended her hand. "You must be the one the nurses said was coming back from a honeymoon."

Villalobos smiled and sighed, looking wistfully skyward. "I am."

"You still have that honeymoon glow." Rebecca glanced from Villalobos to Carver to Phineas. "So, what can you doctors tell us?"

Phineas circled around the foot of the bed and stood next to Rebecca. "Let's examine your mother. Then it looks like they're ready for her dialysis. If we don't find any new problems, we hope to begin reducing the ventilator settings and to let her breathe more on her own a bit later today. Does that sound good to you Ms. Ada?"

Ada James bowed her head briefly and offered as much of a smile as the tube in her mouth allowed. Ruth clapped once then pressed her hands together. "What wonderful news. We'll pray it all goes as you're hoping." She reached behind her for her purse on the bedside chair. "Jericho wanted me to give you something." She rummaged in the side pocket and handed Phineas a folded sheet of paper. "He wanted to confirm your order for here tomorrow evening."

Carver's and Downs' eyebrows lifted. Carver whispered to Ram Patel, "Looks like you and Sadie get the feast this time."

Phineas examined the paper. "It looks perfect, Ruth. Please give Jericho my okay." He nodded to Carver. "Malcolm, you and Michael are welcome to come back on your afternoon off."

Carver responded, "We just might. It'd be worth it."

⬡⬡⬡⬡⬡

When Phineas arrived for late afternoon rounds, he found Villalobos at the nursing station with a tall stack of patients' charts on the desk in front of her. Lisa, quietly charting next to her, put down her pen. In a spooky, singsong voice she announced, "Dr. Mann, they're back."

Villalobos shot a puzzled look at Lisa.

"Jefferson's son and his nurse friend. They came in while you were in with Ms. James."

Villalobos stood and buttoned her coat. "Okay. Malcolm filled me in on everything with the son. I'm ready to face him."

"I'm not sure I ever am." Phineas answered with a sigh. No one could have told her everything about Zebediah's "nurse friend." He hoped his fellow would never find out. "Lisa, anything new?"

"Still off the paralytic. Responds minimally to gentle stimuli, like cleaning his bottom."

He took a deep breath and pushed Jefferson's door open with Villalobos on his heels. He briefly closed his eyes, trying to hasten their accommodation to the darkness, and wished the visitors would magically disappear. When he opened them, he recognized Zebediah and Angela seated on the far side of the room. He informed Enoch Jefferson that they would be speaking of him.

Angela whispered, "Hey, Dr. Mann. Do we have a new doctor?"

"This is Dr. Morales-Villalobos, our pulmonary fellow."

Villalobos offered her hand. "Nice to meet you."

Angela stood and shook it. "I'm Angela."

Zebediah remained seated, watching. Villalobos turned to him. "I understand you're from Pittsboro, Mr. Jefferson. I went to Northwood High there. Did you go there too?"

"It opened after I left school." He was staring at her face. "Your people pickers or pluckers?"

Phineas felt an immediate urge to react to the insult, to defend his fellow. Villalobos was quicker. "Both. My parents came to Chatham County to pick before I was born there. And they also processed chickens. Then they saved up and opened the taqueria out on 64. You been there?"

"I don't eat Spic food."

She kept a smile through his rudeness. "You should try it. I'll bet you'd like it. It's full of spicy flavors. And it's good for the heart."

"Ain't nuthin' wrong with my heart."

The corner of Angela's mouth twitched, suggesting she'd recognized that Zebediah Jefferson had missed Villalobos' subtle slight, and that she hadn't. "Zeb, we should stop there sometime."

Phineas stomach tightened, and he suppressed an urge to turn and walk out on the pair. "Mr. Jefferson, your father has had a steady day. He's off the medication that was paralyzing him and has had no new problems. If it stays that way, we can soon try to let him come off sedation and wake up. Any questions?"

"Just so's it stays that way," he muttered.

Angela whispered, "Zeb, we should thank the Lord your daddy's making progress. Every day helps his chances."

Phineas pushed open the door. "We'll do our best for him."

In the refuge of the hallway, he turned to Villalobos. "Sorry you had to listen to that."

She shrugged her shoulders. “I’m used to it. He’s just one more ignorant equal opportunity bigot. Some white guys aren’t happy when they realize that if they come into the hospital, their doctor probably isn’t going to look like them anymore.” She stopped walking. “Sorry about the heart thing. It just slipped out.”

“I enjoyed it, and I don’t think he got it.”

“Yeah, but she might explain it to him.”

⬡⬡⬡⬡⬡

Phineas ducked into the physician’s workroom to check out with Carver and Downs before going home. The fragrance of garlic, chilis, and basil filled the confined space. A woman with a substantial Afro and perfect posture sat alone at the desk along the far wall facing away from him. Her black sweater protected against the hospital’s overzealous air conditioning as she bent over a pile of books and papers. The image reminded Phineas of Cornell in the early 1970s when Black student unrest had exploded on campus. When the door clicked shut behind him, she turned to face him.

“Patrice. Hello. I was just looking for Malcolm and Michael.”

“Same here, Dr. Mann. I’m told they’re in Emergency admitting a new patient. I was bringing them dinner.” She nodded at a Tupperware container behind her books. “Seems they have a date with a patient with cirrhosis instead of with me.”

“Smells delicious. I’m sure they’d rather be here.”

“I only brought enough for two, but I can spare a taste if you’re tempted. It’s spicy Thai basil chicken.” She showed him two stainless steel forks wrapped in napkins. “I can wash one before they get back.”

The delicious smell tempted him. “Thanks. I’d hate to trouble you, and dinner should be waiting for me at home.”

“It’d be no trouble, and I could use an excuse to take a break from reading.” She slipped a sheet of paper into the pages of a thick book and closed it.

“Well maybe just a taste. I don’t get to eat much Thai food.”

She popped the top off the container and scooped a forkful for him. He accepted it and offered, "Thanks. I've been wanting to tell you how interesting your paper on the Wilmington Massacre is. I had no idea that happened 100 years ago." He began chewing.

"Glad you like it...I hope it's okay for me to work in here."

"No problem. It's a workroom." Capsaicin began to ignite his tongue. "You did say spicy, didn't you?"

A grin emerged as her posture relaxed. "I should have given more warning. You okay? Can I get you some water?"

His blinked back a tear. "I'm fine." The heat in his mouth started leveling off, and any fatigue he'd felt had melted away. "So, remind me, Patrice. When are you and Malcolm getting married?"

"August. He scheduled his vacation then, and it'll be before UNC's fall semester and my teaching assistant duties."

"How did you two meet?"

Her smile widened. "I was helping organize a charity health event, and he was a first-year medical student there to screen patients. He asked me if he could take my pulse and blood pressure. First time for me with *that* pickup line."

"Clever. I never thought to use that one." Phineas glanced at the empty fork and decided he should be the one to wash it. "How's the month been for the two of you?"

Patrice's smile faded. "It's a tough month. I miss Malcolm every other night, and he's exhausted when he's home. That's why I'm here now. He's better at accepting adversity—even that racist son he's had to deal with. I'm spoiled and don't do so well at not reacting to it."

"Oh? Why do you think that is?"

"He grew up having to fight for everything. Single working mother. City college in New York City then state university. Partial scholarships, student loans, and part-time jobs to survive. I had it easy by comparison." She folded her hands and stared at Phineas' eyes, seeking added respect for her fiancé.

"Where did you grow up?"

"Baltimore. Both parents were high school teachers, so I had two at home tutors from the start. We lived in Elijah Cummings' district, and my folks knew him. Our family was politically quite active, so I had the famous congressman's recommendation. Helped me land a full ride to Harvard. Once you're on that track, once you have that brand, doors open for you—except of course in the South when you're someplace where no one knows who you are."

Phineas was embarrassed he knew nothing about the famous Elijah Cummings. "Malcolm mentioned that he was interested in public health. What are your goals?"

"I want to rewrite history books to tell the truth. Things can't get better for minorities until people know the whole truth. That's why I started with Wilmington. It was pivotal."

"I'm guessing there'll be enough work to fill a career."

"More than one career. There's so much. And there are historical lies in all parts of the country. Among people of color, I grew up advantaged. I'd be ashamed if I didn't make the most of that to change things." She narrowed her eyes. "Where are *you* from?"

"Vermont. Pretty tame there."

"And your ancestors?"

"On my father's side, they fought for the North in the Civil War. My mother's people came from Italy much later." He wondered if saying his people fought for the North would somehow excuse him from blame for racial injustices.

"On your father's side, how far back have you traced your family?"

"My grandmother says one of our ancestors on her side came on the Mayflower." He shrugged. "I haven't seen proof though."

Patrice's eyebrows arched. "And I bet you believe Thanksgiving was a joyous celebration for all involved." Her tone suggested it wasn't.

"Afraid I don't know much beyond that grade school story."

"Well, people should know that the pilgrims exploited the Wampanoag tribe for decades after they were decimated by diseases they caught from settlers. That whole history is terribly messy. Natives were enslaved, murdered, robbed—even in "tame" New England. The Thanksgiving fable was invented so that white New Englanders could feel like they founded the country, and so they could feel good about themselves. For Native Americans, it's a day of mourning."

"I didn't know." On that holiday, he'd always thought about how much he had to be thankful for. It would never be the same.

"That's just the beginning of white man's atrocities on Native Americans. It gets much, much worse." She shook her head.

"I guess you *do* have a lot of work ahead."

She nodded and the two sat in silence. Phineas held up the fork. "I'll wash this and bring it back."

Patrice leaned toward him and plucked it from his hand. "I'll take care of that. Why don't you go check on them in Emergency, so you can get home, and they can get here before their dinner gets too cold?" She stood and took a step toward the door. "It's been nice talking with you, Dr. Mann."

He followed her into the hall. "You too, Patrice. Please send more true history my way."

"Will do. And feel free to share it with others." She beamed with the satisfied expression of a teacher whose student was beginning to understand.

⬡⬡⬡⬡⬡

As Phineas crept down their driveway in his pickup truck, Jacob peeled off his beekeeping jacket. The smoker at his son's feet emitted wisps of white.

An alarmed Phineas braked, parked, and threw open the truck's door. "Something happen?"

"Naw. I peeked under Grace and Charity's covers and saw that their combs were completely full of honey, and there were white wax flakes scattered all over the tops of frames. They needed room to draw comb and store honey, so I lit the smoker and added one honey super each." He sounded proud of himself. It was peak nectar flow, and he had made the decision alone to add boxes of empty frames for the bees to build honeycomb and fill with more honey. Phineas felt a twinge of guilt that he'd neglected the bees' needs.

Jacob's description suggested he'd done the right thing, but Phineas hadn't yet granted permission for him to work the hives alone. Pride in his son's decision making and initiative competed with anxiety that a beekeeping calamity could occur with his young son alone in the apiary. This time of year, especially, each hive box could weigh almost half as much as the boy himself. With the queen laying upwards of 2000 eggs per day, the numbers of workers were rapidly increasing. And the boxes could soon be stacked six to eight high, the top ones only reachable with a step ladder.

"Your mother know you went into the hives by yourself?"

He seemed to take a sudden interest in inspecting his sneakers. "She's making dinner."

"I know you're a good beekeeper, but I hadn't told you that you could be in the hives by yourself yet. What if something dangerous happened?"

Jacob now looked defensive. "It needed to get done—and you're hardly ever home." An angry tone replaced pride.

His words stung Phineas. "It's been a busy month for me."

"May is half over, and it's the bees' busiest month. They needed space, for honey and for the queens to lay more eggs. And *I'm* also busy this month!"

Phineas couldn't fault Jacob's logic, only his impatience. "Let's discuss this over dinner. Your mother needs to know."

Jacob groaned. "You know what Mom will say. She doesn't care about the bees. And she's sooo cautious."

It occurred to Phineas that he might be able to score points with Jacob, to gain back some of what he's lost after Jacob's damaging Internet searches. "Let's see what I can do for you on this."

⬡⬡⬡⬡⬡

After Phineas mentioned Jacob's correct and insightful beekeeping actions, Iris put down her knife and fork and stared at her dinner plate then their son. "Jacob, really?"

He scowled. "It needed to get done—and who knows when Dad would be here next during daylight? Sometimes a person just needs to take action, without waiting...and waiting...for permission."

Iris was still staring at him. "If it's not an absolute emergency, *you* can wait."

Phineas searched for a middle ground. "Jacob's assessment of the hives, and the steps he took today were correct...and this *is* Jacob's second season of beekeeping...and he did pass the certification tests..."

Iris' lips tightened into a thin line before she responded. "Where are you going with this?"

How do I move this forward while keeping myself out of the doghouse?

"When the hives are shorter after the honey harvest, how about we say he can go into the hives with me watching him from a window, but only after he's convinced me he has a good reason. And maybe...maybe somewhere further down the road, if I'm at work, and he pages me and explains his thoughts, *you* can watch him from the window? He can always just run away from the hives, in the unlikely event that he needs to. I think he's ready. What do you think?"

Iris returned her gaze to her plate. "You and I will talk about this later."

Jacob and Martha looked at each other with raised eyebrows and kept silent, but Jacob did appear satisfied with his father's effort, at least for the moment.

⬡⬡⬡⬡⬡

Martha's eyes closed and her breaths lengthened. Iris closed *The Secret Garden* and laid it on the nightstand. She eased herself off the bed and onto her feet then switched off the lamp. In the darkened hallway, light escaped under Jacob's closed door. She tapped lightly on it. "Jacob, lights out in an hour."

A soft grunt acknowledged her command.

The familiar sight of Phineas in his recliner studying a medical journal greeted her in the living room. He peered up at her over his reading glasses. "Martha asleep?"

"Yeah." She lowered herself into the chair across from him. "We should talk about Jacob." She spoke softly and gestured toward the hallway. "He's awake with his door closed."

He closed the journal over his finger, keeping his place. "I got the feeling you're not entirely happy with me."

"Yeah. You guys and your bees are the first thing. They still scare an outsider like me. I'm okay with him messing with them when you're right there, but when you're not..."

Phineas nodded slowly. "I get it." He took off his glasses and leaned forward. "He surprised me today too, but when he explained it, I realized how much he wants to be allowed to make his own decisions and to act on them. It's the first time it really hit me how much he's growing up."

"Good of you to notice. And that leads me to the second thing."

"Second thing?"

"During the months when you're not around much, I'm the one here having to deal with his growing independence. Before you tell him he can do something that I might be uncomfortable with, we should talk." She had to remind herself to keep her voice down.

Phineas stared at the floor. His silence and the tight line of his lips suggested he felt chastised. Had she overreacted? Was the stress of her end of semester workload, her obligations to the children's increasingly hectic schedules, and Angela's sudden, unexpected return and attachment to a scary racist wearing her down?

Her husband had always preferred to avoid all disagreements with her. He met her gaze. "I'll do better."

⬡⬡⬡⬡⬡

Before Tuesday evening rounds Phineas opened the windowless ICU workroom door and was greeted by the now familiar bouquet of Gramma's Cookin's fried chicken. A seated Ron Bullock pointed a chicken wing at him. "Hah! I guessed right."

"And what profound insight are you referring to?"

Bullock set the wing on a paper plate. "I knew you wouldn't short-change the other resident team, so I came expecting another Tuesday feast. You didn't let me down. This middle-aged bachelor knows how to forage in the wilderness."

"What? We're already middle-aged? When did that happen?"

"Looked in the mirror lately, Buddy?"

Must have aged this month.

Ram Patel and Sadie Goldschmidt grinned at Phineas over heaping paper plates of Gramma's Cookin'. They mumbled with full mouths, "Thank you, Dr. Mann."

"You're welcome. I'm expecting Gramma's Cookin' to save me Saturday night for my son's birthday."

Bullock raised his eyebrows. "Got room for one more?"

"You want to play video games with a bunch of sixth graders, or hang around with Sarah Jane?"

"Maybe I'll get my own order and call Chelsea. I'll need their number."

"Better idea. Business cards should be in the box." Phineas waited for Ram to swallow. "Anything new since morning rounds?"

"Ada James seems to be tolerating less ventilator support."

"We should turn it up a bit overnight, to rest her. Maybe we can give her a trial off support in the morning. And Jefferson?"

"Fingers crossed. No spasms and steady BP. I got him to squeeze my hand on command this afternoon. I've been explaining things to him." Ram looked pleased with himself.

"Progress. Now if we can avoid setbacks for a couple of days, we can try him off the vent." Phineas winced at the memory of how things had unexpectedly worsened the last time he'd thought Enoch Jefferson was making progress. "How about Callahan in 8?"

"No better. Still on high oxygen levels and ventilator pressures. Can we go over him together at the bedside tonight?"

"Ready when you are."

Patel unfolded a napkin over his piles of cole slaw and pinto beans that were smushed against two drumsticks and pushed his plate into the corner of his desk. He pocketed the tiny bottle of hot sauce Phineas had seen him carry all month to liven up the hospital's bland cafeteria food. Survival in the wilderness.

Villalobos burst through the doorway. "Dios Mio! That smell! What am I missing?"

⬡⬡⬡⬡⬡

As soon as Phineas opened their home's front door Wednesday evening, he inhaled the seductive aroma of sautéed sweet Italian sausage. He'd cooked and frozen portions of the tomato sauce weeks ago for easy meals during busy days. Wednesdays were spaghetti nights during Little League season. Iris had explained that Jacob would have plenty of carbs to burn. As if he needed extra energy for sports.

Phineas did a double take as Stella waddled up to him. Her abdomen was so distended it almost dragged on the floor. She plopped down on her side, panting at his feet on the cool entryway quarry tiles. "What's wrong, Girl?" He knelt next to her and began to examine her massive stomach, palpating it gently. Martha skipped ahead of Iris and appeared beside him.

"Something wrong with Stella?" Martha looked worried and sounded like she might cry.

"Look at how swollen her abdomen is," Phineas murmured. Stella emitted a low-pitched groan as he let up pressing on her.

Iris knelt next to him. "This must have just happened. I didn't notice it when I started dinner."

"Did she eat dinner?"

"Scarfed it down as usual—and wanted more, like any Lab—gulped it down till there's nothing left, then licked the bowl."

Stella's eyes opened fully, and her neck muscles visibly tightened. A series of contractions spread from her lower to upper abdomen as she opened her mouth wide and erupted, gushing wave after wave of partially digested dog food. The three jumped back trying to avoid the mess. The sour stench of puke saturated their foyer air.

Martha wrinkled her nose. "Ewww!"

Iris hurried toward the utility closet. "I'll get a bucket and dustpan and start shoveling, if you'll grab the mop and get some soapy hot water."

A decompressed Stella rose to her feet wagging her tail. She attempted an enthusiastic lunge toward her lake of vomitus.

Martha tackled her hind end and struggled to hold her back. "Ewww, Stella! Ewww! Ewww! Ewww!"

During his rush to fill the mop bucket, Phineas noticed the pantry door had been left ajar. A look inside confirmed that the now empty dog food sack on the floor had been nuzzled fully open and a few missed kibbles scattered around it. He also noticed the economy size bag of cheddar popcorn on the second shelf had been invaded and then not sealed with its clip.

Jacob's favorite junk food.

He closed the door to defend the little dog food that was left and returned to whisper his findings to Iris.

As Phineas began mopping the scattered remnants that Iris couldn't scoop, Jacob sauntered into the room. "Whew! Something stinks!"

Iris glared at him. "Yes, young man, it certainly does."

Phineas handed a surprised Jacob the mop. "Time for you to learn a new skill, Son, and I'll explain why."

⬡⬡⬡⬡⬡

On Thursday morning Phineas opened the ICU workroom door, and Villalobos raised both fists in a celebratory greeting. "Today will be a monumental day, Dr. Mann. I believe we will liberate both Ms. Ada James and Mr. Enoch Jefferson from the tyranny of their ventilators."

"Lead on Dr. V." He appreciated her growing leadership and had done his best to let her take the reins under his watchful eye.

She gently pushed open Jefferson's Room 10 door and began speaking softly. "I think we should turn up the lights this morning and help him get his days and nights back. I haven't heard of any spasms off the paralytic, and we've been cutting his sedation dose steadily so that he's off it now. Oh, and earlier we began explaining what happened to him." The taped patches over his eyes had been removed and he appeared to be studying her. She raised her voice. "Hello, Mr. Jefferson. Dr. Villalobos here again." She turned to Phineas. "He has the tracheostomy, so we can go straight to a trache collar off the vent. Is respiratory nearby?"

Jefferson's nurse, Lisa, stepped back into the hallway while the team began examining their patient. Villalobos leaned over the elderly man to speak face to face. He raised his brow, indicating she had his attention. "Mr. Jefferson, you're doing better. We turned down the medications that were keeping you sleepy, because you're ready to breathe on your own today. That's great news!" She paused long enough for her words sink in. "Your nurse will stay here with you, and we'll be just outside your room, if you need us."

His facial muscles began forming the first faint smile Phineas had witnessed on him, ever. He mouthed, "Thank you."

Lisa returned with Ava holding up an apparatus sealed in sterile plastic. The respiratory therapist asked, "Did I hear trache collar?"

Villalobos pocketed her stethoscope. "It's time. Go for it, Ava. And when you're done here, please join us in Ms. James' room. Lisa, please keep a close eye on him and find us if he looks other than perfect." She winked at Jefferson.

The team gathered around Ada James. She watched as Villalobos and Carver took positions on either side of the head of the bed. He greeted her. "Good morning Ms. Ada. How are you feeling?"

She raised her eyebrows and pointed at the ventilator.

"Your blood tests and x-ray are better. Dr. Mann will examine you, and if he agrees with Dr. Villalobos and me, we'll give you a test to see if you're ready to come off that machine."

She nodded and gave a thumbs up.

Phineas listened to her heart and lungs and held her hand as he watched her ventilator readings and monitors. "Ms. Ada, I agree with Drs. Carver and Villalobos that we should try today. Ava?"

Ava smiled broadly at their patient as she attached the end of the endotracheal tube sticking out of Ms. Ada's mouth to an oxygen and air mixture and placed the ventilator on standby. Villalobos settled into the seat next to the bed to watch for signs of distress. "I can sit here with her while you all round on someone else. I'll catch up." She folded her hands together and leaned forward. "Ms. James, I'm going to stay with you and talk to you while you breathe. You might notice you feel like you have to do more work, but don't worry, we believe you're ready to breathe on your own."

Ada James bowed her head, closed her eyes, and likewise clasped her hands together.

As Carver and Phineas led the team to the next room, Villalobos declared, "Ma'am, your hair looks really nice for your big day."

⬡⬡⬡⬡⬡

By the time Phineas returned to Ada James' room, Ruth, Rebecca and Jericho had arrived. Villalobos was speaking with them. Phineas paused at the room's sink to wash and dry his hands.

"Good morning, Dr. Mann," Ruth spoke first. "Dr. V. has been catching us up on all your team's good work. We're hearing today's the day for Mother to breathe on her own again."

"Good morning. We're all in agreement that it's time to try. Have you begun discussing plans following our removing the breathing tube?" Phineas asked. "I spoke with Ms. James about it last night."

Ruth and Rebecca looked at each other with troubled expressions. Jericho studied them, seemingly for a response.

"We still want everything done." Rebecca closed her eyes and inhaled deeply. "But Mother told us she doesn't want a hole cut in her neck, and she doesn't want to go back on the ventilator. Ever."

Phineas absorbed their sadness at the admission their matriarch was mortal. He addressed his patient. "Even if you have trouble breathing?"

Eyes wide, Ada James nodded vigorously.

"We can give you medications to help with discomfort—if you need it."

She tilted her head forward again, more slowly.

Phineas lowered his face close to hers and looked into her alert eyes. "Ms. James, would you allow us to put you back on the respirator if it looked like you were dying?"

She shook her head. An unmistakable message.

"We will respect your wishes."

Ruth and Rebecca kept their heads up as tears flowed down their cheeks. Villalobos hugged them, one after the other. Jericho dabbed at his eye.

Phineas blinked back his own emotions. "If everyone's ready, we can go ahead and remove the tube. I'll come find you in the waiting room soon after."

○○○○○

That evening, when Phineas circled back to Ada James' room, he could see her through the door's window holding court. In his mind's eye, he conjured up a sparkling tiara accenting her elegant wig, a scepter in her right hand.

He could hear her hoarse laugh followed by a soft rattle and cough. Her respiratory muscles did not appear to be struggling. She sipped water carefully through a straw. The sisters hovered. Jericho and one of his red-jacketed cousins stood in the background while Villalobos smiled and chatted with them.

Jericho waved at Phineas as he entered the room. "Hey, Dr. Mann. I just dropped off a pan of peach cobbler to celebrate Gramma's graduation."

"His is the next best thing to my cookin'," Ada James whispered after a gentle cough. "He grew up in my kitchen, at my side, you know." She looked at him with pride. "You can see I fed him well."

Villalobos patted the bed next to Ms. Ada's leg. "I told them we're just doing our job and they didn't feel like they needed to bring anything—but that we'll certainly enjoy it."

Phineas soaked in the scene, a warm and loving family in a room filled with cold, lifeless technology. "Thank you for your generosity, Jericho." He scanned their faces. "I suspect you have questions about what's next."

Ruth's head bobbed. "Just about to ask."

"We'll start some gentle rehab here in the ICU, while we advance her diet, adjust her insulin, and settle back into a stable dialysis schedule. Then we talk about a transfer out of the ICU to the kidney service."

"So, we have a few more days here?"

"A few, that is if your mother makes the steady progress we anticipate."

"That's a relief. Hear that, Mother? You've got work ahead." A gentle prod to her mother's shoulder. The child becoming the parent.

The corners of Ada James' mouth flexed up before she whispered, "We'll start tomorrow."

Villalobos touched her arm. "Excellent. We'll see you in the morning."

Her eyes locked on Phineas'. "Ready to see the next patient, Dr. Mann?"

She led him toward Jefferson next door. "I saw the son and VA nurse go in about an hour ago." Her words were barely audible.

"What can you tell me about his afternoon?"

"He's been off the vent since morning rounds. Seems to be tolerating it. I let him have some sips 'n chips." Water and ice chips, the first oral intake. "Ready to face them?" She made a quick sign of the cross.

He was tempted to do the same. "With you as my guardian angel. Let's go."

Villalobos took the lead and pulled the door open. A faint burnt smell competed with the hospital disinfectant. "Good evening. How's everyone tonight?" She took up a position against the bedrail, near the patient's head and touched his shoulder. "Hi, Mr. Jefferson. Dr. Villalobos here again."

The window's blinds were adjusted flat to let in the early evening's sublime and revealing light. Zebediah Jefferson wore his denim Jefferson and Son Welding shirt, now with more burn holes over his chest than when Phineas had first met him.

And this was Phineas' first visit when Angela wasn't immersed in darkness. The intervening twelve years and her weight loss had added lines to the corners of her eyes, but extensive blond highlights in her long, thick hair had replaced the dark mane of Baptist Hospital and Jezebel days and created a distracting, blazing corona.

She studied his face in return. "So, I see you've added a few grey whiskers, Dr. Mann."

"Life does that."

Several more this month, thank you.

Villalobos interjected, "Mr. Jefferson has had a very good day." She paused as Enoch Jefferson smiled at her. "He's been breathing on his own since this morning without any signs of the tetanus toxin's effect."

"Saw y'all through the window goin' into that other family's room." Zebediah Jefferson pronounced the word family as if it had a b in the middle. "Seems we been waitin' on you 'bout an hour." Another invitation to conflict.

Phineas chose to ignore the bait. "Tomorrow, we hope to let your father try a clear liquid diet and start some physical therapy."

Angela's head swiveled to look at Zebediah, her long hair waving. "Now, Zeb Honey, there's good news. Maybe your Daddy can get out of the hospital soon."

"When?" A single word response, a bark. An artery pulsated over his temple.

"Maybe Monday we can find him a bed in our rehabilitation unit, as long as he has a smooth weekend, without any setbacks." Phineas kept his tone even, not allowing his anticipated glee at freedom from Zebediah Jefferson to surface. "He has some leg weakness that will take a while to get better. Sometimes we see that after patients need paralytic medications." The neurologic signs actually weren't classic for the critical care neuromyopathy he referred to, a detail that bothered him. He'd have called for a neurology consult, if this wasn't their usual constant fallback diagnosis for weakness in the ICU.

"So, you just need to make sure there's no setbacks over the weekend?" Angela derailed Phineas' train of thought and made him flinch. He wanted nothing to jinx Jefferson progressing out of the ICU and off his service.

Villalobos had been watching the senior Jefferson and was quicker to respond. "You can be sure we'll do our very best for you, Mr. Jefferson."

⬡⬡⬡⬡⬡

Iris, Sarah Jane, and Martha perched on the top row of the metal bleachers watching the Saturday afternoon Little League's drama unfold. The day was already scorching hot. Iris began shaking her head slowly from side to side while watching her husband and son facing off on the pitcher's mound. "Uh oh. This could be a problem."

Martha turned her attention away from another fan's puppy to look at her mother, waiting for an explanation.

Sarah Jane fanned herself with a church bulletin she had extracted from her purse. "Daughter, what're you thinking?"

"I've seen Jacob get like this before, but not with Phineas in charge of the team for the first time." Iris lifted the bottom edge of her tee shirt to wipe sweat from her cheeks and chin.

She'd brought Jacob to his Cubs' final game of the season, and it would determine the league championship. She and Martha hadn't missed a game. Of all the weekends for Coach to be called out of town, this had to be the worst possible. Phineas had been anointed the team's reluctant coach for the day by default, after he'd arrived straight from ICU rounds. In what now might be the final inning, Jacob was on the mound, pitching on his twelfth birthday. The Cubs were leading 3-1.

Though Jacob's growth spurt had clearly commenced, others in the league were further into theirs, and some were men among boys at twelve years old. Iris knew that Jacob heaved everything he had into each pitch, as he did with whatever else he believed in. His delivery started with an impossibly high kick. Phineas had said it was like Juan Marichal's, a star San Francisco Giants pitcher in the 1960s. As a result of the power he generated by this motion, Jacob's pitches had been almost unhittable. Almost.

This was Jacob's second inning on the mound, and he struck out its first two hitters, neither even fouling off any of his fastballs. He'd either struck out or walked almost everyone he'd faced all season. He was a valuable reliever, the go to guy, when the other team's best hitters were up. Other pitchers with less velocity would give up hits to the good hitters. Jacob didn't. Until Antonio.

Iris' stomach tightened when she saw Antonio leave the Astro's on-deck circle. Deep into his growth spurt, he stood nearly six feet tall. He launched Jacob's first fastball so high into right field that Paul, the right fielder, wandered under it for what seemed an eternity—before he completely misjudged it. A competent fielder would have turned it into a loud and dramatic out. Coach always assigned Paul to right field for a reason. He was their least competent fielder.

Antonio circled the bases while Paul helplessly circled right field under the ball that was scored a home run instead of an error. Jacob kicked the rubber—twice—indicating his disappointment. Then he straightened up, all business.

He accepted the ball from his catcher and retook the mound. Early in the season, Phineas told Iris that he noticed that whenever Jacob began pressing, his mechanics changed for the worse and his control suffered. Was this one of those times? He nodded to the catcher, wound up, kicked high, and let the ball fly.

"BALL ONE!" Just below the batter's knees.

Jacob missed more than found the strike zone and walked the next two batters. The weak part of the batting order was coming up. Phineas called time-out and came to the mound to chat with Jacob. They both nodded their heads and Phineas returned to the bench.

He'd once explained Coach's pitching strategy to Iris, what he'd called the game within the game. Coach started Stephen, a master of control and velocity, for most games. He pitched three to five innings, depending on the competition, and how close he was to the league's allowable weekly innings limit.

If the opposition's good hitters came up to bat next, Jacob relieved. His first pitches were reliably grooved down the middle of the strike zone. If he gave up a walk or two, it was less damaging than extra base hits. He usually struck out more batters than he walked, until his control wavered. By then, the weaker hitters were usually coming up to bat, and Nick took his turn pitching. Nick threw strikes but with less velocity. Weak hitters stood watching or flailed helplessly at his pitches. Strong hitters could crush his pitches. This pitching strategy was successful throughout the season—a part of the reason the Cubs were tied with the Astros in first place.

After today's meeting on the mound with his coach and father, Jacob took the count to three balls and two strikes. The batter's one weak swing missing badly on his only attempt at contact. Each pitch generated an attention-grabbing *thud* as it hit leather in the catcher's mitt, a sound Iris only heard when Jacob was pitching. She could tell her son was pitching without looking. After his pitches, involuntary gasps escaped from the batters' frightened mothers.

The Astros' coach then called his batter over and whispered instructions. Jacob studied the catcher's signal, looked the runners back, and let fly.

"BALL FOUR!"

The pitch had missed, over the plate but high, by two inches. The bat hadn't budged. The batter had clearly been instructed to not swing.

Bases loaded. Two outs. Score 3 to 2.

Iris squeezed her mother's hand. "Wish it wasn't so darned hot." Her pulse pounded in her ears.

Phineas again called time-out and strode across the third base line. He signaled for Nick to come from shortstop to the mound, then held out his hand for the baseball. Jacob glared at him, shook his head, and pushed the ball deeper into his glove, causing Nick to stop halfway to the mound. Phineas again held out his open hand. Jacob shook his head with more vigor. In the intensive Care Unit, Phineas was used to having his orders followed. Immediately.

All chatter in the stands ceased. All eyes focused on Phineas and Jacob. Iris whispered to Sarah Jane, "I don't think Jacob's going to give up the ball."

"I'm finishing this inning," Jacob proclaimed, loud enough for Iris and the other fans to hear.

"This is what I was afraid of," Iris murmured. "Coach usually handles the pitching changes." She shook her head. "I feel sorry for Phineas. I don't know how he's going to get out of this one peacefully." She again wiped her face with the front of her tee shirt.

Phineas put his hand on Jacob's shoulder, leaned over, and said something into his son's ear. Jacob's head tilted back, and he stared up at his father's face, shrugged, and handed him the ball. Jacob trotted to Nick's shortstop position, and Nick took the mound and struck out the next batter on three pitches.

The Cubs stormed the infield and celebrated their championship. Short speeches and iced Gatorade followed.

Iris approached Phineas from behind and, locking arms with him, pulled him aside. "So how did you get Jacob to give up the ball peacefully?"

"I told him that the rule was that if I crossed the baseline twice to speak with the pitcher, I *had* to make a pitching change."

"It's lucky for you there was that rule." Iris cocked her head. "There *is* such a rule, isn't there?"

"I hope so. He'll probably check." He pecked her cheek. "I'll see you back at the house."

After Iris retrieved Jacob from more postgame cheers and backslapping, he claimed the front passenger seat in her sunbaked SUV. Sarah Jane and Martha climbed into the back seats and began fanning themselves. Wishing she could do the same while driving, Iris opened the windows and turned the A/C to full blast. As soon as it began to emit cool air, she exclaimed, "Finally!" and closed the windows.

The odor of Jacob's acrid adolescent sweat began to fill the vehicle—the familiar smell of finding his unopened gym bag stuffed with week old damp tee-shirts and socks. Iris glanced in the rearview mirror and saw her mother and Martha facing each other while wrinkling and plugging their noses.

Martha exclaimed, "Whew, Jacob, you smell!"

Jacob shrugged. "Get used to it. That's the smell of victory."

Phineas arrived at their driveway behind Iris' SUV. Jacob burst from her passenger's side door and bolted for the house's locked front door before he stopped and waited, tapping his foot with an impatient look on his face.

"I'm hungry and I need to pee."

So did Phineas. "Sure thing." He hustled to let Jacob in.

"Me too," Iris declared and slipped by Phineas. "Then I'm taking a long shower."

Stella bolted outside past him and gave Sarah Jane and Martha an enthusiastic greeting, butt-tucking circles around them before squatting to relieve herself in the front yard. Sarah Jane chuckled and shook her head. "I need to do the same, minus the running around. Then you can have your turn, Phineas." Countless drawn-out ICU disasters had shown him that he could hold his urine, if needed.

Martha skipped toward him with Stella at her side. "Grandma wants to see our garden. Tell her I'll be out back." She disappeared around the corner of the house leaving him alone in silence.

His tense confrontation with Jacob at the game was an additional strain on their relationship that Phineas wished he could have avoided. Ever since his son's Angela Portier and Hurricane Jezebel internet search, Jacob had been consistently less willing to open up to him about anything.

Did Jacob pursue those events further after Iris asserted Phineas' innocence and heroism? She'd checked the computer's search history and found it erased. What had Jacob been looking at to learn that trick? As Phineas finally washed his hands in the hall bathroom, he pondered, "Is there any way to erase those negative articles from his memory?" He doubted it. They'd just have to be countered with the entire truthful story somehow, someday, unforced.

A less uncomfortable looking version of Jacob stood flat-footed and stared into their open refrigerator, pushing aside jars and taking inventory. Food preparation was a peace offering Phineas could provide.

"I'm about to make a sandwich. Want me to make you one?"

"Sure. Ham and cheese. Mayo and light mustard...please." His final word a token offer of civility. Jacob hoisted the gallon container of milk and set it on the table.

"Lettuce and tomato? White or wheat?"

"Yup. Whichever you're having." Jacob shuffled from pantry to cupboard to collect a bag of cheddar popcorn, a large bowl, and a tall glass, then finally plopped into a chair at the table.

Phineas assembled two hefty sandwiches, thought better of stopping, and made a third. He cut this one in half and arranged it on a plate he placed between their seats. Jacob, or the two of them, would want it, if someone else didn't hurry in and claim it.

Phineas waited until Jacob had swallowed his second bite before he tried to initiate a conversation. "Think we should check the hives to see if they need more honey supers?"

"Sure." Jacob took a third bite and chewed.

"It's been five days since you added one each. They may have filled them, if the nectar flow's really brisk."

"Yup." Even being a Little League champion wasn't going to make Jacob talkative today, at least with his substitute coach father.

Phineas finished his sandwich in silence. "I'm going to change and gather stuff for the hives. I'll see you there when you're ready."

Jacob was working on the extra sandwich by then. He nodded. "Okay."

Martha and Sarah Jane had quit the hot backyard by the time Phineas lit the smoker and waited at the hives. Bees were launching into foraging flights every few seconds, while those returning with abdomens expanded from loads of clear nectar settled heavily on the landing platforms before being granted entrance into their colonies. He began to sweat under his protective jacket and screened hood. Was Jacob making him wait and pay the price of sweltering in the heat for imagined offenses? Or was he dragging his feet because he was uncomfortable being alone with his father?

He grasped the hive tool and loosened the outer cover from Grace. A whiff of smoke to the entrance and above the top level further calmed these already gentle bees. He lifted one of the newer frames that Jacob had provided for them. It was heavy and nearly full of shiny, clear nectar, as were the other recent additions, a sign of a plentiful flow and a predicter of a robust harvest. He stacked on another topless, bottomless box built to suspend enclosed wooden frames holding sheets of beeswax honeycomb. Worker bees flooded into it from the box below before he closed the hive. Still no Jacob. Charity was also close to full, so he provided her with similar box of frames. Both of his hives were up to six boxes, with brood in the bottom two or three and golden honey above. Phineas had gone as high as eight boxes once in the past, the year that magnificent colony gave him close to a hundred pounds of honey.

He sat in their cedar observation chair at an angle from the hive entrances and watched Jezebel. How long was Jacob going to make him wait? Maybe he was on the phone with a teammate. Maybe Sarah Jane was detaining him to hear his recounting of the game. Phineas considered opening Jezebel. He walked to the back of her and gave her opening a generous puff of smoke. Within seconds, bees poured out and hit the screen in front of his face. No. He'd better not open her without Jacob. Jacob would find that one more reason to be angry with him.

Phineas was about to head back to the house and a shower, when Jacob came around the corner while zipping his beekeeping jacket. Phineas pulled on his gloves, choosing to avoid physical pain on top of emotional, and settled back into his seat. Jacob could take the lead on his hive. His father would watch and try to avoid saying anything that might provoke more friction.

"Jacob, I'm wearing gloves for Jezebel. I haven't seen anything that shows me they're not as mean as before."

"If you say so." Jacob acquiesced to his father's example before delivering a puff of smoke to Jezebel's entrance. He pried off the cover and gave more. The buzzing level rose. He lifted a frame out of the upper hive body. Bees gushed up from the empty space. The noise level increased. "They're filling up the comb. We should add a third box."

Bees formed a loud cloud around Jacob's head. They bombed the screen in front of his face. He settled the frame back into its slot. "Ouch!" He shook his hand. "They got me through my glove."

Phineas picked up the extra box of empty frames and hurried to the hive. "Let's put this on and close up." He felt a searing pain from a sting on his thigh as he positioned the box on top. Jezebel had returned to punish him once again. Would this be the last time? "I'd say that this cinches it. We should order a gentle replacement queen for this colony. What kind do you want?"

Jacob closed the hive and backed away. "Can we get a Carniolan queen? We've never had one, and they're supposed to be gentle...and they'd still be dark, so I could tell my bees from Grace and Charity's golden Italians." Agitated bees still tested Jacob's jacket for openings.

"Good idea. Let's see if we can order one and schedule delivery for the first of June, so I'll have time to help you find the old queen and dispatch her. Do you know where Carniolan bees originally came from?" Phineas couldn't resist a teaching moment.

"Never heard of Carniola."

"They're from Eastern Europe, from Slovenia. Did you know that honey bees aren't native to North America?"

"I know. I know. The white man's fly." Jacob's tone suggested he wasn't interested in more beekeeping history. "We done?"

"Sure." Phineas was done beekeeping for the day, but not "done."

As Jacob started for the house, Phineas strode to catch up. "Jacob, I know you didn't want to leave the mound today, but you've been avoiding me before today. What's going on?" *Does he think of me as a criminal?*

Jacob spun around to face him and blurted, "What if my *friends* find out?"

"Find out what?" Phineas knew but needed to hear it.

"About your murder charges." Almost a whisper. Like he thought someone might be listening.

So that was it. Jacob was worried his friends might learn about the arrest for murder and ostracize him. He'd probably figured that parents would then stop allowing his friends to come out to his rural home, if any friends still wanted to...and they were scheduled to stay over tonight. Would that come to an end? Would Jacob be left alone—or worse, picked on? Carrying a burden for something that happened long ago and with which he had no connection wasn't fair. Angela's return was punishing both of them.

"I won't tell. Your mother won't tell. So, don't tell any of them. How else would they know?"

"I...I guess you're right." Jacob didn't sound convinced that it would never be a problem for him.

"Let us know when you want to look at reports that show I was never guilty of anything." Phineas craved resolution. Having the problem linger was a constant background stress and a wedge between him and his son.

"I'll let you know. Right now, I need to take a shower and get ready for my party—and my friends."

⬡⬡⬡⬡⬡

Phineas doubted he'd manage to get a full night's sleep before Sunday's early morning rounds, and he almost regretted giving Jacob a green light to invite five friends to stay over after his birthday party. Phineas rationalized that Iris pretty much made the decision before she'd asked his opinion anyway, and he agreed Jacob needed friends at this time. At least they'd sleep in the rec room (what Phineas called the 'wreck' room), if they slept at all.

Sarah Jane kept Martha busy at the dining room table with a game of checkers before Jacob's friends began arriving. Iris and Phineas introduced each friend to Sarah Jane and Martha, before the boys deposited presents on the table and scurried off with their sleeping bags to find Jacob, who was sure to be immersed in playing a Super Mario video game in the rec room.

"Glad there were no video games when you and your brother were growing up." Sarah Jane remarked to Iris, as she jumped one of Martha's kings. "So, what's for dinner, Phineas? We eat early at Croasdaile, you know."

Phineas took a seat at the table. "Gramma's Cookin'. Should be here any minute."

"Well, that should be interesting, since *this* grandma ain't cookin' anymore. Are you sure you ordered enough to feed those six hungry wolves—and the rest of us?" She reached over and gave Martha's shoulder a playful poke. "Your move, Martha."

As soon as he heard the doorbell, Phineas hustled to answer it. Stella barked and beat him there, forcing him to clamp onto her collar. Jericho wore his black t-shirt and durag, and one of his cousins had on the red jacket Phineas had seen him in before. Both balanced boxes and cartons. Phineas motioned them into the dining area and pointed at the table. "You can put it all there." He gestured toward the three females, who were suddenly silent. "Iris, Sarah Jane, and Martha, this is Jericho and..."

"Demetrius," the young man in red answered. "Pleased to meet you folks. Hope you enjoy your dinner." He nodded twice and retreated toward the door. Stella's nose pointed up, sniffing audibly.

Jericho flashed his broad smile. "I'll second that. And thanks for orderin' Gramma's Cookin'." Phineas waited for Iris to have Stella in hand, before he and Jericho followed Cousin Demetrius outside. He was already entering the driver's side of a faded Datsun without hubcaps.

Phineas pulled out his wallet. "How much do I owe you?"

Jericho handed him a hand-written bill of sale. Phineas extracted bills to cover the meal and a tip. He lowered his voice. "Just curious. Does the jacket mean Demetrius is in a gang?"

Jericho's sigh suggested frustration and embarrassment. "Naw. Just safer in his neighborhood than wearing blue. No one'll mistake him for a Crip."

"Sorry, I shouldn't have asked."

"No problem. I understand." He took a step toward the car and spun around. "I got something else to tell you 'bout that white guy with the Dixie tattoo."

"Oh no...What'd he do this time?"

"Threatened Demetrius and his brother in the parking deck."

"How?"

"You remember I said my boys could handle themselves? Well, we don't want that to have to happen. The dude was settin' in his truck when they walked by, and he whistled at 'em, loud." He fixed a penetrating stare at Phineas. "When they stopped to check him out, he dangled a noose he'd made with some cord out the window an' said, 'Ever seen one of these?' They said he laughed then. A *nasty* laugh."

"We should report that. What did they do?

"Didn't help the situation. Demetrius' brother pulled his blade and flicked it open, said he'd cut his rope anytime. Then Cracker Man reached down and pulled a piece."

"A piece?"

"Probably a Glock. All those white boys favor Glocks. Name sounds German. He said, 'You wanna play rock paper scissors? Here's my rock.' So, my boys beat it out of there."

Phineas shuddered. "I think I should definitely go to security, and maybe even the police. You okay with that?"

"Don't want my boys gettin' in any trouble." Jericho was letting Phineas know he needed to trust him.

"I won't say he pulled out a knife."

"Just be careful what you say. Cops don't always treat us the same, you know." His gaze lingered on Phineas face before he reached out his hand. Phineas grasped it, hoping to absorb its strength.

He found Sarah Jane and Martha at the table each gnawing on a drumstick. Iris was setting out piles of paper plates and plastic utensils. Sarah Jane dabbed at her mouth with a paper napkin. "Do we *have* to call that pack of wolves to join us for dinner?"

⬡⬡⬡⬡⬡

On Sunday morning, Phineas found Villalobos waiting for him behind the ICU doors and wearing an alarmed look. "Dr. Mann, it happened again!"

Phineas slipped his backpack off his shoulder. "Let's talk in the workroom."

As he entered, the two residents and two interns looked up from their desks and turned to face him. Ram Patel's brow was deeply furrowed and his hair uncombed. "It was the same as last time, Dr. Mann!"

"What was?"

"Jefferson. He'd been off the respirator yesterday, and awake. I had explained everything to him again. Then, around 2 AM, he suddenly was confused and began writhing in pain and clutching his abdomen. Then diarrhea. Labs and x-rays were unchanged. We gave him morphine and re-attached his trache to the ventilator."

Phineas did his best to control his emotions. Frustration was next to the top, but the knowledge that he had to tell Zebediah that his Daddy had another setback, filled him with dread. He muttered, "let's save some of his serum and blood in the lab again. We may come up with an idea that we want to test for later."

He picked up a piece of chalk from the blackboard tray and wrote Symptoms, Signs, Labs, at the top of three columns. "Okay, let's really brainstorm this time. Start with a list of the symptoms during these episodes."

Patel answered, "abdominal pain."

Phineas wrote it down. "Is there pain elsewhere?"

Resident Sadie Goldschmidt shrugged. "Hard to tell...and we couldn't ask, since he was suddenly hard to communicate with." Concentration wrinkles formed on her forehead. "He did seem to be reaching for his legs—but they looked fine. He was agitated and really confused."

Patel again. "Diarrhea. Lots of it."

Phineas added: "Diarrhea (Gastroenteritis?)" and "Acute Confusion" to the forming list. "Anything unusual about these symptoms? Blood in his stool? Seizure activity?"

Patel and Goldschmidt shook their heads.

"Any other symptoms?" Villalobos asked.

More head shaking. Patel raised a hand. "Nothing he could tell us. His urine output went down for a few hours, so we gave him fluids. I guess that's a symptom."

Phineas wrote "decreased urine output" under Symptoms and moved over to the Signs column. "How about his exam?"

Patel answered, "hyperactive bowel sounds and generalized tenderness, but no signs of a surgical abdomen, and his x-rays and white count were normal. There was nothing else on his exam, except his agitation—enough that we had to sedate him."

Phineas printed the exam and normal x-ray findings on the board. "Lab work?"

Goldschmidt raised her eyebrows. "Same as before. Another slight drop in his hemoglobin level, and a positive test for hemoglobin in his urine. Otherwise negative."

Villalobos' eyes opened wider. "When I came back Monday and reviewed his chart, I saw the tests for hemolysis ordered after his first setback finally returned and were weakly positive, then negative when repeated the next day. Did something cause a single, brief episode of damage to his red cells?"

Phineas wrote "Hemolysis?" and answered, "I saw that too, but since he got quickly better, I didn't suggest we order the incredibly broad range of autoimmune, genetic, and other labs to pursue it then. I guess we need to start ordering some of those studies now."

They all nodded except Malcolm, who was writing on an index card while displaying an expression suggesting deep thought. He looked up at his colleagues. "How do we tie it together?"

Blank looks all around. Then slow head shaking.

Phineas held up his hands, palms up. "It's hard to fit it all together. A rare genetic condition popped into my head, acute intermittent porphyria, but I can't imagine that showing up for the first time at eighty years old. It usually runs in families—and I've never heard of a case here. It's a *real* long shot."

Malcolm was writing again. "Haven't heard of that one since first year med school biochemistry. I'll look up how to test for it."

"I know I came back later in his course, but why isn't this part of his tetanus, a late manifestation?" Villalobos raised her eyebrows and shrugged.

Goldschmidt answered, "We wondered about that, but what we saw was different, and what we read about tetanus doesn't explain it." The other resident, Downs, nodded his agreement.

Villalobos folded her hands over her lap. "I've got nothing else." The others echoed her words, one after another.

Phineas studied the blackboard. "Everyone keep thinking, and write down anything else you come up with later."

Too many of the puzzle's pieces were missing to recognize the picture, and frustration was the meeting's consensus. It was especially so for Phineas, whose temperament wanted everything organized and in its place fitting together. *Mise en place*.

Then, the gut punch of the anticipated hostility from Enoch Jefferson's son, who would pounce on them for the second major hiccough in his father's recovery. He would heap blame on Malcolm and Ram and would lash out at all. Punishment for hard work.

Phineas put the piece of chalk back in the tray and brushed dust off his hands. "Shall we go look at our patient?"

⬡⬡⬡⬡⬡

Later that afternoon, Phineas and Villalobos returned to the unit to look for visiting families and to check on their patients once more. At the top of the stairs, he held the door to the hallway of the ICU floor open. "Gabby, we still need to talk more about how you're going to involve yourself in my research project—Wait. What's this?"

Malcolm and his fiancé, Patrice, faced Zebediah Jefferson down the hallway in front of the ICU doors. Malcolm's gleaming scalp and Patrice's towering Afro rose over the shorter Jefferson. He spun away and muttered, "uppity bitch."

Patrice's spine stiffened. "Can't say it to my face?"

Jefferson twisted back around, rage creasing his face, his mouth hanging open. He then locked eyes with Phineas and chose, instead of responding to her, to aggressively push through the double metal doors into the ICU.

Phineas hurried to the couple. "What just happened?"

Carver looked at the floor. "Patrice and I were talking out here when he came out of the elevator. So, I told him I'd be coming to his father's room and could talk with him. He said that he'd wait for you, and that Patrice and I should 'just go back to whatever s-hole place we came from.'"

Damn! Can that racist make things any worse? And I still need to contact security about him threatening Demetrius.

Patrice kept straight arms and tight fists pressed against her sides. "Malcolm didn't answer the jerk, so I did."

"And what'd you say to him?"

She hesitated a moment before answering, long enough for Phineas to feel both admiration for her audacity and trepidation for the anticipated consequences.

"I looked the creep in the eye and said, 'You mean Harvard?'"

Was that a hint of a proud smile?

"Then he called me an uppity bitch." Her lips tightened and posture remained defiant. Malcolm bowed his head, his eyes closed.

Phineas took a deep breath and slowly exhaled, his cheeks puffing out. "I was on my way to try to find him. I left a message earlier that we needed to update him on his father. I haven't told him of his father's latest issue."

"Sorry," Carver whispered.

Villalobos put her hand on Carver's shoulder. "This wasn't your fault."

Phineas paused outside Enoch Jefferson's Room 10 to collect his thoughts and summon his courage. The most contentious interaction with Zebediah yet waited behind the door.

Villalobos watched him patiently. "Why don't you let me go in before you?"

"No. I should face him alone."

"But I can be part of a show of strength." She tucked her chin in and stood at attention, while she probed his eyes.

He tried to absorb *her* strength. She had so much.

"You can rescue me, if I don't come back out," Phineas murmured.

His attempt at humor felt feeble, as he pushed through Jefferson's door and closed it behind him. Stale tobacco stink permeated the darkness. Angela's bright white uniform was distracting in one seat, before he could make out Zebediah Jefferson's face in the other and see his flared nostrils. Phineas let Enoch Jefferson know he was at his bedside and talking about him.

Angela's hair had been pulled forward and arranged over her rising and falling chest. "Zeb's upset about his Daddy. When we left here last night, he was breathing on his own. And today he's back on the respirator, and the nurse said he had another setback last night." Her voice was matter of fact, even.

Phineas directed his words at Zebediah. "I called again today and left a message that I needed to talk with you."

Zebediah coughed, then grumbled, "Well that other doctor said he was a-goin' to talk with me, and I told him I'd wait for you. Course, he was busy playin' 'round with his wench instead of workin' anyway."

Barely tamping down his anger, Phineas considered whether there was anything to be gained by arguing and defending. "We have nurses and residents here 24 hours a day. Our residents were right here at his bedside last night when your father worsened."

"An' why weren't you here?" Zebediah lifted his chin and pursed his lips, clearly wanting to quarrel.

"It happened late, well after I'd gone home, like last time." Phineas knew this wasn't going to satisfy him.

"Well, I 'spect you to be here."

"I can't be here all the time for the whole month. That's one of the reasons we have residents staying in the ICU."

"Well, I'm purty sure I can find out where you and your family live, if'n you need someone to drag you back here." Zebediah's jaw muscles clenched and his eyes narrowed.

That's enough!

"Mr. Jefferson, did you just threaten me?" Phineas' squeezed his hands into fists to stop them from quivering.

Zebediah leaned forward in his chair. "You're callin' it that. I just call it a fact. I can find you, if'n I want to."

Phineas' chest was pounding. After all the years, the thousands of hours, the horribly sick patients he'd agonized over in the ICU, he'd never felt threatened until this moment. And his family!

"I'm going to call security now and ask them to escort you from the hospital. From now on, I will call you with reports when I need to. It would be best for all, if you don't even *try* to visit here again."

Zebediah shot to his feet. Angela grasped the bedrail and leaned forward, looking from Phineas to Zebediah. "Aw, Zeb, now look what you've gone and done."

"And Angela, you need to leave also. Now." Phineas was surprised by the fury in his tone.

Zebediah stomped around the foot of the bed like he meant to charge Phineas. Instead, he clutched the door's handle and turned back to glare at him. "You can tell your security to keep sitting on their asses. I'm leavin' on my own. I hates this hospital and its so called doctors anyways." His eyes narrowed. "You're a-gonna regret this, Dr. Ma-ann. Y'all ain't seen the last of me."

Angela shouldered her purse and trailed Zebediah through the room's door, glancing back at Phineas. Was that the beginning of a smirk forming? A chill shot from Phineas' neck down his spine when the ICU's metal entrance door slammed against the wall. He stepped around the foot of the bed and dropped into the chair Angela had occupied. Her body's heat remained in the cushion. Was this finally the last he'd sense of her, or would she appear again, another unwelcome surprise to torment him?

Villalobos burst in from the hall. "Dr. Mann, what happened? Zebediah was cursing all the way down the hall. Lisa called security."

"I threw them out." He kept his words even.

She leaned against the bed's rail. "Why? What did he do?"

Phineas tilted his head back to look up into her wide-open dark brown eyes. "Threatened me and my family." He shifted his focus to Enoch Jefferson. "I hope you're sleeping, Mr. Jefferson. If you heard all that, I'm really sorry."

⬡⬡⬡⬡⬡

It was after 5 PM when the ICU workroom door opened, and the security officer's shaved head poked inside. "Are you doctors ready for your escort to the parking lot?" The baritone voice matched the rugged arms stretching his uniform's sleeves, and his skin was so dark, it gave off an indigo tint in the room's fluorescent light. Phineas took note of the holster on his hip.

"Yes, sir. Thank you." Phineas shouldered his backpack. "Ready, Gabby?"

Villalobos finished stuffing papers into hers. "Ready."

Phineas turned to Carver and Downs, who were finishing the day's notes. "Before you guys leave tomorrow, make sure you call for security."

Downs let out an uneasy sounding chuckle. "Seems excessive for me."

"Not to me. That dude is mad—both angry *and* crazy." Malcolm held up his pen like a dagger. "I called Patrice a while ago to be sure she was okay. She was still upset, even after she jogged back to our place."

On the walk to their parked cars, Villalobos was uncharacteristically quiet, and Phineas couldn't think of anything worth breaking their silence.

"Dios Mio!"

She came to an abrupt stop next to a silver Honda Civic. Opposite corners of the back window displayed Harvard and BU decals. "This has to be Malcolm's car." A crude white hood fashioned from a pillowcase had been fitted over the top of the car's antenna. Surrounding it at the bottom, was a noose tied from clothesline. The letters N-I-and part of a C or a G were scratched on the trunk.

"He's either a bad speller, or he heard someone coming," Phineas murmured.

Villalobos shook her head. "That's a word he knows how to spell."

The security guard freed his walkie-talkie from his belt and pressed a button. "I need campus police on the third level of the parking deck, in the back. An act of vandalism. And I need them now!" His eyebrows pinched forward in undeniable fury.

Villalobos scanned the other cars. "Dr. Mann, is that your truck?"

Another hood was draped over his truck's antenna.

Warnings in material form, more than angry words. Did they also come from other racists than Zebediah? Did he have help? Probably. Phineas had to assume his whole team was at risk. And that threat of finding where he lives. His family. What had Phineas unleashed? As the person in charge, should he have been more restrained? The protective shield of his white race had fallen to the ground because of his words. They were now all targets of malevolent racists. He struggled to control this new fear, a fear Malcolm had lived with daily.

"What can you do tonight, Officer?" Phineas stared into the glistening eyes of the furious guard.

"Watch hospital grounds. You gave me a name when you called earlier. Campus Police will want a description." A siren in the distance made him pause. "They'll probably send reports to the Chapel Hill Police and Orange County Sheriff." He sighed and shook his head. "To be honest, I doubt anything will be accomplished tonight, since we don't have a witness to this." He frowned as he gestured at the noose and shrouds. "You'll need to follow up with our Chief Vickers first thing in the morning."

Vickers!

The guard's arched eyebrows suggested that he also had doubts about his chief.

⬡⬡⬡⬡⬡

Phineas had waited all that evening for the right time to tell Iris about the new nastiness at the hospital. Long ago, he'd learned that his face was an open book, that he was incapable of subterfuge. Patients usually suspected when he thought something was very wrong, and Iris could read him better than anyone. Before he could figure out how to start, she had planted herself, standing rigid with hands on hips at the foot of his recliner and bored a hole in him with her glacial blue stare. "The kids are in bed finally. So, what is it you need to tell me?"

There was no denying her an answer. He closed the medical journal article he'd been staring at without reading. "Things with Zebediah Jefferson went totally to shit today."

She stood stock still, mute.

"I had to ban him from the hospital after he threatened me."

"He threatened you? Just how dangerous is he?" Her pitch and shoulders rose simultaneously.

"Can't say. Don't know enough yet. I had Security escort Gabby and me to the parking deck. I'll follow up with their chief in the morning." He wondered whether to mention the hoods.

He resisted an urge to squirm when Iris squinted hard, peering inside him through his eyes. "Tell me all of it," she commanded evenly.

"There were hoods on Malcolm's and my antennae."

"Hoods? Klan hoods?" Her volume cranked up. Fully.

The feelings of helplessness and vulnerability were maddening. He looked down. "Yes—and a noose on Malcolm's." He purposely lowered his voice to suggest she follow suit.

She knelt in front of him, bringing her gaze to his eye level. "You need to go to the police."

"Security already has. I'll see their chief in the morning and check in with him."

The soft steps of bare feet down the hall were barely audible. A door clicked shut. Phineas sprung out of his recliner and hurried into the hallway, just in time to see the light go out under Jacob's door. When Phineas opened it, he found only darkness and the form of his son under the covers facing the far wall.

Iris slipped by Phineas and sat beside Jacob on his bed. "Jacob, what were you doing up?" She peeled back the sheet from his head.

He rolled toward her. A sliver of light from the hallway illuminated a slice of Jacob's worried expression. "I couldn't fall asleep. It sounded like you two were fighting. I thought I might need to protect you from Dad."

His son's words crushed Phineas. How could he think that? "I'd never—"

Iris reached out to place her hand on Phineas' arm. "You know your father would never hurt me. Just what did you hear?"

"Is Dad in danger?"

Phineas sat next to Iris. "We're going to sort it all out with hospital security in the morning. Maybe talk to the regular police too."

"Should *we* be scared?"

Iris put her hand on her son's shoulder. "Let's all be careful until we know more. It would be best to avoid strangers—and you look out for Martha. Okay?" She bent to kiss his forehead.

He pulled his sheet up under his chin. "Does this have anything to do with Angela Portier?"

Iris pivoted on the bed to look at Phineas.

He held up his hands, palms up.

WEEK FOUR

A Bee for Mount Hymettus, the queen of the hive, ascended to Olympus, to present to Jupiter some honey fresh from the combs. Jupiter delighting with the offering of honey, promised to give whatever she should ask. She therefore besought him, saying, "Give me, I pray thee, a sting, that if any mortal shall approach to take my honey, I may kill him." Jupiter was much displeased, for he loved the race of man; but could not refuse the request on account of his promise. He thus answered the Bee: "You shall have your request; but it will be at the peril of your own life. For if you use your sting, it shall remain in the wound you make, and then you will die from the loss of it."

From Three Hundred Aesop's Fables, trans. Rev. Geo. Fyler Townsend

The lower level security officers, who had gathered at the hoods on the parking deck, promised an audience with their chief the next morning. Phineas dreaded his second visit to the head of hospital security, the desk-bound Alton Vickers, but as soon as Monday's early rounds concluded, Phineas hurried to the basement office. When he stepped into the open doorway, the desktop computer cast a glow on Captain Vickers' face. He was focused on the screen and keyboard, where he tapped one index finger at a time.

Phineas cleared his throat. "Excuse me, Sir."

"Hey. You're back. Sit down. Let me save this. Then remind me why you're here again." He tapped a few more keys before he took off his reading glasses, turned to Phineas, and sighed. "What's happened this time?"

Phineas lowered himself into the faux leather chair. "Zebediah Jefferson happened. First, he threatened members of the James family with a gun. I heard about that Saturday night and was instructed by your officer to tell you this morning."

Vickers groaned and closed his eyes. "Same African American family?"

"Same." Phineas clenched his jaw muscles.

"When and where?"

"Late last week, on the parking deck."

"Details?"

"I was told that he dangled a noose out his truck window when two of the patient's grandsons walked by. One of them said something back. Then he pointed a pistol at them."

"I'm guessing the brothers beat a hasty retreat." The trace of a smile formed then left him.

Phineas felt his temper surfacing. "They did."

Vickers glanced at his Joe DiMaggio Mr. Coffee on the credenza behind him. "I need another coffee. You want a cup?" He rotated in his desk chair and poured a cup into a UNC mug, then ripped three sugar packets at once and shook them into it.

Phineas had begun to taste his earlier coffee for the second time, this time sour and flowing uphill against gravity. "No thanks."

Vickers sipped and swallowed. "You said 'first'. Was there something else?"

"Jefferson threatened me and my family."

"What did he say?" Vickers' mouth stayed open after the question.

"Said he could find where my family and I live, and drag me back to the hospital, 'if'n' he wanted to'."

"I'm not sure that's a threat. He might just have been upset. Let his emotions get out of hand." Vickers lifted his coffee to his plump lips.

"It was a threat. Then there were the hoods and the noose on our cars. Your officer didn't tell you about that?"

Seriously?

Vickers slammed the mug on his desk and leaned forward, trying to stifle a coughing fit with his fist. A flushed face replaced his pasty complexion. He shuffled through the pile of papers in his basket marked 'In', extracting a sheet from near the top. "Here's something." He traced his pudgy index finger across the page from top to bottom, his lips moving. He muttered, "This guy's reports still need work. I've been trying to train him." His expression unexpectedly brightened when he looked up. "Well, this is beyond us. You'll need to take this one downtown."

"You can't take care of any of it for me?" Phineas sensed that Vickers had realized a "not my job" opportunity.

"They'll want details from you. They'll need to see if he has a record, if he's a prior felon. And there's the ethnic intimidation issue." Vickers first began flipping through the ring of cards on a Rolodex then gave up and began tapping on his keyboard. "I'll call and get you a name and a time, then I'll page you. You know where the station is?"

"I drive by it every day." The opportunities to complete the bulk of that day's hospital work had just evaporated, but at least someone on the Chapel Hill Police force *had* to be better than Alton Vickers.

⬡⬡⬡⬡⬡

Detective Vincent DiCenzo at 1 PM. Not a name from the old south. This was the first time Phineas had been in a police station since he was booked then bailed out of a New Orleans city jail in 1985. The clean, modern, and uncrowded Chapel Hill Police Station was nothing like that terrifying place. He settled his jitters at the memory and let it pass before he began searching the office listings on the wall of the empty reception area. No Vincent DiCenzo. The bored-looking grey-haired woman behind the desk called over, "You looking for someone, Hon?"

"I have a 1 PM appointment with Detective Vincent DiCenzo."

A blank look. "Who?"

"Detective DiCenzo. Is he here?"

"Let me make a call." She dialed an extension. "Looking for a DiCenzo. Oh, him. Okay. I have someone to see him." She looked up at Phineas. "What's your name?"

"Phineas Mann."

She dialed another extension. "I have a Phineas Mann to see you." She hung up. "Sorry I forgot his name. He just started last week. Room 214. Up those stairs and all the way to the back." She pointed toward the door with the neon STAIRS ceiling sign.

214 was indeed at the far end of the long hallway. Phineas tapped on the heavy wooden door. It opened with such vigor, that he felt like the suction pulled him in. On the other side stood a shorter, barrel-chested man with light olive skin and thinning, slicked-back, wavy, grey hair. His black dress shirt was open at the collar and sprinkled with white cat hairs. A loose black and blue striped tie had been pulled off center. A hint of English Leather cologne hovered above him.

"I'm DiCenzo. You the doc from the hospital?" The pressured New York tempo so familiar to Phineas from college in New York.

"Yessir. Phineas Mann."

DiCenzo studied Phineas' face while he grabbed his hand and shook it with vigor. "Should I call you Doc or Phinny?"

When the handshake ended, Phineas felt his hand bones settle back in their normal positions. "Doc is fine. Never been called Phinny."

"Sit down, Doc." He gestured toward a generic metal chair and retreated behind an almost empty matching desk. Only a framed picture on a stand facing DiCenzo, and a pen and pocket-sized pad sat on its surface. "God, it's good to have something to do. Just got here last week, and you're my first new case."

"Er—um, how long have you been a policeman—if you don't mind me asking?"

DiCenzo let out a belly laugh ending with a soft wheeze. "Thirty years. Retired from the NYPD after thirty." He wiped his eye with the back of his hand where a gold watch sparkled. "Then, see, my wife gets tired of me around the place pickin' up my pension check. She saw this article of great places to live with Chapel Hill near the top. See, Theresa, she's a beautician, so she can work anywhere. Next thing I know, she types up my CV and sends it here—then BOOM, here we are—I'd hardly been south of Jersey, and now I'm livin' in Dixie."

Phineas was about to mention that Chapel Hill wasn't exactly Dixie, when the image of Zebediah Jefferson's tattoo came to him. "Welcome to Dixie."

"So whattaya got for me?" DiCenzo was poised with his pen and note pad in hand.

Phineas described everything he could about Jefferson in the hospital leading up to the parking lot Klan hoods. As he told it, he felt himself beginning to question his handling of the recent Sunday conflict. "Detective, do you think I overreacted when I banned him from the hospital?"

"Doc, sounds like if you'd tried to sprinkle water on that fire, it still would have flamed up again sometime soon."

"So, what do we do next?"

"Okay, here's how I see it. First, I need to find out more on this Jefferson character, see if he's got a felony record. Then he'd be breaking the law owning a firearm. I'll check with the state and feds, and I'll visit his local cops in Chatham County. See what they know about him. See if he's just talk—or actually dangerous."

"That sounds good. What about me calling him with reports on his father?"

"Imagine he's pretty pissed off, after you stopped him from visiting his Daddy. Let me check him out before you try to call him for anything." He held the point of his pen to his pad and stared at Phineas expectantly. "I need to know where I can find the young men he dangled the noose in front of."

"Not sure they'll want to see you."

"I get that a lot."

"Thing is, they live in Durham, in a neighborhood with gang problems. They wear colors, but I'm told they're not active in a gang."

"Geesh! I was hoping I left that behind in New York. Got an address?"

"Just a phone number. They deliver for their cousin's cooking business." Phineas took out his wallet and handed over his only Gramma's Cookin' card. "Fried chicken is amazing."

DiCenzo studied it. "Card's nothin' too fancy. Think those guys'll deliver here?" He wrote down the number and returned the card. "Theresa and I love good fried chicken."

"Won't hurt to ask."

"Lemme get back to you after I sniff around. Can I page you through the hospital?"

"Yessir. Unfortunately, I'm on page all month." Phineas was still looking at the cat hairs sprinkled over DiCenzo's shirt. It was something he'd learned to notice on his asthma patients, since so many were allergic. "So, how do you and your family like North Carolina so far?"

"It's just me and Theresa. No kids...only Cannoli. He's our cat."

Leave the gun. Take the cannoli... What kind of cop names his cat after a scene in a Godfather movie?

DiCenzo turned the picture frame around so Phineas could see the professionally posed image. A flashy middle-aged blond woman cradled a kitten on her lap. The cat's fur coloring made the word 'calico' pop into Phineas brain. "How was the move for them?"

"A different world, Doc. We have a yard. Never had one before. I had to get the salesman to show me how to work a lawnmower. Theresa loves sitting out on our patio and watching Cannoli play. She found a salon that's renting her a chair part time, so she's had a chance to explore the town some."

DiCenzo didn't strike Phineas as a cat person. "Had Cannoli ever been outside before?"

"Don't think so. Never thought we'd have a cat. That's a good story, Doc. See, I had a murder scene to investigate. Someone hit a guy in his apartment. It'd been a coupla' days earlier, so we opened the door to his tiny balcony to air the place out. *Whew!* I left my overcoat out there, out of the smell. While we were looking around, we found an empty saucer and tuna can, and a litter box—but no cat." DiCenzo grinned. "It was still warm outside when we left, so I carried my coat out and tossed it in my car's back seat. When I got home, the tiniest kitten you've ever seen was squirming out of the pocket. Theresa about went nuts, he was so cute. Can't deny that woman anything, and he's grown on me. Purrs when I'm stressed."

Phineas needed to get back to the hospital. He shifted onto the front of the chair seat and planted his feet.

"And you'll love this one, Doc. I'm in the bathroom one evening, and I hear Theresa yelling from the kitchen, 'Cannoli's brought a mouse in the house!'. So, I come out to investigate. Theresa's prancing, and Cannoli drops the mouse in his bowl, like it's dinner. The mouse must've been playing dead, 'cause soon as he's dropped, he takes off. Almost made it to our bedroom before Cannoli got 'im again. I showed 'em both the door. Figured he could dine outside that night."

Phineas stood and offered his hand. "That's a good story. I bet you've got more."

"I know, Doc. You've got work. I'll be in touch."

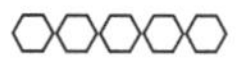

Jacob wasn't the only one who could do an internet search on someone. Back at the desktop computer in his office, Phineas typed 'Vincent DiCenzo NYPD' into Internet Explorer's query box. The page filled quickly and 'More Results' appeared at the bottom of the screen. He selected the first entry, a *New York Times* article from 1988, headlined 'Detective Solves Cold Case'. DiCenzo had unsuccessfully investigated the rape and murder of a young woman in 1979, his first big case after he'd been promoted to detective. When DNA testing became available in the late 80s, he'd retrieved her evidence buried in department storage and obtained warrants to collect specimens from possible suspects. DiCenzo had to pursue one man all the way to a new, secluded residence in rural Florida. That man, the victim's neighbor, matched. The accompanying photo showed a younger DiCenzo with jet-black hair beside a balding, unkempt man in handcuffs coming out of a jetway at JFK Airport.

The next article explored DiCenzo's retirement after thirty years, reviewing several high-profile cases he'd worked on over his career. Mysteries solved. Violent criminals brought to justice. No mention of him having to kill anyone, but it didn't say he hadn't had to along the way. The picture was of him receiving the sparkling gold watch.

Detective Vincent DiCenzo, the new guy in Chapel Hill, was the opposite of a rookie.

Phineas emerged from a deep sleep to Iris poking him between his shoulder blades. "Phineas, your beeper's going off."

The bedside clock displayed 3:20 in two-inch red numerals. He rolled out of bed and shuffled into the bathroom to empty his full bladder. Then he settled into the chair at the vanity and dialed the operator.

"UNC Hospital. How may I direct your call?"

"This is Dr. Phineas Mann. I was paged."

"I have Dr. Villalobos on the line for you."

A bit of static followed by a scratchy voice. Was there a siren in the background? "Dr. Mann, someone tried to burn my parents' taqueria."

Jefferson! "Is everyone okay?"

"We're all fine. I'm sorry to wake you, but I thought you should know—for your safety."

Her warning hit him hard. His ICU team's safety was being threatened outside the hospital. "Is their place badly damaged?"

"Not at all. Someone tried to throw a Molotov cocktail through the window, but the iron bars stopped it from going inside. I'd told my father about the hospital parking lot, so my brother decided to spend the night and was sleeping in the back. He woke up when he heard tires screech and was able to put the fire out right away."

"What'd the police say?"

"They said they'll analyze the pieces for prints—and they'll patrol nearby more."

"Sorry for your family."

"My people have faced worse. This pitiful act is not going to hurt us, but it's a warning for all." She sounded more determined than afraid.

He'd have to let DiCenzo know first thing in the morning to again connect with the Chatham County police. He doubted he could fall back asleep tonight.

⬡⬡⬡⬡⬡

Phineas was yearning for a much-needed Tuesday evening freedom from the hospital and to be at home with his family, as he hurried by the ICU waiting room door.

Almost home—but not a word from DiCenzo.

A lone figure sat hunched forward in one of the vinyl chairs facing a window. She appeared to be studying passersby seven stories below. Ruth. He should stop by and touch base with her. She was bound to want an update and was always appreciative and uplifting.

He slipped through the open door and was about to greet her when he noticed a headline on the *People* magazine among the reading material scattered across the glass coffee table.

BLACK WIDOW EXECUTED

Black Widow?

Sounded familiar. A distant memory.

The *People* issue was from April 1998, last month. The subtitle read, "Judy Buenoano Electrocuted in FL for Multiple Murders."

The memory of a "black widow" emerged from somewhere buried in his memory cortex, a North Carolina woman who was arrested for murdering husbands. He and his colleagues had chuckled about female spiders killing their males after the mating act—killing them then eating them.

Ruth turned from the window and graced him with one of her beatific smiles. "Dr. Mann. How kind of you to drop by. How's Mother?"

"Uh, fine." He looked up from the magazine and made eye contact. "She remains on low levels of supplemental oxygen and seems to be eating better."

"That's wonderful. And I saw her with physical therapy today. We're *very* encouraged."

Velma Barfield!

The name surfaced from that deep region of his brain. Seems she might have been a patient at UNC after she was arrested. Or was it one of her husbands—before he died? But seems there was another woman who later on followed Barfield's example and earned the moniker 'Black Widow'.

Blanche Taylor Moore.

"Dr. Mann?"

"Yes?"

"Was there anything else?"

Arsenic!

Barfield's and Moore's husbands had been to hospitals before they died at later times from arsenic poisoning—proven only after their deaths, when exhumed some months or years later. None of the doctors who saw their victims had figured out in life what the men eventually died from. And the mistaken diagnosis made by the hospitals' doctors had been 'severe gastroenteritis'.

Phineas picked up the magazine and tucked it under his arm. It occurred to him who else would have thumbed through this April issue of *People* magazine while waiting for him to come by on evening rounds the first week of May.

He needed to bring himself back to the present. "Sorry. Had something on my mind." What if this magazine hadn't been in the ICU waiting room in early May? Would Enoch Jefferson be recovered and out of the ICU? Would Zebediah Jefferson and Angela Portier be out of his life forever? And what if Ron Bullock hadn't asked him to be on television?

"About Mother?"

"Another patient."

"Always thinking about your patients. Thank you for stopping by, Dr. Mann. I'll just go see Mother now. I hope you get to go home to your family soon." She offered another warm smile.

He did his best to return it, as his plan came into focus. "Did you have any other questions?"

Ruth tilted her head ever so slightly. "Are they paying you enough, Dr. Mann?"

"Excuse me?"

"I can bring in *our* old magazines for you, if you'd like."

⬡⬡⬡⬡⬡

Wednesday morning, Malcolm Carver closed the door of the last ICU patient the team had seen on work rounds. As Phineas was breaking off from the group, Nurse Lisa tapped him on the shoulder. She leaned close and whispered in his ear, "Dr. Mann, there's *a detective* waiting for you in the conference room."

Phineas' entire core tightened. "Thanks."

DiCenzo sat at the end of the table, his chin in his hand, elbow on the table, studying his notepad and sipping from a paper cup. His red tie slanted to the left. Black and brown cat hairs were sprinkled on the sleeves of his white shirt. He looked up as Phineas entered. "Christ Almighty, Doc! That's some guy you put me on."

Not taking his eyes off DiCenzo, Phineas lowered himself into the chair next to the detective. "And?"

"First, they got nothing on the fire at the Mexican restaurant. Whoever did it must have been wearing gloves."

"That's disappointing." Phineas had hoped the perpetrators would be caught, locked up, and include Zebediah Jefferson.

"So, I started yesterday with your chicken guys, Demetrius and his shy brother, Isaiah. Walked right into the station with my chicken order—and were good enough to sit and talk."

"They wear their red jackets?"

DiCenzo answered, "Warm day. Must have left them in the car."

"What'd they say?"

"What you said. 'Cracker pulled a piece' on 'em—and they beat a hasty retreat. Said it was your patient's son, like you said—and they mentioned the noose."

"Can you do anything?" *Wasn't a threat with a noose and a gun a crime?*

"I went looking for Cracker. Started with the sheriff over there in Chatham County. Cute town. That old guy's been there since Babe Ruth was a Yankee."

Phineas put on a mock frown. "Since they stole him from my Red Sox."

DiCenzo frowned back. "Hey, Doc, not sure I can work for a Sox fan." He took a swig from the cup.

"Well, did the old gentleman help?"

"Old gentleman! That's a good one." The detective coughed hard and had to reach into his back pocket for a handkerchief. "But he knows our guy, Zebediah. Grew up in the same town with his Daddy, Enoch—What names they give 'em here!"

"Welcome to the South."

"Course, you're the first Phineas I ever met. Well anyway, our guy, Zeb, was a handful as a kid. Lost his mamma young. Then Daddy Enoch was always having to get him out of trouble. Finally dragged him to the Army recruiter—hoped they'd make a man out of him."

Phineas winced at the new information. Zebediah Jefferson with military training.

DiCenzo sipped coffee and continued. "That didn't go so well. Bad behavior got him thrown out while he was in Vietnam. Dishonorable discharge. Rumor around town was he bragged to someone that he fragged his black lieutenant during a combat mission."

"Fragged?"

"Killed him during a battle—to make it look like the enemy did it." He set the cup down. "Gave him instant cred with the local KKK."

"Damn!"

"You're tellin' me. So, you got a guy with a nasty disposition and a new skill set."

Phineas tasted sour remnants of his morning coffee, a sensation occurring daily now. "What'd he do after the Army?"

"The old sheriff said his Daddy took him into the family business. Taught him welding. Daddy Enoch had a pretty good business, solid middle class, regular customers. Then son Zeb started driving business elsewhere. Careless work. Not on time. And you've met him. Some personality, I hear." He shook his head. "Then Daddy got old, and Zeb mostly took over the workload. Now he just gets the scraps that good welders don't want. Blames his downfall on immigrants and minorities undercutting him for the good jobs."

"Has he been in trouble with the law in North Carolina?"

"Nothin' major. Misdemeanors here and there. He's not a felon, so we can't pick him up on weapons possession. If I find him, I can question him on his threatening the brothers—just not sure if I can charge him. You know—he says, they say—and belonging to the Klan isn't against the law neither."

"So, he *is* in the Klan?"

"Sheriff says he's likely been in it since he came back from Nam. And they got some serious bad guys round here, just not jailed on anything yet. And I hear they're not afraid to wear their hoods downtown on special occasions. Jeesh!" He crumpled the cup in his fist.

"He have any other family, besides Enoch?"

"The old sheriff says no woman was ever crazy enough to marry him, if he'd been interested."

"That's no surprise. And that he's latched onto Angela. Maybe she can lead you to him. She works at the VA in Durham. Angela Portier RN."

"I'll see if I can find her." He jotted on his notepad.

Phineas peered at the writing on the notepad, unable to decipher DiCenzo's scribbled notes. "So, what's next?"

"I'm gonna to keep trying to bring him in for questioning." He glanced at the ceiling. "Wish I could talk to him like we did in New York."

Phineas had to ask. "How did you do it in New York?"

"You can't tell anyone this." DiCenzo leaned back with a half-smile and pressed his fingertips together. "You need a bag of chips, a grape soda, and a Manhattan phone book."

"And?"

"First you leave them alone in a room for a while. Then you come in all friendly and ask if they're hungry. By then they always are, so you get them a bag of chips, the saltier, the better. You ask some more questions—real friendly like. Take what they give you and let them sit alone for a while longer."

DiCenzo seemed to be enjoying himself. "See after a while they're gonna be thirsty, so you bring them a grape soda. No one ever turns down grape. And you ask some more—still friendly."

He sat silently, now adopting a serious look, waiting for Phineas to ask, "and the phone book?"

"Doesn't leave marks."

"You're kidding."

DiCenzo's wheezy chuckle settled into a sheepish grin. "Yeah, I am. They don't let us do that, 'specially in Chapel Hill. And besides, your phone book's too skinny." He shrugged his shoulders. "Sorry 'bout that, Doc. You looked like you could use some levity."

What Phineas wanted was to hear a plan. "So, you think you can bring him in?"

"If we can find him. He wasn't at his house or business, and their truck and the old bucket of bolts the sheriff says he cruises around in were missing. Sheriff promised he'll keep his eyes and ears out. And if Jefferson shows up at the hospital, security will detain him and call us."

"Are you checking all the other known Klan members' places?"

"I asked the old sheriff to help me with that, but he said Chatham is a big county. He wasn't free with names."

Fine shakes had crept from Phineas' fingers toward his spine. Levity had evaporated. Reality was back. "Detective, now I'm actually more worried than ever."

"Not sure we got enough to put out an APB yet."

"A what?"

"All points bulletin. Bring in the State Police."

The alarm tremors rose up Phineas' back to the base of his skull. He stared at the detective and murmured, "Maybe it's time for them to be involved now. You know about the Greensboro Massacre?"

DiCenzo's face was blank. "Nope."

"I was a resident here about twenty years ago when it happened. There was a demonstration against the Klan and Nazis, who showed up in numbers and heavily armed. They'd been tipped off by the *local* police. Several of the demonstrators were gunned down—murdered—including doctors. Police were remarkably absent."

"What happened to the shooters?"

"Acquitted by an all-white jury. As I recall, one of the demonstrators might have had a pistol, and the jury believed a self-defense plea."

The detective's head drooped forward. "Jeesh, Doc. I wish we cops were all better than that." A look of sadness came over DiCenzo. "Someday, maybe I'll tell you a story."

Phineas waited a few beats before he broke the silence. "I'm listening."

"Now's not a good time." DiCenzo shot out the words rapid-fire, like he had second thoughts. "Let's get back to why *we're* here."

Phineas accepted the pivot back to his problem. "Okay. So, do you think the Chatham police will do anything against the Klan, or could they be sympathetic to their cause?"

"Let me see what my chief thinks. We'll keep ya' posted, Doc." DiCenzo stood. "And, Doc?' His words hung between them.

"Yeah?"

"That was some mighty fine chicken."

Not the pep talk Phineas hoped to hear.

⬡⬡⬡⬡⬡

With Wednesday afternoon office hours and downtown traffic delays behind her, Iris turned the corner into their rural neighborhood. Her dashboard clock shouted her tardiness at meeting Martha's school bus. On a good day, Iris would deposit her work materials at home and, with a joyous Stella on leash, meet Martha as she descended the bus' steps. Today, she lowered the front windows and scanned the side of the typically empty street for her daughter.

Ahead of her, a beat-up sedan, faded charcoal grey from a spray can or bargain paint job, was stopped on the wooded street a couple of hundred yards from the next opening, their driveway. Martha stood still in the low weeds by the side of the road several feet from it, facing the passenger window. A man's hand inside gestured for Martha to step closer.

No! Iris leaned on the horn with both hands and mashed the accelerator to the floor, screeching the tires of her SUV. She then immediately stood on her brake pedal and deposited strips of rubber behind the man's sedan, stopping after the SUV's front jolted his rear bumper. The rusty heap of a car jerked into a three-point turn and came to an abrupt stop half on the street's shoulder straight across from her.

She heard the wheeze of air brakes behind her, a block away, behind the knoll in the road.

Jacob's bus.

She locked eyes with the sedan's driver under his NRA hat. His face was a portrait of anger and hate before a sinister smile emerged. "Well, you must be the Missus." He spat the words like they contained rock dust. "Figured the doctor'd have a purty wife."

Iris glanced at her rearview mirror and saw Jacob coming into view over the crest on her side of the road. He began hurrying toward her SUV.

The driver extended his arm and motioned for her to approach. "You and your daughter. Get in. Y'all are comin' with me. Move!" His harsh command resonated up and down the peaceful street.

She kept her focus on Jacob's image in the mirror. He was silent and now less than fifty feet behind her SUV. He scanned the ground and stooped to scoop up a dark oval stone the size of a jumbo chicken egg. He bounced it in his hand.

The man reached under his seat then leaned back upright, brandishing a heavy silver and black pistol. He pointed it at her, then toward the front of his car, displaying the gun's profile. "I'm in charge here. I said, 'Git in! NOW!"

Jacob's emotionless expression suggested the practiced nonchalance of a seasoned video gamer and relief pitcher. Then, like a dream memory, the too familiar windup, high leg kick and delivery.

"Jacob! Run!"

The stone found the strike zone of the open car window with the force of Jacob's best fastball and hit the man's cheek with a spongy thud. The pistol fired once, shattering the windshield, then fell loose. The man shook his head, rubbed his cheek, and cursed, one long diatribe Iris couldn't understand. Blood dribbled from his mouth down his chin. He spat what she guessed was a crimson-coated tooth into his hand.

Martha stood frozen in the weeds with her backpack against her feet, hands at her sides, her frightened doe eyes fully revealing their whites. Iris pushed open the passenger side door. "Martha, GET IN!"

The man reached across his dashboard for the pistol. A second stone, this one, white quartz and sparkling in the Carolina sun, also found its target, striking the man's left ear and cleaving it from front to back. He screamed and pressed his palm against it.

Jacob was nowhere to be seen after his second pitch, having vanished down one of the countless deer runs crisscrossing the neighborhood's thick woods. Iris clutched Martha's shirt and pulled her daughter down toward her. With Martha's feet still protruding out the open passenger door, Iris pressed the gas pedal. In the mirror she saw a neighbor's car creep over the knoll behind her

The shooter's wounded sedan lurched forward, spinning gravel and grass from one rear tire and leaving tracks on the asphalt with the other, before it vanished over the knoll. Iris heard a second burst of rubber squealing and fading away seconds later.

She pulled over, releasing her iron grip on Martha's shirt and hugged her daughter against her chest, rocking side to side, struggling to hold back a flood of tears. Jacob reappeared at the side of her SUV and climbed in next to Martha. Iris pulled him into the embrace. He shook so hard she had trouble holding onto him.

"Jacob. Jacob. Jacob." She hadn't seen him wipe his eyes in years. Iris' chest was pounding. She took in a slow, deep breath, trying to calm herself. "Martha, what did he say to you?"

Martha opened her mouth, but nothing came out at first. Then she whispered, "He asked if I knew where the Mann's house was."

"What did you tell him?"

"That that was *my* house."

Iris locked eyes with her daughter, waiting.

"He said I should get in and he'd drive me home. Then I heard your horn."

Their neighbor, Alice, drove up behind them and got out of her car. This mother, still in a formal office pant suit, was also arriving home after school let out. She looked terrified as she approached Iris' open window. "Can I help you, Iris?"

Iris was still clutching her children. "We're okay, but we need the police. Please try to call them and ask them to come now. I'll do the same. And thanks, Alice—thanks so much for being here." Hands shaking, she released Martha and Jacob and fumbled with her purse for her cell phone.

Martha held up her right forearm. "Momma, I saw a flag under his skin."

The racist son Phineas told me about. Iris dialed 911.

"911. What's your emergency?"

"We...My daughter and I...We just escaped an attempted kidnapping. We need police right away!" Iris took a slow, deep breath to settle herself.

"Is anyone injured?" A calming monotone.

"No. We're all okay—but he just drove off. His windshield is shattered—shot out. He has a gun. You need to find him."

"Give me your location and we'll send someone."

Iris spelled their street for the operator and impatiently answered the rest of the questions on the county's 911 call form. She punched in UNC Hospital's number and had Phineas paged.

"Phineas Mann." She could hear an ICU alarm in the background.

His voice was a relief, but her throat tightened when she exclaimed, "*Your patient's son* just tried to kidnap Martha and me near her bus stop. Come home."

"Iris? What? Are...Are you okay?"

"For now. He left. I called the police. Just come home, Phineas."

"I will." He cleared his throat. "Let me call the detective working on his case, and I'll call you right back."

"Okay...Hurry. Bye." Dial tone. Her hand shook as she cranked the ignition. She was still afraid, but her exasperation at Phineas for ending her call now competed.

◇◇◇◇◇

With siren still blaring, the Orange County Sheriff eased his cruiser into the entrance of the Mann's long driveway.

Iris' cell phone buzzed. She flipped it open. "Hello."

"Iris, I'm on my way to the parking lot. I reached Detective DiCenzo. He's on his way." Phineas was breathing hard. "What happened? Is that a siren?"

"Sheriff's just getting here. We're all okay, just shaken up. Jacob saved us. Tell you more when you get here. Bye."

"What...Okay. I'm at my car. Bye."

Once home, she had finally calmed Martha. Iris then paced, keeping a wary eye on the driveway from the side porch, fretting over the fact that the dangerous man was still out there. The sight of the sheriff's patrol car was such a relief.

Martha settled on the porch steps, trying to hug an exuberant Stella. A movement in Iris' peripheral vision caused her attention to abruptly be diverted. There. Only an orange tulip poplar blossom, tumbled from on high into the tree's lower limbs, one by one by one, and onto the edge of the asphalt. Phineas would say a twig girdler beetle had likely performed the amputation. Then he'd go inspect it.

Stella raced to investigate the fallen object with Martha in pursuit. The retriever suddenly jerked her head back and scooted away, growling at the blossom and warily circling back. Martha bent to pick up the open flower and brought it straight to her nose.

Christ no! Iris shut her flip phone. "Martha! Put that down!"

Too late. Martha let out an ear-splitting shriek while furiously rubbing her forehead with the heel of her hand. Iris raced to the driveway to embrace her. Another scream. "It hurts, Momma! It hurts!" As Martha pranced in place, Iris lifted her daughter's hand from her face, trying for a close inspection. The offending stinger was centered between her daughter's eyes, still contracting and squirting venom from its tiny sac.

Iris scraped it out with her fingernail and hugged Martha tight. She wished she could absorb her daughter's distress. "Let's get some ice on that sting, Martha." *My poor gentle girl! And after so much already.*

Martha gasped and sobbed, gasped and sobbed. "Can't breathe, Momma!"

A stocky sheriff appeared next to them. "I'll call in an emergency, Ma'am. Might be an allergic reaction." His words were emphatic and tense.

Please, no.

He circled back to his cruiser at a run, his sidearm and the multiple pouches on his belt bouncing with each footfall.

Jacob stepped from inside the house through the porch's door, a glass of orange juice in his hand. "What's going on?"

"Can't breathe!"

Martha stacked one deep breath after another between sobs. Iris' own throat tightened at the sight of her frantic daughter. She inspected Martha's lips and tongue for swelling, but there was none, thankfully, only a pink puffiness that had spread around Martha's eyes and from forehead to the bridge of her nose.

"Momma, I can't feel my fingers!" Her daughter crumpled toward the pavement. Iris caught her before impact and lowered her carefully.

The sheriff was suddenly back. "They're on their way, Ma'am." He stared at Martha lying on the asphalt, his face advertising his own fear as he leaned close. "Should we start CPR?"

Can't he see she's awake? Martha took deep breaths, and her terrified eyes were filled with huge, black pupils. "No. She's breathing and conscious." *Isn't that obvious?*

A siren in the distance rose steadily to a crescendo as it turned onto their street. A fire engine came into view and pulled over abruptly, lights flashing. The sheriff waved both arms to the two firemen exiting the cab. "First responders, Ma'am. Paramedics should be here soon."

The firemen raced down the driveway, one with a silver oxygen tank, the other with a bulky kit adorned with a white cross. *They look so young.* One had to be barely out of high school, the other in his twenties. In no time the two were hovering over her and Martha.

"Let's give her some oxygen, Ma'am. Help her to breathe." The younger man began trying to fit a mask over Martha's distressed face, while she tried to push it away. His partner attached a blood pressure cuff around the struggling child's upper arm, and the instant he began inflating it, Martha yelled, "Ouch! That hurts! Too tight!"

"BP's 125/80. Probably high for her."

It's fine. Settle down. Please.

Another siren. Tires screeched. The promised paramedic truck lined up behind the fire truck. Two doors slammed. A grey-haired man, carrying more marked baggage, jogged toward the human cluster. Iris guessed this man must be in his fifties. *He has to be better.* The driver, a younger, taller man followed.

"BP's 125/80," the fireman repeated.

The older paramedic set his load on the ground and knelt next to Martha, studying her. The name tag over his shirt pocket said "Wayne".

Jacob stood silently to the side looking helpless and worried. The orange juice glass he cradled remained full.

Iris turned Martha to face the paramedic. "She was stung on her face."

"So I see. Stinger out?" His voice was low and soothing.

"A while ago."

"Any hives or scratching?"

"Haven't seen any."

"Wheezing?"

"Some gasping earlier. She said she couldn't feel her hands or feet."

"Hmm. I see." He glanced at his watch and, in a whisper, counted the child's breaths. Then he pulled a stethoscope from his pocket and listened to Martha's back. After several of her breaths, he stood and placed a hand gently on her shoulder. "Sweetheart, my name's Wayne, and I've got just the thing to make you feel better."

Thank God! Someone who seems to know what he's doing.

The paramedic opened his bulky suitcase and removed a brown paper bag. From it, he extracted a Saran-wrapped white bread sandwich, which he slipped back inside his medical kit. Then, holding the bag lengthwise inside his loose fist, he carefully formed a collar in the open end and inserted a finger to create a neat round entrance.

"Lookee here, Honey. I've got what you need to feel better inside this bag. I'm going to let you breathe into it, okay?"

She tilted her head forward in acceptance, eyes locked on him and his bag. He gently removed the oxygen mask and held the paper collar over her mouth.

"My partner's Jim. He's just started with me and learning the ropes."

The silent young man murmured, "Hey."

Wayne ignored him and turned toward Iris. "What's your daughter's name?"

"Martha."

"Oh, that's a good name. My wife's name. And what's your name?"

"Iris."

"Pretty. My favorite flower." He kept his speech calm, content.

"And this young feller must be Martha's brother."

Iris forced a smile. "That's Jacob." Jacob gave a short wave from the empty hand at his waist. He took a cautious sip of juice and stared.

Stella had been sitting outside the crowd quietly observing, but now stood and wagged her tail slowly. The paramedic smiled at the dog. "And what's your well-behaved dog's name?"

"Stella."

"Like in the Brando movie?"

He's buying time. "Yes, Sir."

Wayne gave Martha's shoulder a gentle squeeze. "Your dog has a really cool name. And I'll bet you're starting to feel better."

Martha raised her puffy eyebrows in response.

"Excellent. I'll let you breathe into my special bag until you feel good as new." He glanced over at the two hovering firemen. "Thank you, gentlemen. I think you can safely return to the station now. Situation's under control. We've got this from here. Sheriff, everything okay with you?"

The stocky sheriff cleared his throat. "Sir, I still need to talk with them about a possible attempted kidnapping."

Paramedic Wayne looked startled. He whispered to Martha, "I'm going to let you breathe without the bag now. If you need it again, I've still got it. Okay?" He removed the bag from her mouth and, cocking his head, displayed a boyish grin to her. "Martha, can you smile for me?"

She allowed a shy smile to surface below her pink and swollen forehead.

Iris' rigid neck and shoulder muscles softened. *Her* breaths also began to come easier in Wayne's soothing presence.

"Iris, why don't you get Martha some ice for that sting, while Stella and I do my paperwork?" He reached past Stella's curious nose into his kit for a clipboard and to rescue his all-too-tempting sandwich.

◇◇◇◇◇

Phineas arrived on their narrow street and had to wait impatiently for a fire engine to make a wide turn in short installments. He hurriedly parked behind the paramedic truck and flagged down the firemen. His heart hadn't stopped pounding since Iris' call. He felt for the crumpled hospital papers in his pants pocket. No, he hadn't misplaced the critical information in his hurry.

The fire engine braked next to him. "I live here. Everybody okay? What happened?"

The driver leaned out his window. "We got a call for respiratory distress. Paramedic's with the young girl now." He waved and motored off leaving a cloud of diesel fumes around Phineas before he sprinted down the driveway.

Iris sat stoically on the front steps with one arm around Martha and her other hand pressing a cloth to their daughter's forehead. His wife shook her head at him. "Glad you're *finally* here. Wish you could've gotten here sooner."

"I—I got here as fast as I could."

A sheriff knelt in front of Iris and Martha, apparently interviewing them. He stood, continuing to jot notes on a clipboard. A grey-haired paramedic crouching off to the side secured his bulky bag and also rose. "You must be Martha's father. She's had a very stressful day."

"I'm a physician. What happened?" *She looks okay.* His heart was slowing.

"She got stung between her eyes. Add to that the reason the sheriff's here, and your sweet daughter had a bout of hyperventilation. She's fine medically now. She still has my lunch bag, if the hyperventilation starts again. Nice kid."

"Thank you, Sir—for everything. I'm glad you got the call."

"You're welcome. I'm off now. Good luck with the rest of it." His young partner hoisted the medical valise and they ambled up the driveway.

Phineas knelt in front of his daughter and lifted the ice pack to inspect her forehead. He kissed the raised, pink spot and whispered, "Ouch" before turning to scan the front yard. His pulse raced again. "Where's Jacob?"

Jacob stepped around the house's corner. "Here, Dad. Glad you're home. You can take over being the man of the house now." A new swagger appeared in his step, before he took a protective seat beside his mother.

A car door slammed on the street. Detective Vincent DiCenzo scanned the scene as he approached, then stopped to question the paramedics. His purple tie had flipped over his broad shoulder. He straightened it as he neared Phineas. Stella charged him before she sniffed and snorted up and down each of his pantlegs. She then appeared satisfied and sat staring at him.

"Hey, Doc. Seems your dog likes the smell of Cannoli."

The detective and Iris studied each other. Her penetrating glare stopped him short. "Cannoli? Really? Now?"

"Sorry, Ma'am. Cannoli's the name of my cat. You must be the Missus."

"Astute deduction. And you are?"

He held up his badge. "Detective Vincent DiCenzo, Chapel Hill Police. I've been working with Doc on a case that might be the guy you and Sheriff here are discussing. So, Sheriff—"

"Johnson, Wade Johnson." His round face was shiny smooth, and a dab of shaving foam was dissolving under his earlobe.

"Wade Johnson, what have you got for me?"

The sheriff handed DiCenzo his notes and began summarizing his interview with Iris and Martha. He concluded with "After the suspect showed the mother a gun, the son hurled two stones in rapid succession, each reportedly striking the driver's head. Then a neighbor's car pulled up as the mother and daughter were escaping, causing the suspect to flee the scene." Phineas' fists clenched, as concern over his family's safety shifted to rage.

DiCenzo knelt in front of Martha. "Hi Sweetie. I'm Vinnie. You feel better?"

She nodded slowly.

"Did the man in the car have glasses, a beard, or anything else on his face?'

She stared at her feet and shook her head.

"Long or short hair."

"Short. A buzz. Old. It was grey."

"Was he wearing anything unusual?"

She looked up at DiCenzo. "He was smoking a cigarette—and he had a flag on his arm."

"On his sleeve?"

"His skin."

"An American flag?"

"No...One with a big 'X' on it."

DiCenzo turned to Iris. "You didn't happen to see any of the license plate, did you?"

"It was all too fast." Her tone suggested frustration.

He stood and turned to Jacob. "So, you're the young lad who hurled the stones. What you did, young man, was brave—and a little crazy. Maybe you can pitch for my Yankees someday. Let's see your pitching motion."

Jacob wound up and flung an imaginary fastball. "Or Dad's Red Sox." He smiled, his pride showing in his bright eyes.

"Hah! Looks great." DiCenzo turned to Phineas. "Listen, Doc, description sure fits our guy. Let me give Sheriff Johnson what I know, and he can get the word out to his people and to our friends over in Chatham County." He pointed at Johnson and gestured with his head toward the driveway.

Iris held up her hand. "Hold it, everybody. Listen, especially Jacob and Martha. You can't tell anyone what happened today. Not for quite a while. For your safety." She stared straight at Jacob. "I know you'll want to tell your friends about your heroics—but don't. For your sake and your sister's. This isn't over yet. Do you *hear* me?"

The detective added, "You did poke a wild animal with a sharp stick, Jacob, or in this case a couple of stones. And he's still out there."

Jacob slowly nodded his reluctant acceptance, a disappointed look replacing pride. Martha's nod followed his example.

With a hand on Jacob's shoulder, DiCenzo looked him in the eye and said, "Someday young man, you can tell your story—and it's a really good one—but not for a while. Not till this is well behind us."

Sheriff Johnson reached into his breast pocket. "Ma'am, here's my card. Call anytime if you need us, or if you think of anything else. I just started my shift and will be nearby till 11 when my replacement comes on." He and DiCenzo then trudged down the lengthy driveway, engaged in animated conversation with the detective gesticulating over its entire length.

"Sorry I wasn't here, Honey. Are you okay now?" Phineas kissed the top of Martha's head. He lifted the cloth again and winced at the welt connecting her eyebrows.

She rubbed the swelling lightly. "Still stings a little, and itches."

Iris was staring at him. Her face displayed an effort to hold back her emotions, to stay in control. "So, this was probably your patient's son?'

"Most likely."

She shuddered. "And this was one of your bees." She pointed her index finger at Martha's face.

That hurt. "Possibly...but you know that bees forage up to three miles from their hives, so it might be someone else's."

She looked at him doubtfully.

His pitiful bee nerd defense wasn't working. "It...Um, it might have been a Jezebel bee."

"Hey, Doc." DiCenzo had reappeared behind Phineas. "We've been looking for this guy, Zeb, for two days now. He appears to have gone to ground. No clues to his whereabouts until he showed up here. Johnson is putting out an APB, so now the state police will also be on the lookout."

"He seems to be good at hiding when he wants to."

"Maybe getting help from his buddies in the Klan," DiCenzo responded.

Iris looked startled, and Martha squinted her puffy pink forehead. "What's the Klan?"

Phineas cleared his throat. They shouldn't be having this conversation with Martha there. "Bad people, Martha. Bad people." He pointed in the direction of the side porch. "Detective, I need to discuss another matter with you." Stella whined as she led the way.

As they reached the porch, Phineas pulled the folded papers from his pocket and handed one of them to DiCenzo.

"What's this?" He pulled frameless reading glasses from his shirt pocket.

"Attempted murder."

DiCenzo was squinting and traced his finger slowly from top to bottom. "What? This looks like some kind of test on Enoch Jefferson. Explain what I'm reading, Doc."

"That's his urine arsenic level after his first sinking spell. It should be zero—and it's off the charts. All his symptoms and findings fit with arsenic poisoning. First case at UNC in 20 years." Phineas handed DiCenzo the other paper. "Almost the same result after his second sinker. We saved his blood and urine when we couldn't figure out what happened."

For the first time since they'd met, DiCenzo was silent. He studied the reports. "I can't remember ever seeing an arsenic case."

"Maybe we have more ants to poison with it here than you did in New York...First case for me too."

"Who would...?"

"I can't imagine anyone working in our ICU would do it. And I don't think Zeb would—or could—know enough to do it. It had to be someone with experience with doses and administering chemicals...and using a feeding tube." Phineas watched the detective process these deductions. "I found an article in the *People* magazine that was in our ICU waiting room about how a woman used arsenic to kill her husbands, and the doctors didn't figure out what was wrong with them until after they were dead and buried. Our culprit had to have read it." He let his words sink in. "It had to be Angela Portier."

"Zeb's nurse friend?"

"Who else? She had access to Enoch when his son took one of his many smoking breaks, and it's likely she figured no one would think to test for it. She had to be the one to do it—to launch Zebediah against me—against us." He paused to collect his thoughts then punched his palm for emphasis. "She was pretending to like him. She used him. She weaponized that violent racist against me, my family, and people in the hospital."

DiCenzo was staring, head bent forward to look over his spectacles. "What's she got against you, Doc?"

"It goes way back." Phineas inhaled deeply and slowly let it out. "After Hurricane Jezebel, she leveled charges against me."

"Charges against you?"

Phineas bowed his head and closed his eyes. "Long story. She claimed I euthanized patients—murdered them. I gave them morphine, because they were terminally ill and suffering horribly, all while we were without power in the hospital for 5 days."

"That doesn't seem like a reason to come after you years later."

"There's more. She was the DA's main witness, and when my attorney found out *60 Minutes* was going to do a show on my upcoming trial, he fed Morley Safer some background on her, background that provided Safer with penetrating questions about her motivation."

"And?" DiCenzo's mouth hung open.

"His questions brought out that Angela believed doctors let her father die, that she felt he should have been kept on a ventilator waiting for a miracle for *his* terminal condition. She went into a rant about doctors giving up on their patients and looked so deranged, that the DA felt he had to drop the charges." Phineas relived both his pain and relief. "She was humiliated on national television and blames me."

DiCenzo looked incredulous. "Jesus, Doc...I remember that show!"

"Unfortunately, I'll never forget it."

"Let me get word out to pick her up and bring her in. I checked at the VA earlier and she wasn't working today. Took a day off."

The *People* article revealed what their Black Widow used for her poison. "You should check around her place for ant poison, and I hope you can find her right away."

"Maybe she's with her Zeb. Doc, he could have all kinds of stuff at his disposal, if he gets crazier and decides to get violent. Stuff the Klan has hoarded, like assault weapons from before the '94 ban. They'd probably love for him to use what they got. Have him take one for their cause."

"I guess anyone could buy those rifles before the ban?" Phineas pictured one in Jefferson's hands.

"In the U. S. of A. losers snatched 'em up. Made them feel like they had power." DiCenzo rested his hand on his shoulder holster. "Those guns *did* scare the shit out of us in New York when we ran into 'em. Excuse my French."

"It's hard to believe the KKK still exists."

"More losers. They get together and blame Jews and Brown and Black people, especially successful ones, for their own failures, instead of blaming their ignorance and laziness—and they've gone after my Italian people, too." DiCenzo snorted his disgust.

Phineas tried to muster confidence in law enforcement but thought again about the Greensboro Massacre and the Chatham County sheriff. Why hadn't that sheriff helped DiCenzo more? "I'd better let you all get started finding them."

"Doc, keep all this poisoning stuff to yourself for now." DiCenzo pocketed his glasses and stepped to the edge of the porch. "It won't help our investigation if it hits the papers. Okay?"

"Sure, but I need to tell hospital administration."

"Just those in charge, okay? Now I want to say goodbye to your family, then you can walk me to my car and tell me everything else you know about this Angela person."

They circled back to Iris, and the detective handed her a card. "Sorry about all you've been through, Ma'am. Here's my number. Call us right away if you think of anything else. Sheriff Wade promised they'll have cruisers in the area to keep an eye on your place." He reached into his shirt pocket and gave her another card.

She examined it and looked puzzled. "What's this?"

He shrugged and smiled sheepishly. "My wife, Theresa. She's a hair stylist, if you know anyone who might need one. She's just getting started in Chapel Hill. She assigns me a quota of her cards. I only have to give out two more this month."

"Err—thanks." She reached up and touched her long tresses.

"Your hair looks great though."

⬡⬡⬡⬡⬡

It was almost 10 PM when Phineas' pager vibrated on his belt. *The ICU's number.* He slipped into the solitude of their bedroom to use its bedside phone. The evening shift secretary's familiar voice answered, "ICU."

"It's Dr. Mann, Abby. Responding to a page."

"Dr. Carver was paging you, Dr. Mann. Let me find him." She placed Phineas on hold, and a popular instrumental tune replaced her.

Phineas tapped his foot and waited. It had been a challenge for Iris and him to settle Martha and Jacob down enough to get them to go to bed. Martha, totally exhausted from the afternoon crises, immediately plunged into deep sleep with Iris lying next to her, but Phineas suspected that Jacob was reading by flashlight behind his closed door. Jacob was still pumped from his heroics.

"Dr. Mann?" Malcolm now.

"Right here, Malcolm."

"Did you see the news?" His voice had an edge that alarmed Phineas.

What now? "We haven't had the TV on. What happened?"

"The Klan held a rally after sunset—over in Chatham County...They burned a cross on a mountain top." His words trailed off.

"Did they hurt anyone?"

"Not as far as we know. It just hit the news. Apparently, it's been quite a while since they've had one."

"You talk to Patrice yet?"

"Yeah. She's okay. She wasn't surprised, mostly just disgusted. She'd predicted it—or *something* public to announce they're still around."

"Well, we all need to stay extra careful. Use security whenever you're coming or going, and the police are on high alert after what happened this afternoon. You gave them your address after we banished Zebediah, didn't you?"

"Of course. And I let them know Patrice is at home." He paused. "Dr. Mann, you just said something happened this afternoon. What was it?"

"Zebediah showed up on our street."

"No! What'd he do?"

"He was dispatched before he could do anything—and before the police got here." Phineas needed to figure out how much he could tell his team. He'd probably tell them most of it, but not tonight.

"Well, I thought I should let you know about the Klan rally."

"I appreciate the heads up. We'll check the news. I hope you can get some rest tonight...and I'll see you in the morning." Rest. When could Phineas get rest?

"Good night, Dr. Mann."

"Good night, Malcolm."

Phineas put the phone down and pounded on his pillow with both fists. First Zebediah Jefferson goes after Martha and Iris, and now racists from all over were crawling out from under their rocks and declaring themselves in a public display. Was their action to show they backed Jefferson, or was it (Phineas desperately hoped) unrelated? What could be coming next? Would the Klan use Jefferson for more? The scene of the ICU confrontations replayed in Phineas' head. Did he provoke a cascade of violence by throwing Jefferson out of the hospital?

By now, Malcolm had to be wishing he and Patrice had stayed up north. They'd never faced this level of danger in Boston. Phineas wouldn't blame them if they left the South to continue their education. They had to be wondering how trying to do good had innocently placed them in such jeopardy.

Phineas was still sitting on their bed staring at the phone when Iris entered. She sat next to him and squeezed his hand. "Phineas, you look like you've heard bad news. I hope you don't have to go back in. We need you here tonight."

"We should turn on the news." He stood, pulled her into a standing position, and led her to the living room. She searched his face as he pressed WRAL's number on the remote.

Chelsea LaFever's usually cheerful tone was replaced by one that allowed anger to emerge. "We're continuing our special coverage with footage from our WRAL News helicopter as it flies toward Collins Mountain in Chatham County."

The TV screen was nearly dark except for a flickering light on top of a mountain, like an enormous candle in the distance. As the image approached, the light became a flame, then a towering burning cross sending up plumes of dark smoke from the open peak of the mountain. The helicopter's camera circled, and the ground around the cross came alive. Scores of white dots scurried away from it and became ghosts that broke like foam in surf flowing toward a thin crease in the forest. The crease became a road when a line of vehicle lights flashed on and began a procession down the mountain, before they scattered onto random routes and dispersed into the night.

In the distance, flashing blue and red lights of police cars and fire engines were drawn to the flame from different directions and merged at the entrance of the now abandoned mountain road. Chelsea LaFever's image returned to the screen. "Our reports appear to confirm the obvious, that the Ku Klux Klan was behind this troubling display. What we don't know yet is what led them to do this tonight. Why, after years in the shadows, have they chosen a public display? Is this a warning? Should we expect more?"

The screen image returned to Collins Mountain where firemen, tiny workers viewed from high above, began dousing the flaming cross and the trees around it with glistening jets from their hoses.

Phineas pressed the mute button on the remote. Iris' eyes were still locked on the screen. She shook her head, her lips pressed into a tight line before asking, "Think this had anything to do with Jefferson and this afternoon?"

"We have to assume it did."

Her eyes became moist as she stared at him in silence.

⬡⬡⬡⬡⬡

The scream yanked Phineas from the deep sleep he'd finally fallen into after what seemed like more than an hour of his mind racing from the new information DiCenzo dropped on him. Phineas spun out of bed and bolted for the bedroom door. Right behind him came Iris' footsteps and distressed voice. "That was Martha!"

He burst into the darkness of his daughter's bedroom and flicked the wall switch. The sudden brightness of the ceiling light made him squint. Martha had been sitting up in bed crying and now covered her eyes with her hands. "I couldn't get the car door open!"

Iris plopped down beside her and hugged her. "It was only a dream, Honey. We're here with you now."

Martha rocked forward and back in her mother's arms. "That man with the flag on his arm—I was in his old car. It was hot and smelled like cigarettes. I couldn't get the door open!"

Phineas noticed that she'd been sleeping under at least two blankets and the cover. He stepped to the curtain. "I can open the window and cool it down some."

"NO! He might be out there!"

Iris pulled her closer. "Oh, Honey..."

A barefoot Jacob in pajama pants shuffled into the doorway, rubbing his eyes. "What's going on?"

"Your sister had a bad dream," Phineas answered. "You can go on back to sleep. You have school tomorrow." Jacob faded into the dark hallway.

Iris waved Phineas off too. "I'll sit with her. You have an early morning and should go back to sleep."

"You sure? I can stay longer."

"I've got a light office day tomorrow, and I'm going to keep her with me. I'm not sending her to school—for her sake and her classmates. Not with *him* still out there."

My poor, gentle daughter. And after her horrible day. Now it's nightmares. One more thing he couldn't fix for her. Phineas kissed the top of Martha's head. "Night, Honey."

The digital clock next to their bed read 12:45. It felt like he'd barely fallen asleep when Martha awakened them. The last several days began churning through his consciousness, and he found it impossible to shut it down.

Phineas had called DiCenzo after they'd watched the Klan news. The detective reported that Angela was nowhere to be found, that she'd cleared out from her apartment—at least the address the VA Hospital had on her. He'd also mentioned that her daughter, Marie, was gone. *Her daughter?* The detective found school paperwork scattered on the studio's kitchen floor with the name Marie Portier, and sixth grade, neatly penciled in the upper corner.

Sixth grade! The same grade as Jacob.

Angela never mentioned a daughter when he spoke with her in the ICU. Of course, he did his level best to keep their conversations to a minimum. He didn't want to know her any better.

He asked DiCenzo what he thought Jefferson's motive was. The detective doubted Jefferson was after ransom when he tried to take Martha alone, or Iris with her. They wouldn't have been bargaining chips for anything, and kidnapping doesn't offer takebacks. So, what sort of payback did he have in mind, if he'd succeeded? Torture? Murder? Did that sick son of a bitch have that level of cruelty in him? Probably. He'd murdered his lieutenant in Vietnam.

Another troubling thought gnawed at Phineas. Was it possible that Jefferson just came looking for him, like he'd said he could, if he wanted? Did he arrive on their street with sinister intent, or was he, a simple man barred from the hospital, only wanting to talk? Had it all gone terribly wrong when he offered Martha a ride home, and Iris ran her SUV into him? Had the whole thing spiraled out of control from that point?

And now, it was likely that Angela abandoned Zebediah—probably not the first time that miserable bastard had been abandoned. His anger could fester into desperation. Yesterday, Jefferson crossed a one-way line and couldn't go back. And now the Klan. Would they use him for something awful? Phineas felt his guts twisting into knots.

He glanced at the clock again when Iris slipped between the sheets; 2:00 AM.

"She asleep?"

Iris inhaled deeply and let it out. "Finally."

"I could have sat with her. I couldn't fall back asleep anyway."

"If she does it again, you can take a turn. He *is your* patient's family."

That stung. "This isn't my fault."

"And I know all the trouble *we* went through after Jezebel wasn't your fault either. Maybe you should consider other career options *this* time." Her words sounded exhausted and testy.

They were also punishing. "Maybe I will."

Had she reached her limit? Had the miseries he brought into their life finally become too much for her? She'd always had his back. Until now?

"Sorry...That wasn't fair." She gave his shoulder a gentle squeeze and leaned against him. "Now let's try to get some sleep." She rolled onto her side facing away from him.

Her apology was a relief. He struggled to think of something else he could do about Zebediah Jefferson and came up empty. He recalled the feelings of powerlessness he'd felt after his Jezebel murder charges. This was how Jefferson and the Klan wanted them all to feel. Powerless. Their threats negating hard work and achievement.

He tried to concentrate on relaxing his feet, his legs, his hands and arms. He desperately needed sleep for the day ahead.

Another scream. 4:10 AM. Phineas rolled out of bed and through their bedroom door. On his way to Martha's room, he made out a pair of headlights creeping past their driveway out on the street—hopefully the sheriff on his regular rounds.

⬡⬡⬡⬡⬡

A soft knock on Iris' UNC office door lifted her eyes from the manuscript on her desk. "Come in." Martha was perched silently, pencil in hand, a stationary fixture on one of the two chairs in the corner behind the frosted glass door as it opened. She looked up from her school workbook, undoubtedly pleased to be given a break.

The young Black woman in bright white slacks and a satin blouse of multiple citrus hues looked like she'd stepped out of a fashion magazine. Stiletto heels lifted her to an elegant height. With the hallway light directly behind, her full Afro created a solar eclipse.

"I'm Patrice. I'm so glad you emailed me, Professor Mann."

When Iris stood to shake hands, she felt a touch of embarrassment. She'd revealed the ragged jeans she'd thrown on for her attempt at a quick and covert office visit before her planned escape from town. At least she'd covered her t-shirt with a nice jacket against the air conditioning that was always excessive in her office. Today it was helping to keep her awake after the mostly sleepless night.

"Please call me Iris, Patrice. I emailed you last night to warn you about our common problem. And then the Klan had their miserable display. Sorry you had to see that—that you have to live with it." Iris frowned and shook her head.

"It's what I study...Iris...why I came to North Carolina. I hope it'll emphasize how important my work is." Patrice looked and sounded defiant. "And Malcolm and I are being careful."

"Oh, and speaking of your work, I wanted to tell you that I've been reading your manuscript about the Wilmington Massacre. It's illuminating and very well written. I can see why you chose the topic for your thesis."

"Thank you. That means a lot to me...and if the common problem you mentioned has the name Jefferson, you must have heard that I had an unpleasant confrontation with him at the hospital." She closed the door and opened her eyes wide when she noticed Martha. "And whom do we have here, studying as quiet as a mouse?"

"Martha." She seemed unconcerned about *her* attire of a faded green hand-me-down Cubs t-shirt and old cargo shorts. Their vibrant visitor had her full attention.

"I kept her home from school," Iris explained. "We had such a bad day yesterday." She gestured to the seat next to Martha. "Please, sit down."

Patrice swung her backpack under the empty chair and lowered herself into it, while her focus stayed on Martha. "What are you studying, Martha?"

"Subtraction. It's not hard. Multiplication's next."

"I bet you'll figure that out too. Is today a better day?" Patrice's voice was soft butter.

Martha nodded slowly while studying Patrice's vivid blouse and lime green fingernails.

Iris felt relieved to be seated back in her chair, the four-inch hole in her jeans' right knee concealed behind the desk's panel. "I don't know how much you've heard, but Jefferson paid us a visit yesterday. He tried to pick up Martha after she got off the school bus. Then he tried to kidnap both of us. Fortunately, he was interrupted."

Patrice gasped and covered her mouth with her hand, her eyes fixed on Martha. "That must have been really scary, Martha."

"Jacob saved..."

Iris silenced her daughter with a single crisp shake of her head.

Martha cleared her throat. "Jacob's bus came, and our neighbor came, and the man left."

Her mother offered a quick tilt of her head to show her approval.

"Then I got stung by a bee!" She pointed at the barely visible residual swelling between her eyes.

"*What?* Wow! You *did* have a bad day."

Patrice leaned closer to Martha and inspected her face. "Girl, I *thought* there was something about you. You have the most beautiful blue eyes, and I don't see *any* lines in your forehead. Course you're still young, but when a girl gets older...might be something to help with wrinkles...We could call it BeeTox!"

Iris traced her finger lightly down her own deeply furrowed brow.

Martha had perked up at the animated young woman's attentiveness. "His gun went off and blew up his windshield, and we had police, and firemen, and an ambulance—and then Daddy came home with a detective. I breathed into a bag to feel better, and then they put ice on my sting."

"Wow! After all that, I hope your night was better."

"Oh, I had the worst dreams. That man was in 'em. Momma and Daddy came in twice. And Daddy slept the rest of the night on my floor next to me."

Well! That's the most she's said in a while!

"We're hoping last night was a one-night event." Iris yawned and stretched.

Patrice's shoulders slumped and she leaned back into her chair. Her expression shifted from captivated to subdued, and she looked like she was weighing a troubling admission. "I...I think I owe you an apology. I'm really sorry that all happened to you, because I may have been at least partly responsible. Malcolm took that man's insults and stayed calm, but I let my temper get the better of me and fired right back to him."

Iris shook her head. "Patrice, you should *never* feel like you need to apologize for standing up to abuse. This is all on *him*."

"Thank you for saying that, Iris. That makes me feel a little better. After hearing what happened, I do feel partly guilty." Patrice leaned forward and placed her hand gently on Martha's. "Martha, I know a way to make bad dreams stay away. My grandmama showed it to me."

Almost at the same time, Iris and Martha asked, "How?"

"Well, when you take off your slippers, or your shoes, if that's what you got on when you go to bed, you put them on the floor, heels next to the middle of the bed, toes pointed straight out. The toes will keep the bad dreams away." She slipped her high heels off and demonstrated.

Martha stared at Patrice's matching polished toenails. "What about the good dreams?"

"The shoes will let them in."

Iris felt grateful watching Martha's spirits lifted. "Thank you, Patrice. We'll definitely do that tonight."

Patrice put a hand on each of Martha's shoulders and drew her face close. "Girl, you got through all that and can still do subtraction while looking fabulous! You *have* to be a strong young woman, strong enough to get through *anything*!"

Martha's chest expanded at the words, and her head rose up to a new height. Her eyes were locked on Patrice's, while she absorbed her energy and her power.

Iris, a reverent and transfixed spectator, stared until Patrice removed her hands, releasing Martha from the spell.

They needed to pick up Jacob at his school, and Iris' watch read 2:20. She pushed DiCenzo's business card across her desk. "In case you don't have the number of the detective my husband's been working with on our problem. We're worried about you and Malcolm."

"I already have the detective's number." Patrice pushed the card back to Iris. "Your husband gave it to everyone at the meeting he called this morning with the ICU team and security to warn everyone. Malcolm called me right after."

⌬⌬⌬⌬⌬

As Iris' SUV crawled along the entrance drive behind the other parents, she could see Jacob staring at a sheet of paper and displaying a puzzled expression. He waited, as instructed, at his middle school pick-up location, backpack at his feet. He had on his Cubs' team t-shirt, the one he donned whenever it was clean enough, ever since they won the league championship.

When Jacob saw that Martha had already claimed the front seat, he flashed his mother a disappointed look then pulled open the back door. "Mom, why did the teachers give me a list of work assignments for the next couple of days?"

"Because we're heading to the coast. Now get in and close the door before we fill up with exhaust fumes." She tried to sound more relaxed than she was.

Martha pivoted in her seat, a warm smile displayed for her brave brother. "Hi, Jacob."

He slammed the door and fumbled for his seatbelt. "When did you decide we're going away?"

"This morning, when I found a place for us. We'll be staying with the Beckers. I think we might even get to the house before they do."

After the miserable night and several cups of coffee, she had concluded that she just wasn't going to be able to sleep in Chapel Hill with an armed kidnapper still loose. She'd then remembered that, many weeks ago, friends had invited them to share a too large house on Bald Head Island over an extended weekend. At the time, she'd grudgingly declined, knowing Phineas couldn't leave town while on the ICU service. When Iris called back this morning, her friend, Sarah, sounded pleased that she'd changed her mind.

When she called Phineas, he sadly agreed that it would be safest for her and the kids to disappear for a while. And Bald Head Island seemed as secure a spot as he could think of—with access limited to those registering and arriving on a scheduled ferry—and no cars allowed. They'd only had happy memories of vacations there, but she acknowledged the guilty privilege, that her family could afford such a safe and pleasant getaway.

For now, Phineas would have to hold down the fort at home with the cops and Stella keeping watch. When May was over, it would be a relief for him to hand off the ICU's burdens to someone else.

DiCenzo had called her in the morning. It was right after she'd gotten off the phone with Sarah to confirm they were still invited to the Becker's sizable Bald Head Island rental house. Iris had hoped his call wasn't Sarah apologizing that she had the dates wrong, and the house wouldn't be ready for the Mann's today.

"Hello?"

"DiCenzo here...Mind if I call you Iris?"

"Of course not. We're almost family, right...Vinnie?" The detective was beginning to grow on her.

He cleared his throat. "That's the nicest thing anyone's said to me in a while." A pause. "I wanted to give you an update on Zebediah Jefferson."

"What have you got?"

"They found that beat up sedan of his ditched and covered with branches down a dead-end dirt road not far from your house. Windshield was gone like you said, and blood was smeared on the driver's seat."

"So, he's still out there." She spoke softly, hoping Martha wasn't listening from the living room.

"'Fraid so. And someone had to pick him up, so he has help."

"Well, I'm not going to hang around here and wait for him to come back. I'm taking Martha to my office soon, and we're going to pick Jacob up after school and head out of town." Her hands were trembling.

"Where are you going?"

"Bald Head Island. We have a friend there, and you can't get on the island without a ferry reservation. I can't think of anywhere safer."

"Maybe the police station, but that might get old."

"We'll pass, thank you." His humor calmed her.

"Listen, I'll have our patrols keep an eye on Jacob's school—and look for my car when you pick him up." His tone was fatherly. "I'll follow you out of town to make sure no one's watching you...and Iris, don't stop until you're at the ferry, okay?"

"Thanks, Vinnie. See you this afternoon."

Iris scanned cars in the school's parking lot and then on the nearby streets. A hand waved from a black unmarked sedan. DiCenzo, there as promised. The detective pulled in behind her and followed at a respectable distance. He had said he'd make sure no other vehicles seemed interested in her SUV and forbade her to stop until she was unloading their luggage at the island's ferry port.

After she merged onto I-40, she peeked up at a sullen looking Jacob in the rear-view mirror, before she refocused on the highway. With a single soft groan, an exhausted Martha drifted off, her head bowed, her breathing relaxed. Iris was always the protective mother bear, and now it was time to relocate her two Cubs to a safer den.

"Subway sandwiches, sodas, chips and cookies are in the cooler on the floor next to you. And now, we're off to Bald Head Island."

"Bald Head and Subway! All right!" He pounced on the cooler, pulled open the lid, and began rummaging through its contents. Jacob held up one of the sandwiches. "Mine must be this twelve inch one."

"Of course. Martha and I can't eat more than half that."

"Club with bacon, mayo and light mustard?"

She nodded. "You might want to save it. It could be your supper. Why don't you have a cookie and some water for now?" His shoulders slumped in her rearview mirror image. "And I have something for you to look at without messy fingers."

"What kind of cookies did you get?"

"Some oatmeal, and some white chocolate chip with macadamia nuts."

"Can I have two of the chocolate chip?"

"Sure. And when you're settled, there's something for you to read in the tote bag on the seat next to you."

"The new X-Men comic?" He sounded hopeful.

"Hah! No. And it's best for you to look at what I brought while Martha sleeps."

He raised an eyebrow when he looked at her eyes in the mirror. "Why? What is it?"

"It's a scrapbook your grandmother made after Hurricane Jezebel. I still want to wait till Martha's older to explain everything that happened there to her."

He pulled the thin album from the cloth tote and opened to the first page. "I'll have cookies after. Wow! You and Grandma sure looked young back then, but Amos still had a white chin. Where were these pictures?"

She didn't think she'd aged *that* much. "Those first ones were in Memphis. Your grandmother took them. We escaped New Orleans while your father went to work at the hospital. It was the first motel we found with a room."

"Who's this young guy with the buzz cut you're hugging?" His tone was suspicious.

"Your father. He shaved his beard and had his hair all cut off when he was evacuated from New Orleans to Houston after the flood. He said it felt too disgusting to keep." He'd located her after calling his mother in Vermont and then shown up in Memphis in the middle of the night after a long bus trip. It had taken her a minute to recognize him.

Jacob pointed at a double-page glossy photo. "Where are these circles someone drew on this picture?"

That's an aerial photo of the day after the levees broke and flooded the city. One is your grandma's old house where I grew up, and the other—the one under water—is where our apartment was. We had to live with Grandma when they finally let us back in the city."

He turned the page and traced his finger along the tiny print of a newspaper article, then a second.

"You must be at the part where they wrote about your father's arrest."

He nodded and read more. "Who's this guy on the card, Simon O. Serine, Esq?"

"Our attorney. He figured out how to convince people that Angela Portier was not a reliable witness for the case."

"This article says she went crazy on *60 Minutes*." He turned the page to a spread of colorful photos. Iris knew them well. *Life* magazine's 1985 Jezebel aftermath edition on the Baptist tragedy, including photos of the main participants.

"Dad's picture in *Life* magazine...So, this is what Angela Portier looks like. She does look a little crazy—and scary." He perused the next two pages, those of Baptist Hospital's awful state after it was finally evacuated. "Looks nasty there."

"Those are the conditions your father worked under. No electricity, plumbing, phones. It was dark and incredibly hot—and smelly after the toilets all backed up. I had no idea what he was going through at the time."

"Dad really worked through all that?"

"Five long days and nights. Wore his headlamp in the dark hospital. He hardly slept. Then he caught a ride in a flat-bottomed boat to an evacuation area where they put him on a bus to Houston. He found out where we'd gone, and he came looking for us on a Greyhound bus." She waited until Jacob turned the next page. "Your grandma took those pictures after all charges against your father were dropped."

"Who's the bald guy playing a violin on the steps?"

"That's Dr. Kornberg, your father's UNC chief. He came to help defend your father. Those are some of the people he worked with around him on the courtroom steps."

"He has his beard back."

"It took six months until he was cleared after he was charged." Those were six long and scary months. "Read the article where they interview Hilary, the ICU head nurse. It's on the next page."

She could see him in the mirror silently tracing his finger. He was taking his time, going over some parts twice.

Iris had avoided reliving the painful episode until it was a necessity. Maybe soon it could be buried forever. "You'll see how the hospital staff considered your father and the other doctors heroes for all they did."

Jacob nodded and continued reading. After several more minutes he closed the scrapbook and inserted it in the tote bag. "I'm ready for cookies now."

As Iris sped along the nearly vacant interstate highway, she felt another pang of guilt. The scrapbook was a reminder that today was the second time she'd escaped danger and left Phineas to face it without her. In August of 1985, she'd fled the frightening approach of Hurricane Jezebel with her husband's seed still fresh inside her and their son's embryo beginning to take shape, while Phineas returned to Baptist Hospital to face the devastating storm and its brutal aftermath.

Most of Louisiana also fled the approaching destruction that day in 1985 and, unlike on North Carolina's nearly empty I-40 today, traffic crawled bumper to bumper all the way to Memphis. There they spotted a neon vacancy sign in the dark a block from the highway. When the clerk first saw Amos, he'd told Iris there was no room in his inn. Her mother had calmly entered the lobby and put the obedient dog through his basic behaviors, giving the impression that Amos might be a trained service dog. Then her tenacious mother had stared down the clerk, and they got the last room "under the extenuating circumstances".

Phineas then showed up six days later, barely recognizable, filthy and with his head and beard shorn. The four refugees had to share that one room for several weeks until Jezebel's flood waters receded, and it was safe to return to a barely functioning New Orleans. Phineas was arrested at dawn the next morning, and six miserable months followed before he was free from the prosecution Angela brought down on him.

⬡⬡⬡⬡⬡

While the ICU team was finishing Thursday morning rounds, DiCenzo paged Phineas to say he was eager to question Enoch Jefferson. Jefferson was only off the ventilator a day this time and still had his tracheostomy tube in place. Speech would be a challenge, but DiCenzo was waiting for Phineas in the conference room.

"Detective, I'd better prepare him for your visit first. He's been through a lot."

"I'll wait, Doc." DiCenzo began reviewing his notepad.

Carver was writing orders at the nursing station. He looked up at Phineas. "Malcolm, let's go see Jefferson. We need to let him know the police want to question him about his son."

Carver pocketed his pen. They knocked on Jefferson's door and entered. The elderly man was sitting up and staring out the window at the sunny day. A smile formed when he locked eyes with Carver. Phineas washed his hands and extracted a fresh pair of latex gloves from the box on the back of the room's bathroom door.

Phineas approached the bedside. "Hi Mr. Jefferson. Everything okay?"

He nodded and mouthed "fine".

"I'm going to show you how you can speak." Phineas lifted the collar providing humidification from the tracheostomy. "Take a deep breath, and when I put my finger over the hole here, you should be able to speak." Jefferson inhaled deeply, and Phineas plugged the opening. "Now, is everything okay?"

"Jes' right...You?" A throaty squawk.

"Well done. Now, I need to explain that someone is here to ask you some questions." The old man shrugged before Phineas continued. "He's a detective. He wants to ask you about your son."

Jefferson's brow formed deep furrows and he closed his eyes. He mouthed something Phineas couldn't decipher. He replaced his gloved finger over the tracheostomy opening and instructed, "Take a breath and talk."

"What's he done?"

"Can we send for the detective?" Phineas asked.

Jefferson nodded. He blinked several times and stared at his folded hands. Carver slipped out the door and returned with DiCenzo, who offered a compact wave. "Mr. Jefferson, I'm Detective DiCenzo. I need to ask you a few questions." He appeared at ease, as if he was used to being in an ICU questioning someone.

Jefferson reached for his tracheostomy and felt around until he had his finger over it. "What's he done?" A raspy growl.

"Sir, we need to find him to ask him some questions. We've been to the house you share with him and checked around places your sheriff suggested but haven't located him. Do you have any idea where he might be?"

The old man scanned his bedside table and windowsill. "Paper."

Phineas located the room's clipboard with tethered pen and handed it to him. Jefferson wrote two names in wobbly block letters. "They might know." He held it up. "Now...what's he done?" The muscle along his jaw twitched.

As DiCenzo squinted at the paper, he said, "I regret to inform you, Mr. Jefferson, that he's a suspect in an attempted kidnapping." Patient and detective locked eyes. "I'll look for these two men and come back if I have more questions. I'll let you rest now. Thank you—and I hope you have a speedy recovery." Jefferson closed his eyes and slowly shook his head. DiCenzo nodded at Phineas and turned to leave the room.

Phineas peeled off the gloves and tossed them in the bedside trash can. "I need to talk with the detective. I'll be back in a bit."

Carver pulled a chair to the bedside. "I'll sit here with you for a while, Mr. Jefferson. We can talk some more, Sir, if you want."

⬡⬡⬡⬡⬡

Carver and Downs closed the door of their new admission and stepped into the ICU hallway, ready to report on her to Phineas and Villalobos. Downs muttered, "That poor lady has been one stumble away from a crumble for years—and then it happened."

Phineas winced. Villalobos whispered, "Michael, it's best if we keep our terminology professional, especially while we're in the hospital."

"Sorry." The resident's blush suggested embarrassment on top of his fatigue.

It has been a long and tiring month.

Carver took over the patient summary. "Dr. Mann, we have an 88-year-old Caucasian woman, an ex-smoker, whose dog tripped her while she was carrying groceries, causing her to fall on a bag of cans and fracture six osteoporotic ribs and two thoracic vertebrae. On arrival in the ER, her right chest was collapsing during inhalation, consistent with a flail chest. She had severe carbon dioxide retention, so the ER team intubated and ventilated her. It looks like she'll be on positive pressure ventilation for a while to let her ribs heal and stabilize. At least her x-ray didn't show a pneumothorax."

Phineas felt sadness for the "poor lady" to have such a miserable injury at this stage of her life. "Let's take a look at her now, and we can see how her chest wall looks off positive pressure in the morning. If it looks as the ER described, we can discuss a tracheostomy and feeding tube with her and her family. Healing her ribs could take several weeks. For now, let's control her pain and let her settle in overnight."

Nurse Lisa closed the conference room door and approached the three. "Dr. Mann, you're needed in the conference room." She added more softly, "Security, your chief, *and* the hospital CEO are waiting for you."

Villalobos looked startled. "I'll go over the new patient with the guys. Dr. Mann, you don't want to keep *that* group waiting."

When Phineas walked into the conference room, no one stood to shake his hand. CEO Sheldon Fields said, "Shut the door, Dr. Mann, and take a seat."

Fields had come on board UNC Hospital in 1997, promoted from the Chief Operating Officer position at Johns Hopkins. In his forties, clean-shaven and always seen in a tailored suit, he had shaken Phineas' hand only once previously, during his welcome reception last year.

Phineas' Pulmonary Division chief wore an expression of concern bordering on panic. A decade after Phineas' hiring in 1986, Dr. James O'Riley had replaced Dr. Kornberg as division chief. Unlike his predecessor, O'Riley seemed to relish the administrative side of running a division more than practicing medicine. His crisp white coat was buttoned all the way up. Its pockets lacked a stethoscope. He pushed clenched fists into those empty pockets.

Security Chief Vickers, his uniform shirt buttoned and tie straight, sat at attention staring at Phineas, then at CEO Fields.

Fields began the meeting. "Dr. Mann, let me come straight to the heart of the matter. The hospital is being sued. The complaint alleges that you have refused visitation to a family member. I'd like to hear your explanation."

"You should have brought any difficulties you were having to my attention." O'Riley jumped in. "Maybe we could have prevented this."

Are they blaming me for Zebediah Jefferson? Phineas remained surprisingly calm. "Are you aware that this family member has threatened me, *my* family, *our* staff, and other patients' family members—and that he is probably a member of the Ku Klux Klan?"

CEO Fields cleared his throat. "Well that explains one thing."

"Explains what?"

"Why the person who filed the suit, according to our hospital attorney, happens to be the Grand Dragon of the North Carolina KKK."

Shit. Now they're definitely behind Zebediah Jefferson. "And I don't believe you are yet aware that his father, my patient, was being poisoned with arsenic in *our* ICU." Phineas reluctantly revealed his trump card. "I've just started working with the police on this matter. They told me I could call you today with this new information."

The three sat across from him in stunned silence, mouths hanging open. Vickers shifted his ample rear end in his chair.

⬡⬡⬡⬡⬡

The last Friday morning in May. Three more days on service. The home stretch. Phineas felt a surge of energy as he stepped through the double ICU doors. Villalobos, Carver, Downs, and two fresh faces stood next to the nursing station waiting, almost at attention, for their leader's final push. Phineas offered his hand to the young woman in the short white coat, who appeared the only tense one in the group.

"I'm Dr. Mann. Welcome aboard."

She shifted her stack of index cards from her right to her left hand. "Tina Chung. *Obviously,* the intern."

He recognized the other fresh face. It was no secret that the lanky junior resident Earl Mangum was seriously interested in a pulmonary fellowship after completing his internal medicine residency. Two months ago, he'd met with Phineas and several other members of the division to let them know. His performance on this rotation would be critical for his chances to secure one of the three coveted specialty training positions at UNC.

Carver took two steps toward Jefferson's room before he looked back. "Almost there, Dr. Mann. Monday is June—and freedom for you—until your next rotation. And WOW! Last night was my last night as an *intern* on the ICU."

Phineas wished he would really be free Monday, but there could be no true freedom until Zebediah Jefferson and Angela Portier were found. "This month has been a bit of a blur for me. What's next for *you,* Malcolm?"

"Nephrology inpatient service. And my *last month* of internship."

"Well, you had the opportunity to learn about dialysis with Ms. James. I went by last night and visited her on the nephrology ward. She seems to be getting stronger, but she'll still be there when you go on service. It's good you know her so well."

Carver paused in front of Jefferson's door and glanced at the index card in his hand. "Mr. Jefferson continues to improve. He's been off the ventilator for three days now. We pulled his trache tube two days ago, and the stoma is almost fully closed. He was able to eat a soft diet yesterday, so his gastrostomy feeding tube can probably come out today." He beamed with well-deserved pride.

"How about his peripheral neuropathy?"

"Physical Therapy has started working with him, and they've recommended that he be transferred to rehab as soon as we say it's okay. I think he's about ready, and social work says there's a bed in a skilled rehab facility not far from his home. He'll still need braces until his foot drop improves, and maybe the chelating treatment for the arsenic will help speed recovery from the nerve damage." Carver shrugged. "I wish we'd figured it out before the second poisoning."

"It's lucky we figured it out at all." The April issue of *People* magazine with the answer was now tacked to the bulletin board in the house staff workroom.

Villalobos punched Phineas lightly on the shoulder. "Come on, Dr. Mann. Kudos to you on identifying that rare bird—and happening in the hospital! That's got to be a first. I hope I never forget to think of arsenic, if it visits *my* ICU."

"The lab director *did* tell me that it was the first positive arsenic test in almost twenty years." A minor consolation. *And where is the perpetrator?*

Tina Chung held up a tentative hand. "Chelating for arsenic?"

Carver answered, "It's to bind the arsenic, so his body can remove it. Unfortunately, DMPS works best when given early after the poisoning, so it may not have helped Jefferson's neuropathy that much. His foot drop should improve eventually though."

Carver pushed open Jefferson's door. The morning sun filled the room through the wide-open shades over the solitary window. Chelsea LeFever's voice greeted them from the blaring TV mounted high on the wall across from the foot of the bed and wished her viewers a safe Memorial Day weekend. Enoch Jefferson was sitting up in bed and leaning over a plate of breakfast. He set his forkful of grits down on it and pushed the remote's button to mute the sound. A teardrop patch of egg yolk hung on his white chin stubble.

"Figured I'd best be catching up on what happened in the world while I was gone." His voice was just above a whisper, and a barely audible hiss escaped from the bandage over his tracheostomy site. He scanned the eager faces surrounding his bed. "I feel like I know some of y'all. I couldn't see ya', but I could hear y'all talkin' 'bout me some those weeks."

Phineas took a position at the foot of the bed under a TV commercial. "How's your breakfast, Mr. Jefferson?"

"Jes' right. How was yours?"

"Not as appetizing as yours looks."

"I'd offer you some, if'n I hadn't already ate most of it."

Carver leaned over the rail in front of Jefferson. "Is anything giving you any trouble this morning, Sir?"

"Nothin' I can do anything about, young man. How 'bout you?"

"I'm fine, Sir. The big news today is that we're thinking you're about ready to move to a rehabilitation facility where you can have physical therapy on a regular schedule, and our social worker says there's one close to your home."

"Suits me."

Phineas marveled at the easy connection between the young Black man and Jefferson. Carver had spent time in emotional conversation with him after DiCenzo's questioning. The intern had confirmed why Jefferson's son wasn't visiting and comforted the old man as he wept.

Phineas announced, "Mr. Jefferson, Dr. Carver and I will come back to examine you. We'll let you enjoy the rest of your breakfast."

"I'll be here—and thank you. I'll miss y'all." A tear glistened from the corner of Jefferson's eye then trickled over his cheek and splashed on his plate. "I'm so grateful, grateful you saved my life."

The old man sniffed and swallowed, his protruding Adam's apple lifting and settling. "And I'm sorry ma' boy caused so much trouble. Just never knew what to do with him after his Mama passed away. He was jes' four, you know." He reached out, trembling, and gripped Carver's hand. "I 'member that evenin' like it was yesterday. God, how I loved that woman! An' I *still* miss her."

Jefferson stared into Carver's eyes. "She was a-goin' to make a quick trip to the store. It was rainin' an' slippery—and she musta' took that corner too wide and slid—'fore she had the head-on with that Black fella'... Killed him too."

He coughed twice, once for each death, his healing neck wound hissing his heartache. "After the police called, I had to take Zeb with me to the wreck. He set in my truck and watched while they pulled them outta' their crumpled cars. Was never the same after."

He began sobbing into his crumpled napkin. "So sorry...I'm just...so... sorry. Sorry I couldna' done better by him after we lost her."

The team of doctors stared at the old man, their eyes beginning to glisten in the room's bright light. Villalobos reached out her hand to his heaving shoulder. "Mr. Jefferson, you did your best. We *know* you did your best."

Phineas shared in the collective sorrow, and he hoped he never felt the need to apologize with such despair for *his* son. Yet, it was clear that the childhood seed planted in Zebediah Jefferson one awful night had to have been cultivated during later years by others with sinister motives, others who wouldn't hesitate to use him.

WEEK FIVE

Know thy enemy and know thyself, find naught in fear for 100 battles.
Know thyself but not thy enemy, find level of loss and victory.
Know thy enemy but not thyself, wallow in defeat every time.
SUN TZU FROM THE ART OF WAR

After Saturday ICU rounds, Phineas lingered in the hospital longer than usual. Being surrounded by busy people seemed preferable to the emptiness of his house, but Stella's mealtime was approaching, so he decided he'd better head home and check on her. Her stomach would surely be growling by now.

Nights alone had become especially miserable for him with trouble falling asleep, staying asleep, and frequent trips to peek out the window at real and imagined sounds and shadows. Stella absorbed his tension and was also on edge, racing to the door, growling at ghosts in the gloom each time Phineas rose from his chair or bed. Whenever he let her out, he fretted about her safety.

When he finally reached home, she whined and pestered him until he fed her. He figured he'd get around to ordering a pizza delivery at some point, if only for some brief company.

A sated Stella at his side, Phineas attacked the swaths of weedy invaders in his vegetable garden with a scuffle hoe. He noticed for the first time how the garden's location gave a vantage point to monitor most of their property and keep an eye out for uninvited visitors. When the fur along Stella's spine abruptly stood erect, he was on alert before he heard the approaching vehicle. A black Lincoln Town Car, its wax job gleaming, crept down his driveway and stopped next to the side porch. Stella charged it, barking furiously and circling its perimeter. Phineas, with hoe in hand and his grimy t-shirt drenched in sweat, followed at a distance.

A blond woman peered over the steering wheel at the ruckus. Next to her, a smiling Vinnie DiCenzo was waving. Phineas commanded Stella to, "Sit. Stay."

Stella lowered her rear to the pavement and stared at him with blue eyes that asked, "Are you sure?"

The woman lowered her window. "Is it safe?"

"It's safe. Hi. I'm Phineas." He patted Stella's swiveling head. "It's okay, Girl. Good girl."

DiCenzo's companion pushed open the driver's door and stepped out in black slacks and a white silk blouse that draped over her full figure. "I'm Theresa, Vinnie's better half. He thought you could use some company."

Vinnie joined her and held up a bottle of wine and a loaf of crusty bread. "We come bearing food."

Theresa extended her hand, with its manicured candy apple red nails, to Phineas. He shifted his hoe to his left hand and wiped his soiled right hand down the front of his jeans. He started to extend it to her, complete with dirt caked under his nails, then held it out for her inspection. "Sorry. I'm pretty filthy. Been in the garden."

She shook it gingerly. "Maybe we'll take up gardening too someday soon." Her expression brightened. "There's rigatoni with meatballs in the back."

"Wow! What a nice surprise. Thank you so much."

She let out a hearty laugh. "Just keep Vinnie entertained while I go impress a new hair client, and we'll call it even. You're just about the only person he's gotten to know since we moved here, other than that old sheriff over in Pittsboro. How about I come back in a couple of hours?"

Phineas' spirits were lifting. "I promise we'll finish dinner by then."

DiCenzo retrieved a foil covered baking dish of a size appropriate for a family reunion. He somehow also managed to pin the wine, bread, and another narrow brown bag under his arms despite the pistol in his shoulder holster. "Give me a hand here, Doc." A tuft of grey chest hair emerged from the open collar of his red sports shirt. White cat hairs dusted black pants covering legs that Phineas suspected never saw the sun. Stella's active nose was pointed at the evening sky. Her tail wagged with purpose. Cat smell and rigatoni.

Theresa settled back into the driver's seat and turned the ignition. She waved before deftly backing the Lincoln back out the curvy driveway and into the street.

Phineas relieved Vinnie of the hefty dish. "Let's put these inside then grab some fresh vegetables from the garden to go with them."

DiCenzo slipped a bottle containing a sunny yellow liquid from the bag. "I also brought limoncello for dessert. Don't know about you, Doc, but I'm getting hungry. Smelled meatballs all the way over here."

After Phineas filled a colander with greens, zucchini, snap peas, and carrots, he found DiCenzo studying the three beehives from a cautious distance. "What are they doing, Doc?" Thousands of bees marched in and out from each hive entrance over the sloping landing platforms and hung off each other in shimmering masses.

"It's called bearding, because it looks like each hive has one. They're cooling off, sitting out on the porch on a warm night." Phineas could smell their fresh honey.

"Those are some lumberjack beards, Doc. How many bees have you got there?"

Phineas smiled at the question everyone asked. "They're still building up in May. Maybe forty thousand workers per hive."

DiCenzo shook his head and let out a whistle. "Don't you get scared working with 'em?"

"At first, my heart pounded every time I opened a hive. Now I know how to stay in control—when I can take a hive totally apart—and when it's time to get the hell out. When they get revved up, you can hear it, and it's time to get out, even with smoke that ordinarily quiets them."

"Someday, on a really calm day, maybe you can show me what's inside?"

Phineas nodded. "Be happy to after all this mess is behind us."

The two men watched for several minutes in silence before DiCenzo began sniffing, like he'd noticed the hives' enticing aroma. "What's that smell, Doc? Now I'm even hungrier."

"Honey. It's the peak time for them to gather the nectar to make it."

"Smells delicious." He patted his stomach. "You hungry yet?"

"Famished. Let's go."

While the two were stuffing themselves, DiCenzo lamented a complete lack of progress in locating Zebediah Jefferson or Angela Portier, keeping their somber feast from being any kind of a celebration. "And there's something I haven't told you."

Phineas halved his last meatball with his fork. "Oh, what's that?"

"Something the Chatham sheriff said about Jefferson. Let's see if I can say it the way he did. 'Always suspected his bread ain't done.'"

Phineas put down his fork. "What's that supposed to mean?"

"Said it means 'soft in the middle'—his brain, that is. Thought I'd heard every way of sayin' someone has a screw loose. We used to collect those sayings on the force in New York, we had so many crazies there."

"I've heard a few. Not playing with a full deck."

"Old one, Doc. Not the brightest bulb in the chandelier?"

"One fry short of a happy meal."

"Hah! Hadn't heard that one, Doc...But if the old sheriff's right, it means that our Zeb could be easily manipulated."

"As he was by Angela."

"And as he could be by the Klan for something else, something they'd give him up for—make him expendable for something bigger."

The final stage in the cultivation of a violent racist? Phineas' gut all at once felt overstuffed. "I think I'm ready for a taste of that liquor you brought."

DiCenzo slipped a piece of paper from his pocket, unfolded it, and smoothed it on the table with his meaty hand. "So'm I."

Phineas sat up and peered over at it. "What's this?"

"Doc, you have to keep what your patients say private, right?"

"Of course. Patient confidentiality." *Where's he going with this?*

DiCenzo pulled out his wallet, extracted a dollar bill, and pushed it across the table. "Here's a dollar. The document says that I, Vincent DiCenzo, told you, Dr. Phineas Mann, that I have no known lung problems, and that you received one dollar as payment to hear that. You sign it, and you're my doctor. Now I can tell you that story I mentioned before, and you *have* to keep it to yourself."

Phineas crossed his heart. "I promise, Detective."

"Christ, Doc. Call me Vinnie."

Phineas got up from the table, found a pen and two crystal tumblers and sat back down. He leaned over the sheet, read it, signed it, and pocketed the dollar. "Okay. I'm listening...Vinnie."

DiCenzo poured three fingers of limoncello into each tumbler. "You remember when we were talking about bad cops?"

"Yeah." Where was he going with this?

"And I told you I retired after thirty?"

Phineas nodded and sipped. Tart and sweet led to a pleasing fire that slowly descended from his palate to his stomach.

"Well, I had to—or they'd have arrested me."

What? How could that be?

"But everything I read about on the internet was good. Glowing." Phineas immediately felt embarrassed to admit that he'd checked up on DiCenzo.

"Smart to be doing your research, Doc." DiCenzo didn't seem put off by Phineas admission. "See, I noticed a couple of officers in my precinct were skimming from drug dealers in return for turning a blind eye." He sipped and swallowed. "Oh, that's a good batch...So, I went to my superior and laid it out for him. Didn't realize he was in on it. Dumb. Should have guessed that." He swirled the yellow liquid and stared at it.

"Next thing I know, I'm being cuffed in the precinct parking. There's crack under my car's spare tire. Bastards took it from evidence and planted it there." He looked up at Phineas. "Then my 'Superior' shows up." Air quotes. "Tells me if I keep my mouth shut, take my gold watch, and find somewhere else to retire, no one will ever hear about my arrest—and nothing will happen to my Theresa." He pressed his napkin to his eye. "Dirty bastards! What could I do?" His gold watch caught the overhead light.

"Nothing. Well, I'm glad you found Chapel Hill, Vinnie."

"Me too. So, you see, Doc. We're both victims. You had New Orleans, and I had the NYPD." He downed what remained in his glass. "And we both had to move on."

We both had no choice. "I'm still not over the bitterness of what happened to me. My nightmare followed me here and showed up in my ICU in the form of Angela Portier." Phineas drained his tumbler.

DiCenzo offered more limoncello like it was hope. "Maybe this will be the last chapter with her, and you can move on for good."

Phineas signaled 'yes' to the offer with two horizontal fingers pressed together. "We'll see. I'm not holding my breath. What'll it take for you to finally move on from the NYPD?"

DiCenzo poured. "I dunno, Doc. Maybe those bastards getting what they deserve? Either from the system or the criminals they're in bed with."

Stella growled, pushed herself to her feet, and raced to the door. A cruiser had entered the driveway and parked. Wade Johnson emerged in uniform.

Phineas cracked the door enough to yell without allowing an excited Stella to escape. "Sheriff, come on in. Detective DiCenzo and I are just finishing dinner. You hungry?"

Johnson grinned and quickened his pace. "You bet."

"You got any good news for us?"

The young man's smile faded, and he shook his head. "Wish I did."

Phineas fixed him a plate, and the three leaned over the table and commiserated over the frustrating situation. Phineas took another sip of the liquor. Its sweet vapor filled his throat. "Looks like I'm the only unarmed one here." *Should I be?*

DiCenzo put down his glass. His cheeks had taken on a rosy glow. "You ever handle a piece, Doc?"

"I grew up with guns in Vermont. Learned gun safety from NRA material. I was a good shot back then." A long time ago in a faraway place. "Sold all my guns after we married. Iris wanted nothing to do with 'em." He wanted to comment on the NRA's shift from gun safety to gun sales and political influence but decided it might be a loaded topic in present company.

Johnson paused his voracious consumption of rigatonis and swallowed. "Ever kill anything, Doc?"

"Shot a deer when I was fourteen." Phineas remembered what it felt like to kill a creature nearly his size and the hollow space that formed in his core. He'd gotten that out of his system. Could he kill Zebediah Jefferson, if it came to that? As an intensive care doctor, he made decisions and recommendations to patients and families as to when they should push on with aggressive measures—and when to pull back, if there was no hope of recovery. But those weren't decisions to actively *end* a life. That decision had been made by a terrible disease and maybe by a higher power. Those choices were between a drawn out, agonizing death on invasive artificial life support and one providing all measures of comfort.

But should he arm himself, and could he use a gun on another human being, if it came to shooting someone threatening his family? *Hell, yes!* Wait. Was this the alcohol talking? Could he really?

His dinner guests studied him, waiting for him to say more. "Studies that I've seen say a gun in a home is more likely to harm the residents than protect them." And Jacob is curious and clever, a risk no matter how a gun is secured. An instrument of death at hand could still be more dangerous than the undefined threat of an evil man out there somewhere.

Johnson responded, "From all I've seen, what you're saying might be so. But I bet Jefferson'll be expecting you're armed now—after everything."

He would. "If I bought a gun, my wife would take the kids and move out." Iris had made that absolutely clear to him many years ago.

And the corrupt NRA would have won; and the savage Jefferson, perhaps an Army murderer, wannabe kidnapper, and potential KKK instrument, would have won.

⬡⬡⬡⬡⬡

On Monday, June 1st, Phineas rounded early in the morning and turned over the ICU service to his replacement attending. He felt less relief than he'd hoped he'd feel. Zebediah Jefferson was still out there and probably plotting trouble with other violent Klan wackos. Phineas felt such helplessness that he couldn't think of a thing in the world he could do to fix the situation. Sitting on his hands and waiting was so frustrating. And where had Angela gone? And *a daughter*?

As he left the hospital, he felt the end-of-a-month-on-call urge to shut off his pager but decided against it, in case Iris or DiCenzo needed to reach him. Iris had already paged him earlier to let him know they were going to catch the ferry and would be home late that afternoon. He was apprehensive about his family's return from the island's protection, but he could at least be there at home with them now. Their island hosts' rental had ended, and they couldn't continue to stay away with no end in sight.

Yesterday evening, Sheriff Wade had stopped by again to sit on the stoop, chat, and pet Stella. He'd assured Phineas that until Zebediah Jefferson was brought into custody, his office would continue to have someone close by at all times. How long could they keep that up? The clever Angela remained at large, and the police had found no evidence at her place to tie her to the arsenic poisoning.

Phineas decided to busy himself with grocery shopping for his family's return. Their refrigerator was empty. He'd finished off its contents including the pasta that Vinnie and Theresa DiCenzo had delivered to him in his solitude. Their easy affection with each other had reminded Phineas of how much he missed Iris—and Jacob and Martha too. He'd pick up essentials and all he'd need to make one of Iris' favorite Cajun dishes, jambalaya—the one that he'd prepared the first time he'd wooed her with his cooking. Maybe that would lift his spirits out of the dumpster.

⬡⬡⬡⬡⬡

Phineas was rhythmically rasping his paring knife against a sharpening steel when the kitchen phone rang. He placed his tools in parallel on the cutting board next to the precise grid of herb and spice piles. *Mise en place. Everything in its place. Words to live by—or satisfying last words.*

Phineas Mann
R I P
Mise en Place

He answered on the fourth ring. "Hello."

"Dr. Mann?" A harsh male voice, quivering with excitement.

"Who's calling?"

"Officer J. D. Brockwell here. We have a situation at your hospital."

"A 'situation'?" Dread was already replacing his methodical cooking mood.

"Yessir, an emergency situation. I'm told you know a Zebediah Jefferson."

Now what? Phineas' jaw muscles twitched. "His father was on my service in intensive care. He transferred to a rehabilitation facility yesterday."

"Sir, Zebediah Jefferson's an active shooter with a truckload of explosives at the hospital entrance—and he's asking for you."

Jesus!—What?

Phineas lowered himself onto a kitchen chair and pressed the receiver to his ear. "Sorry. Did you say shooter—and explosives?" His last image of Jefferson's furious face flashed before him. He'd threatened that he'd be back.

"Yessir. He's barricaded himself in the parking deck's booth in the front of the hospital. He shot up one of our cars, wounded two officers, and now he's taking potshots at us."

"How...?" A fleeting tightness in his throat interrupted him.

Officer Brockwell pressed on. "He showed up in the parking area outside the emergency room and backed his Jefferson and Son Welding truck against the ambulance unloading platform. Our Officer Bradsher was nearby, and saw Jefferson was wearing a flak jacket and getting ready to roll a suspicious looking pallet off his truck." Brockwell paused. "It was fully loaded with acetylene and oxygen welding tanks, propane tanks, and gas cans. And our guy thought he might also have seen a sizable package of dynamite." Phineas heard the officer take a deep breath. "Jefferson pulled a pistol and shot Bradsher in the leg before he could reach cover."

Phineas tightened his grip on the phone after all his other muscles suddenly felt limp. He was usually greeted by that friendly man, Jameson, working in the kiosk when he left work. "What about the booth attendant? Is he okay?"

"Escaped out the back, right before Jefferson smashed the booth's glass and climbed inside with his weapons and ammunition. He's got what looks like an AR-15 assault weapon trained on us, and who know what else in there? And he also grazed one of our guys answering Bradsher's call. They took Bradsher and him to Emergency."

So why the hell are you calling me? "You must have ways to flush him out."

"We might ordinarily fire tear gas canisters or have a sniper try to bring him down, but any spark from metal on pavement or concrete could ignite his explosives. It smells like he's doused it all with gas...We just don't have any good options." Brockwell's keyed up tone had faded off. He sounded defeated.

"And you're calling me?"

"He wants to talk to you and an Angela Portier."

At the mention of her name, a chill crept from the base of Phineas' skull down through his spinal cord, like someone had reached inside him and touched sensitive nerve tissue. "What's he want from me?"

"Don't know. We're hoping you can talk him down."

Like talk will change him. "I'd be surprised if it'll do any good—but I guess I can come in...You really should find Angela Portier. He won't blow things up, if she's there."

"I hear we've been looking for her for days. Can you come to the back of the parking deck, where we set up our command center?"

"Have you called Detective DiCenzo?"

"He's on his way."

"Then so'm I."

Zebediah, you evil son of a bitch. Come after my family? Yeah, I'll come after you!

He imagined Jefferson's surly response mocking his words. *Yeah? You an' what army?* The old middle school bullies' taunt. The one Phineas had heard before his adolescent growth spurt; before he was big enough that bullies in his blue-collar hometown left him alone. *Well, I do have an army.*

Phineas hurried to the garage, donned, and zipped up his hooded bee jacket. He grabbed a screened cardboard bee transport box, typically known by beekeepers as a nuc for nucleus colony, but today it could be his personal nuclear option. He pulled on his long calfskin gloves.

Gloves for you, Jezebel, because there'll be no smoke today. I don't need my meanest bees gorging on honey. I need you hungry—and mean!

He pried open Jezebel's lid and began hurriedly shaking frame after frame of bees into the nuc box. Furious workers swirled over him, dive-bombed and head butted his gloves and the screen in front of his face. "You call yourselves social insects? Well, this is your chance to do something good." His voice trembled with rage infused with fear.

He banged the box on the ground over and over, knocking the bees to the bottom, while loading more and more angry bees—more and more live ammunition. The buzzing grew into a jet engine roar. He closed the hive and nuc box and raced for his truck, trailing a frenzied cloud of furious bees, then secured the box in the truck bed with bungee cords and slipped into the driver's seat where a sting penetrated his pant leg, then another. *Stinging me once again, Jezebel?*

He opened the windows, turned the A/C to blow on him at full blast, and began speeding toward the hospital, his truck trickling live bees out the windows. Obstinate worker bees clung to his jacket and the seat upholstery. Countless stingers, with their venom sacs left behind by dead attacking bees, but still rhythmically contracting, dotted his gloves.

Two Carolina blue fire engines blocked one lane of Manning Drive near the hospital. Phineas maneuvered around them and approached a circle of cruisers behind the parking deck, each with lights flashing. Clusters of police eyed him suspiciously in his bee jacket and hood.

"I'm Dr. Mann. Officer Brockwell asked me to come. Said Zebediah Jefferson wanted to talk to me." He exited his truck cab and began unfastening the cords that restrained the nuc box. A few remaining free bees seemed keenly interested in it, exploring its cardboard top for an opening. *They're looking for the swarm queen. She must be inside.*

The officers stepped closer. One drew his pistol and yelled, "Hold it! What's in the box?"

Its buzzing was attracting everyone's focus. Phineas held it up. "Angry bees."

"What the hell..." They had him completely surrounded.

"He said you couldn't use tear gas." Sweat dribbled down Phineas face and into the corners of his mouth. He tasted salt.

"Your point is?"

"Bees have been used in battles throughout history."

The officer lowered his pistol. "How on earth...?"

"I drive by the parking booth every day. It's concrete on three sides and a window in the front. If it doesn't look like he's going to surrender, and you have no way to flush him out, I'll toss the bees through the window."

The officer took a step back and grimaced, undoubtably imagining being stung repeatedly by the numerous furious bees they could only hear. He holstered his pistol. "I'm Officer Swaringen. For Chrissake, at least talk to the crazy bastard first."

Phineas took off his bulky bee jacket, cradled the noisy nuc box under his arm. "Just curious. How'd Jefferson get from the ER into the parking booth?"

Swaringen cleared his throat. "After Bradsher and his partner returned fire, Jefferson tried to drive away. They flattened two of his truck's tires right away. By the time he got near the street, he was on rims, so he had to pull over against the parking deck's booth."

Too bad he didn't get farther away.

The officer was studying Phineas, like he was questioning the decision to call him in, before he asked, "You sure you want to be here?"

"Let's go before I change my mind."

Phineas followed Swaringen around the parking deck's back to its front and behind more patrol cars lined up in front of the hospital's main entrance. At least a dozen uniformed officers wearing expressions ranging from purposeful to terrified crouched behind their vehicles. The odor of gasoline hovered in the air. Phineas spotted a white van with WRAL in bold letters on its side inching toward them before it was halted by the police. The media had arrived. Cameras. He groaned.

Swaringen announced, "I have Dr. Mann."

They all stared at Phineas. A lanky grey-haired uniform gripping a bullhorn gave a quick wave with his free hand. His tall frame was folded behind the cruiser next to the one where Phineas had been delivered. "J. D. Brockwell here. What's in the box?"

Swaringen shook his head and shrugged. "Angry bees."

"What the hell...?"

Phineas put the buzzing box on the ground. "Did you want me to talk to him?"

"Yeah. But why bees?"

"Let's see if we need them first. Where's Detective DiCenzo?"

"Over here, Doc." The detective, in white shirt and Carolina blue tie, gestured from two cars away. "Damn, Doc, this job in gentle Chapel Hill was supposed to be my mellow retirement gig."

Brockwell motioned Phineas to squat next to him. "Detective DiCenzo filled us in on Jefferson, and you can see his tanks." He eyed the buzzing box suspiciously. "He could even have C4 and other powerful explosives from the Klan's stores. If it blows, it could level this whole area."

"He might still decide it's not worth dying for."

Brockwell shook his head slowly. "He's sounding more and more irrational. Going on about the doctors hurting his father...about not being able to reach his girlfriend...that we must have her hidden somewhere. He says it's all to 'get' him."

Phineas' hopes sank. Zebediah Jefferson had been used by Angela and abandoned, then wounded by Jacob, and now was being used as an expendable pawn by the KKK. He was desperate, likely suicidal. "Can't we try to wait him out?" His question felt foolish after he uttered it.

Brockwell frowned. "He's already threatened to go ahead and blow everything up before you got here. He might just have enough explosives to bring down half the hospital—like those terrorists did in Oklahoma City a few years ago. As a welder, he surely knows how to set it all off. We're running out of time and options."

Phineas now truly regretted agreeing to be dragged into this mess. Despite the heat, he felt a drop of cold sweat dribble down his spine. "Shouldn't...Shouldn't everyone move back?"

"No time for that." End of discussion.

Brockwell lifted the bullhorn to his mouth and slowly advanced its cone around the car's grill. "Mr. Jefferson, we have Dr. Mann to talk with you." The booming echoes off the concrete deck startled Phineas and silenced all ambient chatter.

A snarl came from the booth. "Put that sonofabitch on, and y'all remember, you send any fire my way—an' blowin' up this hospital's on you!"

Phineas stole a peek at the booth from under the cruiser's front bumper. Jefferson's pickup truck's cab blocked the empty window frame except for a sliver. Light glinted off a rifle muzzle poking out from it.

Phineas accepted the bullhorn. "Mr. Jefferson. Dr. Mann here." He waited for a response. Silence. "You wanted to talk with me?"

"Hah! Guess I got your 'tention now. I told you I'd be back." An agonizing pause. "You tell me why every time Daddy starts gettin' better, he gets worse again. You been tryin' to kill 'im?"

"We just got tests back that answer your question. Come out and I'll explain and show you the reports."

"'Splain away. I'm stayin' right here."

"This isn't going to be easy to hear."

"I'm listenin'. I ain't deaf."

Phineas swallowed hard. "The tests prove that someone gave your father doses of a poison." His amplified words reverberated across the gap between them.

Jefferson's rifle barrel tilted up for a few seconds before sweeping across the line of cruisers. "Probly one of them coloreds or furriners workin' there. Place is full of 'em. They don't like my kind—and I don't like theirs."

"The police have identified a suspect. It's not someone who works in this hospital." How would Jefferson respond to hearing who it was?

"Well, who'n Hell is it?"

Phineas looked at Brockwell. "Can I tell him it's Angela Portier?"

Brockwell shook his head. "Not till we question her."

Phineas squeezed the bullhorn's trigger. "Mr. Jefferson, the police need more information before they name the suspect."

"Where 'n Hell is my Angela? I need to talk to her." His words contained despair layered with anger. The rifle's muzzle was trained on the front of Brockwell's car.

Doesn't everybody? Phineas turned to Brockwell. "Still haven't located her?"

Brockwell shook his head. "The officer who just went back to her place radioed that it looked like she hasn't been back. We've had an APB out for her."

"Have them search around her place one more time for ant poison. Maybe also her locker at the VA Hospital. That'd unequivocally tie her to the poisoning." *She's probably too clever for that.*

Brockwell took the bullhorn back and inched its cone around the car's grill. "Mr. Jefferson, Officer Brockwell here. We haven't found Angela Portier. It appears that she's packed up her possessions and vacated the area."

"Liars! She can't be gone. What've you done with her?"

The bullhorn's cone exploded with a resounding bang that echoed down the street. Brockwell grimaced and wiped blood from his split lip. "That sonofabitch."

A burst from Jefferson's automatic weapon pounded the side of the squad car. A rear tire hissed and went flat, shifting the back of the squad car toward the pavement.

"Come on and git me! Blow everythin' up. I ain't goin' to no jail."

I'll come.

Phineas' thigh muscles twitched. His front pants pocket buzzed. He placed his fingertips cautiously over it. *Cell phone—Not angry bees.* He flipped it open. "Hello?"

"Phineas." Iris' voice. "We just got off the ferry. I've been worried about you, and...I miss you."

"I miss you, too." He kept the phone pressed firmly against his ear. "Glad you're back on the mainland. Can't wait to see you."

"Any progress on finding Jefferson? Is it safe to come home?"

"The police have him located—nowhere near our house. I can promise he won't be there." Ever again. *Just hope I will.*

"That's great news. Well, I need to get the car now. See you soon...I love you."

Phineas blinked and swallowed. "I love you too. Bye." *And hope I see you soon. Gotta go now.*

He tapped Brockwell on the shoulder and said, "I think I can get him out of there. I'm going to him." Another burst of bullets hit the squad car.

Brockwell shook his head. "Too dangerous."

Phineas felt a hand on his arm. DiCenzo squatted behind him. "Doc, you got a plan?"

Phineas pointed at the noisy box of bees. DiCenzo nodded. "Got it." He turned to Brockwell. "Cover him. He knows what he's doing."

Do I? Really? Phineas picked up the bee-filled nuc and jogged behind the squad cars and around the back of the parking deck to its side, where he had a full view of the windowless back of the kiosk. He assumed he was alone there, until he felt a tap on his shoulder. The industrial shoes first, then the tight black jersey over a familiar muscular torso materialized from the shadows.

"Jericho! What are you doing here?"

"Waitin' to see my gramma. They won't lemme cross."

He looked up into Jericho's eyes. "You should take cover—far away—now."

Phineas sprinted to the back wall of the parking deck's concrete block kiosk. He crouched to gather his thoughts and courage then gently tried the back doorknob. *Locked.* He crept down the left side and stole a glance around the corner. The rifle's muzzle still poked out from the shattered window. The reek of gasoline was overpowering.

He heard the click of Jefferson inserting another ammunition clip and then bellowing, "If'n you ain't got the guts to end this, I will!"

A long cord extended from the back of the truck to the window. Then Phineas heard a sizzling sound. A whiff of smoke. *A fuse!*

He removed the nuc box's cover, stepped around the corner, and hurled the box high up into the window. As he dropped to the pavement, he jerked hard on the burning fuse and pulled it loose from the truck's bed. Scrambling on all fours to the back of the kiosk, he stood up, waiting.

Jefferson's gravelly voice erupted. "What the fuck?" Silence. Then the screaming began. "Shit! Ow! OW!"

A swarm of bees in June is worth a silver spoon. "Best not to mess with a beekeeper, Zebediah."

The back door burst open. Zebediah careened out, peppered with bees, swinging his arms and swatting at the cloud surrounding him. He locked eyes with Phineas and reached for the pistol in its belt holster. Before Phineas could move, Jericho launched himself into Zebediah, tackled him, and wrestled for the gun. He smashed Zebediah's hand onto the pavement, causing the Glock to skitter three feet away. The powerful Black man rolled off Zebediah, grabbed the weapon, and stood tall, aiming it at Zebediah with both hands. "How's it feel now, Cracker?"

"Put the gun down or I'll shoot!" Two white officers had their service weapons trained on Jericho. Bees circled his bare scalp. He froze, arms still outstretched, the Glock still pointed at Jefferson. More police began surrounding and yelling at him. "Put the gun down! Now!" They too aimed their pistols at him. Jericho grimaced in obvious pain.

Time stood still as Phineas, stretching his hands to the sky, rushed to place himself between the police and Jericho. He stood face to face, inches away from him. "Jericho. Slowly put the gun on the ground. We're done here...You're a hero."

A chorus surrounded them. "Put the gun down, now!"

Jericho slowly crouched, Phineas with him, and laid the pistol on the asphalt. He stood and stepped back; his hands were now raised high over the scene. After the sudden silence, he cautiously began lowering one hand and rubbing his scalp. "Hey, Doc. I got stung. Mind taking a look?"

Phineas glanced back over his shoulder. Zebediah was being handcuffed, his blotchy red face pressed onto pavement. Phineas winced at Jacob's handiwork, the nasty gashed ear and the gap from missing teeth exposed in Zebediah's grimace. Jacob's role, unseen by Zebediah, would need to stay a secret for the foreseeable future, for the boy's safety.

Black and brown bees marched across Zebediah's uncovered pale skin and inspected his camouflage clothing for entry points. He twitched and swore at intervals after each sting. Phineas smelled the bees' alarm pheromone released with their venom, the bouquet of a freshly peeled banana, its purpose to mark a threat. This threat had been neutralized. *My army. Posthumous medals for you brave warriors who sacrificed all.*

Phineas felt his hostility toward Zebediah Jefferson melting, felt it turning to empathy for a man cheated out of one of life's greatest treasures at a tender age. *Pitiful, pitiful man.* How would his life be different, if he'd been lucky enough to feel a mother's love? What if the weather had been fair on that fateful night so many years ago?

⬡⬡⬡⬡⬡

With Zebediah Jefferson secure in jail, Iris watched the local news regularly. The WRAL cameraman had caught prime footage. The station couldn't seem to run enough of the story, and clips of Phineas and Jericho's actions played over and over.

As she poured her second cup of coffee, she heard a news segment begin with, "This is Chelsea LeFever bringing you more on the incredible drama that played out earlier this week at the University of North Carolina Hospital. First, WRAL has *breaking news* that the Grand Dragon of North Carolina's Ku Klux Klan, Herman 'Skinny' Arnold, has dropped his lawsuit against UNC. WRAL has learned that Arnold sued the hospital administration, claiming doctors had prevented UNC bomber, Zebediah Jefferson, from visiting his father in the hospital's Intensive Care Unit. Jefferson remains in Central Prison without bail where authorities have been questioning him about the others involved. Stay tuned to WRAL for more on this developing story." She paused before a mischievous grin emerged. "Now, let's relive the scene once again, as Dr. Phineas Mann heaves his bees into the parking kiosk to root out the terrorist bomber."

Martha appeared out of thin air for an instant in front of the screen. "I'll tell Daddy he's on again." She raced down the stairs to the garage accompanied by sounds of her light steps descending and trailed by Stella's padding in her four-beat rhythm. The door opened, closed, reopened within minutes, and the beat of their familiar steps ascended.

"He and Jacob say they can't come up. They're in the middle of extracting, and they've got honey all over their hands and shoes. Daddy says they're 'a sticky mess.'"

Iris couldn't help but marvel at the transformation in Martha after she'd bonded with Patrice. Her daughter had insisted on a shopping trip on their return to Chapel Hill. She wanted fresh new clothes to replace her faded, dull wardrobe. Martha was now interested in being part of the visible world.

And Jacob. Iris was convinced that after consuming the contents of his grandmother's scrapbook, Jacob was satisfied and proud of his father. She also knew how much he wanted to tell *someone* of his own heroic act. She'd promised to let him know when it would be safe for him to release his story. It would be quite a while before he could tell just anyone, but she let him tell one person she knew they could trust.

After they'd settled into rooms in the beach house, Iris called her mother to tell her where they were and all that had happened before handing her cell phone to Jacob with the words, "Why don't you tell your grandmother about how you saved us?" It was the first time Iris had heard his version and, despite no preparation, he'd told it well, and his chest had swelled with pride. Martha had sat transfixed in admiration.

Feeling immense relief to be home and have that whole frightening chapter behind her, Iris plopped onto the sofa to finish watching the news segment. She wished she'd thought to pop a tape into the VCR before Chelsea LeFever gushed, "Isn't Jericho James amazing here?"

Then there were the well-worn lines from Phineas' later interview with Chelsea LaFever that had also played over and over.

Chelsea LaFever: "Where did you get the idea to flush out the terrorist with your bees?"

Phineas: "I read a book about honey bees' roles in history, including combat."

Chelsea LaFever: "Your usual light reading?"

Iris grinned again at the words that had transformed her husband from warrior to honey bee nerd. She wanted to keep him that way, the man she knew so well and loved.

The piece concluded with, "This is Chelsea LeFever, and I am excited and, to be honest, a little nervous this morning, because I'll be attending Dr. Mann's annual honey extraction celebration later today. It'll be my first time, and I suspect there *will be* bees there. I've been promised that Jericho James is bringing food from his brand-new *Gramma's Cookin'* food truck and catering business. *I'll* be bringing videotape copies of our newsreels for our two-legged heroes. It's the least I can do to say 'thank you' for their bravery."

Her face took on a solemn look. "But let's not forget the heroic bees that sacrificed themselves when they drove the would-be UNC Hospital bomber from his concrete fortress. Dr. Mann tells me they were all females." She folded her hands on the desk in front of her and smiled sweetly into the screen. "To all our listeners, have a great weekend and stay safe."

Iris and Martha stared at each other with mouths hanging open, after Chelsea LaFever announced she'd be their guest today. Iris stomped down the garage stairs, her footfalls announcing that she meant business, with Martha close behind. They entered a busy scene fragrant with scents of honey and beeswax.

A neighbor friend vigorously cranked the extractor handle. The extractor, a four-foot-tall gleaming stainless steel can with a spinning centrifuge inside, spit golden honey from a spigot, through a screen strainer, and into a five-gallon white plastic bucket.

A grinning Gabriella Morales-Villalobos displayed a live bee in her open palm. "Hi, Dr. Mann. Your husband tells me this one is called a 'drone'. What a name for the male bee, eh? And this little man has no stinger. Only females can sting." She offered it to Martha, who let it walk onto her hand.

Phineas was supervising Jacob, who wielded a hot electric knife with intense concentration and sliced off the wax cappings from a frame's honeycomb to free the honey from its storage cells for the extractor.

She planted her feet in front of the pair. "Phineas Mann! Chelsea LeFever just announced, *on TV*, that she's coming here today—to *our house!*"

Phineas' expression shifted from one of intense concentration to one of surprise. "Sorry, Hon. Ron Bullock asked if he could bring a date. I didn't ask who it was." Phineas had to have known.

Jacob's eyes grew wider open than Iris could recall seeing. "Chelsea LeFever! Coming here? Whoa! She's hot!"

Phineas, now grinning playfully, winked at Jacob. "Never noticed. Iris, do you think Chelsea LeFever is hot?"

Does this mean I'll have to deal with two adolescent males now?

Iris stared at her son, then at Phineas, scowled and shook her head. "Now we've got to really clean up this place. She might bring a camera... You men!"

Jacob began prying another frame of capped honeycomb from its wooden box. "Mom, don't forget the mess in my room. I'm really busy here."

"Hah! Your room is *your* problem." There was so much to do now.

⬡⬡⬡⬡⬡

Phineas and Jacob finished returning the extracted frames to the hives Grace and Charity. Their typically gentle golden bees buzzed around them and pinged their jacket's face screens with uncharacteristic hostility.

"They're never docile after we rob them of their honey." Phineas kept up his teaching. He stepped behind Jacob's Jezebel. "As long as we're here, want to see if they've chewed through the sugar plug and accepted your new and improved queen?"

"You bet." Jacob pumped the smoker twice to confirm it was as ready and willing as he was.

He and Jacob had introduced a purchased Carniolan queen—advertised to produce gentle workers—in her special cage the day after Zebediah Jefferson's honey bee takedown and arrest. Jezebel's bees, missing a queen's pheromone, had appeared jubilant at the new queen's arrival, dancing over the tiny screened wooden chamber she'd been transported in. Phineas had felt relieved at their friendly greeting, telling his son, "If Jezebel's old queen was still here and hadn't joined Zebediah in the kiosk, her workers would try to kill a foreign royalty."

Jacob puffed a gentle cloud of smoke at the bees on the hive entrance and pried the outer and inner covers off. The tops of the frames were lined with worker bees menacingly pointing their stingers at him.

Phineas looked over his son's shoulder. "Same spicy workers, daughters from the old queen. But it looks like she was a good egg layer, and you have plenty bees left to make it through a transition, until the new queen's workers emerge as adults from their metamorphosis."

Jacob teased the ribbon handle stapled to the queen's temporary chamber from between the frames and lifted her container free. It was empty, and a tunnel eaten through the sugar plug documented her exit path.

Phineas couldn't help himself. "No more mean queen genes."

"Hah! Good one. Shall we comb the comb for her?"

"Best to exit now and let her settle in, but you do wax eloquently."

Jacob groaned. "And you drone on."

"Okay. Enough bee puns" Phineas would have preferred to see how far they could take the pun match then and there, but less clever jokes were sure to pop out as they straightened up their mess. "You may need to rename your hive, once it's filled with gentle bees."

"Naw. It's going to stay Jezebel—a reminder of everything we did." His son wasn't going to let this chapter go.

"Your call. Time for garage cleanup."

Jacob slouched and groaned. "Clean up. Yuck." As they approached the garage his pace quickened. "Dad, let's hurry and get it done. I need to take a long shower. Chelsea Lefever is coming *here*."

When did Jacob start to notice the opposite sex? It seemed that every time Phineas was consumed by work for a stretch, his son took another step toward adulthood.

⬡⬡⬡⬡⬡

Tables were set on the porch and two five-gallon honey buckets had been stacked next to them. Three dozen glass jars of crystal-clear light amber honey lined the tables, favors for the guests. Family members, including Sarah Jane, were scrubbed and waiting.

Phineas heard the sound of car doors slamming followed by cheerful voices out on the street. He recognized Ruth and Rebecca chatting with Ron Bullock and Chelsea LeFever, as they marched down the Mann's driveway.

Bullock waved. "Hey, Finman, when's the food coming?"

Stella made a beeline for the group and began an olfactory inspection. Phineas grabbed Stella's collar and commanded her to sit. Jacob had been standing at attention next to him, and Martha, in new jeans and blouse, leaned against her father's leg. Her long hair had been freed from its perpetual ponytail and brushed out. Iris strode past the three. "We really are glad you could come." She offered her hand to Chelsea, Ron, and the James sisters, one after another. Jacob cleared his throat. *When did he start wearing cologne?* His mother laughed and stretched her arm toward him. "And this is our son, Jacob, and our daughter, Martha. You all know Phineas."

Rebecca stepped to Phineas and hugged him. Ruth followed. "Indeed, we do. And we've been giving thanks for him every day. Mother keeps getting better and may come home soon."

Jacob shuffled toward Chelsea and held out his hand. "Hi. I'm Jacob."

She pumped his hand twice then ruffled his hair. "Well, I'm pleased to meet you, Jacob. You're even more handsome than your father. Bet you're proud of him and his heroism." Jacob's mouth fell open. He directed a pleading look at his mother.

Iris shut him down with 'the look' and a barely noticeable pantomime of a zipper across her mouth. "Jacob will have his turn someday."

Chelsea put her arm around his shoulders. "Jacob, I'm sure you will. Make sure you let me have that story first." Jacob leaned into her ever so slightly and kept his wistful gaze fixed on her face.

Martha started bouncing up and down. "Patrice is here!" She sprinted down the driveway.

Ram Patel and Sadie Goldschmidt were walking ahead of Michael

Downs, Malcolm Carver and Patrice. She bent and hugged Martha. "Look at you, Girl!"

Two more car doors slammed out on the street. DiCenzo held up a bottle of wine in each hand, and Theresa carried a cake dish. Stella bolted toward Vinnie and completed her obligatory olfactory inspection of Cannoli's hair sprinkled over his pantlegs.

They all turned to the emphatic hum of a diesel engine. A gleaming stainless-steel van crept down the driveway, parting the growing crowd of guests, and parked next to the porch. After a moment of silent anticipation, the metal shade on the van's side rolled up, revealing a smiling Jericho and his two cousins. They unfurled a banner from the van's window that read:

Gramma's Cookin'

Come and Get it!

Jericho's booming voice greeted them. "What'll you have, my good partners?"

Iris turned a puzzled expression toward Phineas. "Partners?"

Phineas felt his face flush from chin to scalp. Was he about to be in trouble? "I was going to get around to telling you. Chelsea, Ron, and I are limited partners. Minority partners. *Silent* partners...We all think Jericho's a solid investment."

Jericho made a sweeping gesture toward Phineas. "And Phineas has agreed to be a guest chef one day for a New Orleans menu."

Phineas looked from his shoes to Iris' face. "Guest cook. I'm not at the guest chef level."

Martha grabbed his hand. "Daddy, you can wear one of those big chef hats, and, just like in the Wizard of Oz, it'll make you a *real* chef."

"Can I get some courage with that?"

Chelsea gushed, "Iris, haven't you *always* wanted to be in the restaurant business?"

Iris covered her face with both hands before sliding them open and half smiling. “I hadn’t even considered it—till now. Guess we’ll find out. Jericho, what do you recommend?”

“For you, young lady, I’d recommend Gramma’s Carolina Mixed Platter. Give you a taste of everythin’ good.”

ACKNOWLEDGMENTS

I am grateful to my coach and editor, Dawn Reno Langley of Rewired Creatives, Inc., for her encouragement and words of wisdom as *A Swarm in May* came together.

Christy Collins and Maggie McLaughlin of Constellation Book Services, for designing my book's cover and interior as well as ebook production and printing support.

Martha Bullen, publishing consultant, for guiding me through the complex publishing and book marketing process.

Jeremy Avenarius, for designing my website.

Damon Tweedy, for his memoir *Black Man in a White Coat.*

Ian Burris, founder of the popular Dankery food truck, was my inspiration for Jericho James' culinary aspirations, and thanks to *Duke Chronicle* for writing about him.

My Osher Lifelong Learning Institute (OLLI) novelist group workshopped this novel in its entirety. We are led by Carol Hoppe and include Bonnie Olsen, Ro Mason, Phil Goldberg, and Sara Strassle. An extra thanks goes to our retired microbiologist, Bonnie Olsen, who examined my words under her high-powered lens.

I also recognize OLLI teachers Elaine Taylor, Samantha Shad, and Paul Deblinger, my first writing teachers since Cornell University's creative writing classes, and especially Linda Hubbard Curtis for her Black Experience in America: 1950 to Present class. My writing classmate Katharine Bartlett provided helpful observations after reading an early draft of this novel. Rick Johnson opened my eyes to the world of independent publishing in his OLLI course.

The University of North Carolina trained me in Pulmonary and Critical Care Medicine, and Duke University hired me for their faculty later in my career. David Ryu, Duke medical student and an editor of the literary journal *Voices*, took time from his busy schedule to provide insightful comments.

Several Orange County Beekeepers generously offered to be beta readers and gave me important feedback. They include Kim Talikoff, John Rintoul, Chris Apple, Cynthia Speed, Celeste Mayer, and Carrie Donley. Randall Austin has been continuously generous in sharing his encyclopedic beekeeping knowledge with all of us.

My mother, Irene Powers, taught me to read and insisted that I continue. Hi, Mom! She and my sisters, Jan and Vicki Powers, shared their positive thoughts on my work. My son, Luke Powers, found some scattered last-minute typos. My father, Norman Powers, inspired, even as his health declined, by still telling stories as easily as most of us breathe.

And to my wife, Karen Lauterbach: Without your love, encouragement, and gentle but honest feedback, I would not have had the temerity to write a novel.

ABOUT THE AUTHOR

Mark Anthony Powers grew up in the small town of West Lebanon, NH. At Cornell University, he strayed into Russian and Creative Writing while majoring in engineering. After receiving his MD from Dartmouth, he went south to the University of North Carolina for an internship and residency in Internal Medicine, followed by a fellowship in Pulmonary Diseases and Critical Care Medicine.

After almost forty years in clinical practice and teaching, he retired from Duke University as an Associate Professor Emeritus of Medicine and began his exploration of other parts of his brain. Writing, gardening, IT, and magic courses were just some of the enjoyment that followed. A deep dive into beekeeping led to his presidency of the county beekeeping association and certification as a Master Beekeeper. Two cups of coffee and two hours of writing most mornings produced *A Swarm in May* and other works. To learn more or connect with Mark, please visit www.markanthonypowers.com.

Made in the USA
Columbia, SC
22 September 2022